Fela Dawson Scott writes
romance that deeply touch

UNSPOKEN LOVE

"You're still planning to marry Harrington?"

"Of course I am."

The anger on Dylan's face confused Ariel. What had he expected? He said their lovemaking should never have happened.

"Why? Why would you marry him? After last night I thought...."

"You thought what, Dylan? Are you proposing marriage?"

It was so direct, so stunning, Dylan couldn't speak. "Ariel, I...." For the second time, he was unable to finish.

As if paralyzed, Dylan merely stood there as Ariel walked away. His heart told him to follow her, to catch her and tell her. What? He loved her? The thought further disabled him, and in the end, all he could do was watch until he could no longer see her.

Other *Leisure Books* by Fela Dawson Scott:
GHOST DANCER

THE TIGER SLEEPS

FELA DAWSON SCOTT

To my agent, Natasha Kern,
for believing in me and encouraging me to be different.

Book Margins, Inc.

A BMI Edition

Published by special arrangement with Dorchester
Publishing Co., Inc.

Printed in the United States of America.

Digest format printed and distributed exclusively for Book
Margins, Inc., Ivyland, PA.

In what distant deeps or skies
Burnt the fire of thine eyes?
On what wings dare he aspire?
What the hand dare seize the fire?

"The Tyger"—
William Blake

The tiger sleeps within . . .
Awaken and run free.

Prologue

India, 1866

Ariel lifted her head and listened. The water she held cupped in her hand dripped through her fingers and back into the lily-choked pool. The sweet smell of the flowers drifted to her nose, but her head was filled with another scent, a stronger more powerful one. The tiger's cry echoed through the jungle. Monkeys coughed, and peacocks screeched in fear. A small herd of deer stopped browsing on the tender shoots of bamboo that edged the small clearing. One stamped a delicate forefoot, and they all scattered for the safety of the forest, tails raised in alarm. All but Ariel.

She remained at the water's edge, her eyes intensely studying the bamboo tracery rising in a wall around her. Long, feathery foliage reached out, brushing the green grass carpeting the earth, its weight carried by yellow stems. Her gaze moved to the giant pug marks in the bank, her fingers tracing the indentation the tiger's paw had left in the mud. She knew he was near.

Again, the tiger called to the oncoming night. Still, Ariel remained waiting, watching. She studied the trees, so tall and dark their tops were invisible. Vines clung to them, winding upwards, then dropping down out of view, caught up with each other, twisting and knotting together so tight she could not see through them. A flash of color warned Ariel, and the tiger stepped out of what seemed an impenetrable maze. Slowly, he came toward her. The gold and black striped animal moved with stealth and grace, his golden eyes never leaving her. He bunched his hind legs beneath him and crouched low, his muscles taut as he prepared to strike. Suddenly, tail erect and ears forward, he exploded in a powerful leap.

She did not move when the beast came upon her. Ariel's gaze locked with his. He raised up on his hind legs in front of her and clawed the air above her head. His muscles flexed and stretched, ridging beneath the thick fur. His roar filled her head, his strength and power pulsing around her. The tiger loomed above her, his massive frame threatening, even when his roar softened, gentled. Ariel stretched up on her toes, smiled, and rubbed him on the chin.

"Kala Bagh," Ariel whispered, "I've been waiting for you, my friend."

Kala Bagh dropped down on all fours, and together they walked over to a large banyan tree. Ariel's hand rested on his broad back as she dug her fingers deep into his fur, causing him to growl happily. She sat down with her back against the tree's trunk, and Kala Bagh lay beside her. The bark felt rough against her skin, but she welcomed the feel of it. She buried her bare toes into the soft mat of peat and leaves covering the ground, the dampness deep in the vegetation causing the dirt to cling to her feet.

With a sigh, Ariel watched the sky darken from powder blue to coal. In the jungle, the temperature dropped quickly when the light faded. Ariel knew she should go back.

She had missed dinner. Aunt Margaret would be furious with her for being late, especially since they were having guests tonight. Ariel liked seeing her aunt, and their visits were few; yet the visits were made so difficult by her aunt's persistence.

"She doesn't understand, Kala Bagh."

At the sound of his name, Kala Bagh turned his head toward Ariel. Slowly, he blinked his golden eyes, as if nodding in agreement. He yawned and stretched lazily. The danger had passed, and jungle movement and sound returned to normal. The hunter was at rest. The evening chatter of the birds eventually quieted, and the monkeys scurrying about the branches high above settled into their beds. Sambars returned to drink, no barks of fear sounding as Kala Bagh continued to ignore them. In that moment of silence, those who roamed the day gave over their jungle to the nocturnal watchers.

Slowly, new sounds awoke and touched Ariel with their music. Owls came out to hunt, their silent flight broken only by the squeals of their prey. Bats emerged from the dark caverns and filled the blackness with the flutter of wings. The grunt of a wild boar, the scurrying of a mongoose, the drip of moisture gathering upon the broad leaves of the palms all carried to her. The moon came out, its light showing Ariel a spider that loomed above her. She watched it crawl up a fine thread of its own making, reaching the intricate web that glistened from the moisture clinging to its pattern.

This was the time Ariel and Kala Bagh treasured, the darkness of night and the wild freedom it gave. Soul mates of the night with its special magic, their hearts belonged to the black jungle. This was their home.

Ariel laid a delicate hand upon the cat's head, her touch bringing an immediate rumbling purr. She felt the nick in his ear, the scarred flesh now covered in soft fur. The white markings on his face stood out in the darkness, and she knew his eyes were closed in contentedness. She touched the velvet of his broad nose; then his whiskers tickled the tips of her fingers. A special warmth and joy filled Ariel, as it always did when she was with her lifelong companion.

"I suppose we are a unique twosome, you and I. I don't think Aunt Margaret will ever understand we are a part of each other. What we share . . ." Ariel shook her head. "Perhaps it is something she will never know."

Ariel stood and stretched, slow and catlike, then drew in a deep breath of damp, night air. "It's going to rain." Ariel smiled, then laughed, the sound carrying in the quietness. "I can hear her now. 'You'll catch your death, Ariel. A young lady doesn't allow herself to get caught in the rain. Just look at you . . .'" Her words faded, along with the good humor with which she mimicked her aunt. "I'll surely be in trouble, my friend."

Together they left the small clearing and rock pool, disappearing into the jungle. Ariel sensed the green-black swallow them, as if they had walked into a tunnel, the damp walls of foliage cloaking the light of the moon. It felt familiar, comfortable, like coming home. Peacefulness permeated her soul, the jungle giving her life in its raw, purest form. The jungle and her soul mate, Kala Bagh.

Dylan Christianson stepped out onto the veranda, the fresh air reviving him. He loosened his tie, wishing he could discard his dinner jacket altogether, perhaps even his shirt. Of all the people in all the world to end up having dinner with, why did it have to be Bryce Harrington?

His dark eyes glanced back toward the doors through which he had come. He heard Margaret Witherspoon's high-pitched voice rattling on and on. In spite of his initial annoyance with her, he laughed. She talked too much and seemed too nosy, even pushy at times, but he liked her. She seemed to care for people, in her own odd sort of way. So, here he was, having dinner at the estate of Jason Lockwood, an old friend of his father's.

It was almost a year since Dylan had seen his father, and then it had been by accident. A small pang of guilt struck him, but it was quickly doused by frustration. Every time he saw Nathaniel Christianson, they fought. It seemed easiest to avoid his father, yet he was glad he had not put off Jason Lockwood. Even the unexpected presence of Bryce Harrington couldn't take the pleasure from the evening.

It looked to be a beautiful plantation, nestled at the edge of a jungle. The lush growth of vines and trees crowded in on the carefully tended gardens, stretching along the back of the large two-story house. The red brick laid in geometric artistry contrasted with the rich green tapestry surrounding it, reflecting a constant vigil, man against nature, the jungle at bay. Even the smells were at odds, the sweet scent of cultured flowers mixing with the pungent odor of jungle earth and rain.

Jason Lockwood had worked hard for his wealth, and his cotton empire was proof of his success. Dylan's ships had hauled plenty of the precious cargo during the war between the states in America, and both men had profited much during those years.

Dylan struck a match on the bottom of his boot. Holding it to the tip of a cheroot, he drew on it until the end was red-hot. Mrs. Witherspoon seemed upset with her brother tonight, something about her niece missing dinner. He wondered what

Jason's daughter was like and why she would risk displeasing her aunt. He certainly wouldn't want the woman angry with him. He laughed at the picture this thought drew in his mind.

He watched the rain pour down in sheets, just a few inches from the shelter of the roof where he stood. The dark line of shadows shifted, and it took a moment for Dylan to recognize movement from the tall blackness of the trees. Something was coming toward the main house.

He took a step forward to see better but stopped in amazement. Dylan blinked, hardly believing what he saw, but plainly the form of a young woman appeared. Then, in utter disbelief, he noted that a tawny-coated cat striped with black walked at her side. His focus intensified, enthralled by the sight before him.

The beast must have weighed at least 500 pounds, all muscle in its graceful movement. The woman and the animal drew closer. The rain muted their image in a misty veil, the wetness obviously of no concern to them. Enough light cascaded from the windows of the manor to show Dylan the animal's great head rubbing against the woman's hand, much like a house cat nuzzling for affection. The glow of the moon cast silver light through fast moving clouds and onto the enormous fangs of the tiger. Dylan felt the quickened beat of his heart as exhilaration spread through him. Still, he made no move when they neared. Hidden in the building's vast shadow, he stood and watched. The rain apparently prevented the tiger from catching his scent. Dylan held his breath in anticipation.

"Wait in the jungle, my Kala Bagh. I'll join you later, after I've appeased my aunt's anger."

The cat growled softly, then raised up on his hind legs and stretched his paws high into the air. The girl looked slight against its giant form.

Respectful fear prickled the back of Dylan's neck. Yet, in the young woman's presence, the tiger seemed meek. Then, to Dylan's further amazement, the magnificent cat reached out an enormous paw and caressed her cheek. Dylan felt his heart tighten, a strange feeling overcoming him. He had just witnessed an expression, at most of love and devotion, at least of affection or trust. The animal was much more than a pet, she much more than his mistress.

The tiger twisted and bounded off, disappearing into the night. Dylan released a long-held breath. The girl's movements brought his gaze back to her. She turned and crossed to the veranda, stopping when she saw him standing at its edge.

Dylan found himself staring into wide, golden eyes—eyes like the tiger's. Her dark, auburn hair hung in wet tangles about her bare shoulders, giving her a wild, unkempt look. The word uncivilized came to his mind. She dressed like an Indian native, not in the traditional English garb he would have expected. The bold print wrapped about her snugly. Its dampness outlined every curve exquisitely. Yet an innocence underlined her natural sensuality. She was like an orchid unaware of its own beauty. The rain ran down her face and washed away bits of mud that clung to her cheeks. Matted, dark lashes framed her magnificent eyes, wide and tilted upward at the corners—exotic. Full, wet lips parted as she studied him in return. She stood still, as he did.

Dylan thought it a dream, a vision. His gaze locked with hers in some shared intimacy. Without thought, he reached out and touched his palm to her cheek, as he had seen the tiger do. He felt his pulse throb with each hurried beat of his heart, charged with something spiritual or heated with the same wild fire he'd sensed in the tiger.

He pulled his hand away and closed his eyes against the lure of her beauty, but her image remained clear in his mind's eye, giving him no respite. When at last he opened his eyes, she was gone. He searched the darkness, but she was nowhere to be seen. He looked down at his hand, remembering the warmth of her flesh against his. Had he dreamed it all? Was the beautiful girl and her great beast a figment of his imagination and nothing more?

A strange sadness washed through Dylan, and he turned back to the house. Bryce Harrington stood in the patio doorway, the look on his face telling Dylan it had been no dream. Harrington had been there long enough to see the young woman, too. His stare was one of greedy lust, not admiration.

Dylan had known Harrington since they were children, and he had always disliked him. The feeling surging through him now was as close to hatred as any feeling he had ever known. Dylan wanted to strike the lewd smirk from Harrington's twisted mouth. Had Harrington not turned and gone inside, Dylan knew he would have hit him.

It took a few minutes for Dylan to rid himself of his anger, a few more before he went back inside to join his hosts in the parlor. Deciding to stay only long enough to be polite, Dylan entered the room.

The room itself was soothing, a medley of color and style, from formal rich-toned woods to lighter informal rattans and wickers. Green plants of all sizes and shapes graced corners and shelves, delicately scenting the room. Tapestries, needlepoints and paintings added color and texture. Dylan liked it, and this made him smile—especially when he saw the disgust on Harrington's face when he looked about him. So far nothing in the house struck him as very traditional. That was what appealed to Dylan. And he was certain that was what didn't appeal to Harrington.

"My trip to India is twofold, Mr. Lockwood. Politics and pleasure. I've taken care of the politics. Now I'm looking forward to the pleasure—the hunt."

"What do you intend to hunt, Mr. Harrington?" Jason Lockwood asked, though Dylan thought his tone said he was merely being polite. Out of the corner of his eye, Dylan saw the young woman step into the room through the double doors. He realized it was the same woman he had seen emerge from the jungle only a short time ago and found himself unable to pull his gaze from her.

"Tigers, of course." Harrington's voice made clear his amazement that there would be any question at all. "It looks like you have some excellent hunting grounds here."

"We don't allow hunting on our property," the young lady interrupted.

Ariel felt everyone's attention turn to her. She crossed to her aunt and kissed her on the cheek. "I'm sorry I missed dinner, Aunt Margaret."

She read the disapproval in her aunt's eyes but took heart when she gave her a small smile anyway.

"Look at you," Margaret whispered. She quickly straightened Ariel's turned collar, then tucked in a stray lock of hair. Her aunt's lips puckered in disapproval, examining Ariel's wrinkled dress and damp hair, hastily pulled back with a ribbon.

Ariel's gaze moved from her aunt's dismayed look to her father, then to their guests. Her father made the introductions, and Ariel offered her hand. Bryce Harrington took her offering, but she pulled away before his lips actually touched her hand. Unable to stop herself, she wiped the back of her hand against her skirt before directing her attention to the man she had seen outside.

"You have a beautiful place, Miss Lockwood."

She felt the heat rise in her face and flush all through her with its warmth. Never had she seen a man more handsome, nor any eyes so blue. This time, Ariel did not pull her hand away. The fire inside her increased.

"Thank you. You are very kind, Captain. Father and I tend to surround ourselves with what pleases us. It's not quite what you would find in a fashionable English parlor."

Dylan smiled, the whiteness of his teeth stark against his tanned face. "I find it quite pleasing."

"And," Bryce Harrington interrupted, "it would please me very much to do some hunting here, Mr. Lockwood. Would you allow me and my party to hunt tomorrow?"

Ariel saw her father's surprise, but he quickly covered it with another polite smile. "As my daughter said, we do not allow hunting on our plantation."

"I find this quite absurd, Mr. Lockwood." His look was one of incredulity. "You have hundreds of acres of jungle. It's perfect hunting grounds. Surely, you would allow a fellow Englishman to enjoy what you obviously take for granted."

Ariel stepped forward, angry words right on the tip of her tongue. Her father took her arm and replied calmly, "I suppose I do take all this for granted, just as you take for granted all men are hunters."

"Well, I can't say you surprise me, Mr. Lockwood."

Gently, Ariel twisted free of her father's grasp and this time said what was on her mind. "And you don't exactly surprise me either, Lord Harrington. To make it all perfectly clear, just so there are no further misunderstandings, I don't approve of trophy hunting. I find it loathsome you would kill for sport and pleasure, to hang a head on your wall or lay a skin on your fine polished floor."

Harrington's dark eyes watched her closely, but Ariel did not back down.

"Have you ever been on a hunt, Miss Lockwood?"

Ariel countered his amused look with one of her own, right down to the raised eyebrow. "Not your kind of hunt, only the hunt of life and survival. Natural and unforgiving, but honest in its intent. Something you, obviously, would not understand."

"True." He continued to smile, still amused. "I don't believe in such fairy-tale notions. I believe in what gives me pleasure."

"I see you haven't changed over the years, Harrington. Always thinking of yourself."

Dylan's words made Lord Harrington laugh, but Ariel thought she saw him flinch at the captain's failure to use his title when addressing him. "And you still are of a different cut. Odd man out."

Her aunt's voice broke the look that passed between the two men. "Lord Harrington, please forgive my niece's outspokenness."

"Margaret, I see no reason—"

Lord Harrington interrupted her father, cutting off his words. "Mrs. Witherspoon, there is no need for forgiveness. Miss Lockwood merely expressed her feelings. I find it quite charming."

Bryce's charm made her aunt glow, his smile melting away her anxiety. "Mr. Lockwood, I certainly had no intention of disturbing you or your daughter with my request."

"No harm done, Lord Harrington," her father conceded.

Bryce Harrington brought his attention back to Ariel.

"I'll bring a remarkable evening to an end and say good night. It has been a pleasure, Miss Lockwood."

She bristled under his smooth talk. "To say it's been a pleasure would be a lie."

This made Lord Harrington laugh again. "You are quite remarkable. I shall count the moments until we meet again."

"I shall take my cue, and I, too, shall leave," Dylan said.

Ariel watched the two men leave, but her gaze remained on Dylan. A mixed array of emotions ran over her mind, and her body reacted to each strongly, without inhibition. She knew she would see him again.

Chapter One

England, 1868

Ariel's finger traced the path of a raindrop down the windowpane, the dark, dreary day reflective of her own mood. How she missed India . . . how she disliked England. Ariel pushed herself away from the leaded window and let the velvet drapes fall back to block the dismal light. She didn't like remembering. It hurt too much. If only her father hadn't made her promise to stay in England with her aunt for two years. Two long, dreadful years. Like a bad dream, it plagued her mind.

How she wanted to go home, to run away from it all.

It was impossible. No, it was crazy!

Ariel felt the beat of her heart quicken once again at the thought of her intolerable situation.

23

Bryce Harrington. Just his name made her flesh crawl; the man himself disgusted her. For months he had pursued her, even in the face of her continued rejections. How could she bear to marry him? She would never marry him. Never!

Yet she forced herself to sit under her Aunt Margaret's watchful eye and pretend everything was fine. To sit and wait for Lord Harrington to call. Ariel wanted to scream and run from the room, but, of course, she wouldn't. She would speak with Harrington; then she would figure out what to do next.

She tugged at her collar, wishing it wasn't so tight and uncomfortable.

"You'll mess your lace, dear."

Immediately, she pulled her fingers away at her aunt's words and clamped them together on her lap. But within seconds they began to pull again at the constricting fabric.

Ariel knew her aunt loved her, so much that she'd become determined to turn her into a civilized lady of quality and grace. Ariel tried hard to please her aunt, but the harder she tried, the more she failed. The more civilized her behavior, the more she longed for the jungle, the more she desired to run free with Kala Bagh.

Ariel massaged the pain in her temples with the tips of her fingers. If she could just go to the park . . .

To keep from suffocating within the strict confines of her aunt's rules, Ariel had found a secret source of strength—the city park across the street from their home. It was her salvation. By day, she played the demure lady, but under the cover of darkness, all pretense fell away, and she ran wild and free. She felt herself at night. She imagined herself in India once again with Kala Bagh, imagining it as it had been—as it would be.

"Dear."

Aunt Margaret's voice broke into her thoughts.

"Henry and I thought it would be best if you met with Lord Harrington alone. You two have a lot to discuss." Aunt Margaret stood near Ariel's chair.

Ariel saw her aunt's discomfort, the pain in her eyes. Ariel determinedly put her own anger aside. "Of course, Aunt Margaret. You two don't need to concern yourself with this. I will handle it. Now, you go on."

"Thank you, dear." She patted Ariel's hand and turned to leave but stopped. "You will be all right?"

"Of course." Ariel gave her a wide smile. She was getting quite good, even at difficult pretense.

Aunt Margaret put her hand through her husband's arm. "We will be upstairs." She added, much like an afterthought, "Remember . . . remember, we are here should you need us."

Watching them leave, Ariel thought of how much they suited each other. Henry was a man of many weaknesses, one of which was Margaret. Aunt Margaret needed someone to rule over. Despite her aunt's eagle eye, Henry had managed to gamble. Still, Margaret was there to help him through it and, as much as Margaret disliked Ariel's situation, her aunt would not abandon him. Ariel felt like a sacrificial lamb. As long as she married Bryce, all would be well for her aunt and uncle. They were depending on her.

Since she had come to England, Ariel had wanted nothing but to return to the plantation in India. She counted the days; even her father's sudden death had not deterred her. Always, her heart longed for home—and for Kala Bagh. Tears came to her eyes, but she banished them and forced her mind onto other matters, like Bryce Harrington and his reason for visiting.

It was as if her thoughts and his entrance were synchronized. He stood at the doorway looking directly at her.

"Miss Lockwood, I have been anxiously awaiting this moment."

His words were honeyed and smooth, his movements graceful when he stepped across the room, took her hand, and lightly kissed it. Despite her reluctance, she found Bryce Harrington handsome, his looks almost perfect. But she still had the urge to pull away from him. He was not a man who suited her.

"I find myself unable to share your enthusiasm. It's anger I feel."

Gray eyes watched her closely. She stood her ground, determined not to let the chill they gave her show. The smile he so charmingly flashed didn't seem to touch the coldness in his stony eyes. Her stomach twisted.

"And what . . ." His pause was perfectly timed for effect. "Would such a beautiful lady have to be angry about?"

Already she felt her patience slipping. Determinedly, she reminded herself of her promise to remain calm. "You took advantage of my uncle. I find that despicable."

He raised an eyebrow but maintained a tight smile. "Your uncle is a weak man. *That* is despicable."

"Well, the fact remains he owes you a great deal of money. And"—Ariel drew a deep breath and courageously moved on—"I hope, as a gentleman, you won't even consider such an absurd idea as marriage in lieu of payment of his debt."

Still, his smile did not soften. "I most certainly will."

"It's madness! I have no desire to marry you."

He looked pleased by her outburst. Ariel wanted to scratch the smirk off his face. Bryce moved across the room to the sideboard and poured himself a drink. He lifted the crystal decanter in a gesture of offering. When she ignored him, he casually put it down. After tasting the amber liquid, he turned his attention back to her.

"Actually, my dear . . ."

His choice of endearments made her wince.

He saw this and, again, looked pleased. "It doesn't really matter what you desire. I want you to be my wife, Ariel Lockwood, and I'll not be denied."

A red haze drifted over Ariel, bringing a definite warmth to her face. "And if I refuse?"

More than anything she wanted to tell him she would not marry him, not in a million years. But caution calmed her instinct, making her approach the whole preposterous idea carefully.

Bryce laughed, telling her more than his words. "Refuse? Oh, my dear . . ."

There it was again, pushing Ariel just a bit closer to the edge.

"You really have no choice but to marry me. To refuse would be foolish, not to mention hard on your poor uncle."

His callousness burned into her mind the kind of man he was. "You would send him to prison?"

Another question he seemed to find amusing. "Of course I would."

"You're a fiend."

"Of course I am."

"It would kill my aunt." It was a thought she had not meant to say out loud.

"Oh, Ariel..." His voice was smooth, too smooth. "My heart is breaking." Bryce walked over to the fireplace and picked up a small porcelain object. He pretended to examine it, but he still watched her.

Ariel felt a tremor shake her, and she nearly lost the control she'd managed to muster. He looked so at ease, so casual, as if he did this sort of thing every day. "Why me, Harrington?"

She purposely used his last name, avoiding the familiarity of his first and the respect his title Marquise demanded. Everything she said amused him, and his leering grin continued to play havoc with her nerves.

"Why you?" he mimicked.

"Yes," she ground out. Ariel hated, more than anything, providing him with enjoyment. "Why have you decided to bestow me with an offer of marriage?"

"Well, offer seems a bit of a lie, considering..."

The smile grew even wider, but he let it go. "As to why, let's just say I find you attractive. Very beautiful, in fact."

Ariel was sickened that he thought her beautiful. Ugly would have been better.

"And you are a definite challenge, Ariel. You've scorned me in the past. I had to find a way to have you. Your uncle was . . . shall I say . . . handy."

He reminded Ariel of a spoiled child who had never been denied, a child who was now a man. This made him dangerous.

"I have no money." Ariel was desperate for a way out.

"True," he agreed. "You have no money and no home because your uncle lost it all to me at the gaming tables. Your wealth is already mine."

That galled her. He was more than despicable.

"You bastard," she fumed. "I'll never marry you." Her simple words sounded empty even to her.

He looked at her as if she were an errant child caught in a lie. "Now, Ariel, you really do not have a choice."

The threat was real, despite his imitation smile. She saw it in his eyes and felt it clear to her bones.

She replied softly, "For my uncle's sake, I concede I have no choice." *At least for now.*

His laughter rang out, filling the room with its aggravating sound.

"Somehow, my dearest Ariel, I am not so certain I should believe you. Your words are what I want to hear, but your eyes . . . they say other things."

Bryce moved across the room to stand in front of Ariel, drawing her gaze to his.

"Your cat eyes . . . they tell me you despise me."

It was too hard to resist. "I do despise you. Never doubt that."

His hand came up and touched her cheek. Ariel pulled away, but he grabbed her arm and stopped her. "I always get what I want. That's something you'd better learn here and now, my dear. I like the animal fire in your eyes, but do not push me too far."

Before she even thought, Ariel reacted, slapping him across the face. The emotion on his face passed like clouds across a sky. Silence filled the room.

Bryce let her go and slowly rubbed his cheek. A red mark remained when he lowered his hand. He no longer smiled. His eyes flashed steely fury.

"You've been warned, Ariel."

At that moment, she saw the hunter, the part of him she detested, the man who killed for pleasure. *I am just another trophy, another prize for his collection.*

"Yes," she replied, "I've been warned."

The salty spray of the ocean, the move of the ship beneath his feet, the snap of the sails full against the wind stirred Dylan inside. It was always the same—the excitement. The sea was his life.

He thought of returning home. Home. It really hadn't been home for a very long time. The sea was home, not England. A sadness descended upon him when he thought of his father being gone. They had never been close, but it would be strange for Nathaniel Christianson to never be a part of Crestwood Manor again.

The Earl of Crestwood. It suddenly struck Dylan he had inherited his father's title. He was now the Earl; he was now Lord Christy. Only his father had gone by Christy, and though he felt the honor of it all, he was still uncomfortable.

Being the second son, Dylan had never expected it to fall to him. But his older brother, Robert, had died over nine years ago, not long after the birth of his own son, Robert Junior. That was after Dylan had left for sea to seek his own fortune. Or maybe it was his happiness he was searching for.

Now, his father was dead, and he was returning to Crestwood Manor, his inheritance and his title. Dylan wasn't certain he was ready to be bound to it, to give up the life he had made for himself.

Unwilling, perhaps unable, to deal with the many emotions of his past, Dylan sought the solitude of his cabin.

The small quarters were warm and pleasant, the smell of wood and leather mixing with the tang of the ocean air. Along one wall sat a large desk of age-darkened oak, brass knobs and handles worn with use. Golden parchments of all sizes were rolled and tied, each carefully penned to guide the captain across the seas. A brass cargo lantern swung gently from its hook secured in a large crossbeam, its light flickering along the rich wood paneling of the walls.

A sea chest lay alongside the desk, sturdy leather straps and buckles dangling free. A spindle-railed bunk lined the opposite wall, the blankets neatly tucked in. A washstand, a small leather chair and shelves with books orderly placed completed the furnishings. Paintings brought warmth to the walls. Coats and hats hung on an ornately carved rack by the door, and a beautiful Persian rug with its intricate pattern invited bare feet.

Stretching out on his bunk, Dylan tried to relax, but too much worried his mind—mostly, Ariel Lockwood. It was his own father's letter that had sent him back to the plantation to seek the truth of Jason Lockwood's mysterious death. His father thought the so-called accidental shooting suspicious and asked Dylan to look into it. When Dylan arrived, he discovered Ariel had been in England for almost two years.

Dylan knew their first meeting had affected him strongly. Still, he had not expected such disappointment at not seeing her again. Other matters had dominated, and the information he had gathered in India was disturbing.

Reaching out, Dylan picked up a small, leatherbound journal—Jason Lockwood's. He turned to the last entry.

How odd, I have a visitor this morning and, to my surprise, it is Lord Bryce Harrington.

Mrs. Applegate's tale came back to Dylan. The argument and Bryce leaving quite angry. Later, that same day, when Jason Lockwood heard the sounds of a hunt and the angry cries of a tiger, he had run into the jungle afraid it might be Kala Bagh. Later, Lockwood was found dead, shot—not once, but twice. The first shot was likely accidental, as claimed. It had not been severe enough to kill him. But the second was fired at close range, with cold-blooded deliberation, sending Jason Lockwood to his grave with the knowledge of who had murdered him.

"The devil take him." Dylan's anger took hold, and he felt the need to vent it, to strike out at the cause of it. But the man causing his fury was in England, which was perhaps best, for at that very moment he could have killed.

The remembrance of Ariel with her father and the grief she must feel saddened Dylan. In the short time he had visited with Jason Lockwood, he had seen the love they shared. And he'd seen it, too, in Lockwood's journal. Dylan envied their relationship.

Now the sadness he felt was for what he'd never known. Dylan's mother had died when he was young, his memory of her vague. Yet the loneliness remained clear and hurting. His father had Robert, the heir to Crestwood, and when he remarried, a new wife and a second family. Dylan had spent his youth at school.

Carefully, Dylan turned back the pages, going to an entry he had read earlier.

Never had I done anything as difficult as the task I set about tonight. As usual, Ariel missed dinner, putting her aunt in a foul mood. I have never seen my daughter so vibrant and full of life as she was when she bounded down the stairs, her hair wet and dress wrinkled. I felt my heart break into a million pieces when I thought of sending her away. My dear sister, with her persistence, has convinced me I do my daughter a grave injustice by keeping her with me. Ariel's so independent that she never seemed to need a parent. I couldn't bear thinking I've done my heart's delight harm by my own selfishness and lacking. Therefore, I have agreed Ariel should return to England with Margaret. Of course, Ariel does not understand. How could she? She is so young. And Margaret is so determined to make her into a lady, a part of her raising I have failed miserably. God forgive me, but I do it for her.

Dylan set Jason Lockwood's journal on his stomach, giving his mind a moment to understand the man's love for his child, wanting only what was best for her. Dylan admired him.

He continued.

Ariel leaves in the morning, and I think I shall die from the pain in my heart. I know tonight she runs free with Kala Bagh. He, too, shall lose the light in his life.

The next day's entry read only, *She is young, and her pain will lessen. It is best this way.*

A later entry caught Dylan's attention. *Kala Bagh sits in the darkened forest, just beyond the gardens. Night after night, he cries for her, for his Ariel. I have never in my long life heard such sorrow. Never will I get Kala Bagh's pain from my mind, nor the grief from my heart of what I have caused us all with this terrible separation.*

Dylan rose and poured himself a generous portion of brandy. The fire of the liquid relieved some of the cold chill crowding in upon him. He went to the porthole and looked out into the blackness.

"Kala Bagh," he whispered. He saw clearly in his mind's eye the tiger and his mistress, the savage beast touching her face in loving tenderness.

"Lordy," he mumbled to himself, "I'm beginning to think strangely."

He returned to his bunk and again picked up the journal. Then another image struck him, and he set the book aside.

The vision of her walking from the jungle with her tiger clung to his mind, her beauty even now creating a warmth inside him. Even after two years, having seen her only once and so briefly, he remembered all too clearly.

This tender feeling mixed with his anger. He didn't know for certain who had killed her father, but he would find out. Until then, he could do nothing, nothing at all, but in time he would find the evidence he needed to hang the son-of-a-bitch.

Chapter Two

The noise was like a distant buzz, the words beyond Ariel's willing comprehension. Each and every time she looked at Bryce Harrington she recalled her humiliation from the week before when her solicitor pointed out the grim truth of her situation. There was no money left. Nothing. It galled her that she was at his mercy, but her aunt and uncle seemed grateful that he would continue to support them, paying all their living expenses. Even their shame was overridden by their fears, and her stubbornness would only hurt them. Pain clouded her thoughts, but the toast made to them broke through with resounding clarity.

"Here's to Bryce Harrington and to his beautiful fiancée, Ariel Lockwood!"

Glasses were lifted, and everyone drank to their health and future. Ariel was careful not to show her dismay, nor the shudder that shook her. Bryce looked down at Ariel. The obvious pride in his normally composed expression surprised her. She knew how important it was to him they make a striking couple. Bryce was a vain man, one of his many characteristics Ariel disliked.

She continued to study him from beneath lowered lids as an immaculately groomed hand smoothed back his hair. But, as usual, every hair was perfectly in place. He was not exceptionally tall, yet he held himself in a manner that made him seem formidable. Ariel knew, to many who watched them, they appeared a perfect match. This made Ariel ill.

People filed by, shaking Bryce's hand and hugging her. The large room became small, the air scarce and overused.

"My congratulations, Harrington. You've outdone yourself this time."

Ariel felt the deep tone of a familiar voice but couldn't place it as it vibrated through her. She raised her eyes to seek his. Their gazes met, dispelling the coldness that had enveloped her as the heat of their contact stirred her. Her heart raced.

"Well," Bryce drawled, "if it isn't Captain Christianson. What brings you to dry land?"

Bryce's comment drew Dylan's eyes away from Ariel for a moment. "I came to London to see someone," he said, his gaze moving back to Ariel. "Somehow, I ended up here. I didn't realize when it was suggested I come I would find you the center of it all."

Whether he meant Bryce or her, Ariel wasn't

really sure. The only thing she was sure of was the distaste the two men felt for each other. Their mannered talk barely disguised it. Propriety guided them through an exchange of aristocratic civility, each acting with perfect decorum. Ariel was fully aware of the emotion underlining each word.

"Captain Christianson, may I present Ariel Lockwood, my fiancée." Bryce turned his cool, gray eyes to her. "Ariel, you remember Dylan Christianson?"

Ariel managed to offer her hand in practiced politeness, but her voice betrayed the effect Dylan's unexpected appearance had on her. "It's a pleasure to see you again, Captain."

Dylan bowed gracefully, his lips brushing the hand ever so softly. "The pleasure is all mine, Miss Lockwood." When he pulled his hand from hers, his long tapered fingers skimmed her palm.

Her hand tingled, and she felt his warmth rush through her. She wondered how it was his mere touch sent her heart into a flurry, just as it had the only other time she had seen him. The blue of his eyes, bright against his darkly tanned skin, the shape of his face, the set of his jaw, the soft curl of his sandy colored hair—every detail had been etched into her memory. She had put it off as fascination, but she was no longer fascinated. She was enchanted. No, she corrected her own thought, she was on fire.

Bryce noticed the slight color on Ariel's face and wondered what had prompted it. His gaze moved back to Dylan, and he knew the answer.

"Perhaps you should see if your aunt and uncle are enjoying themselves, Ariel." Bryce Harrington was a man used to getting his way, and he intended to make it very clear. He recalled the first time he had seen Ariel Lockwood. He had wanted her, and despite her obvious dislike of him, he had vowed to make her his wife. Something about her stirred his blood; an almost uncivilized quality lurked just beneath her polite manners and cool reserve. The only other time he had ever felt such heat was on the hunt and during the kill.

He reached for her hand and brushed his lips against the softness of her flesh, the small gesture his way of showing Dylan, and everyone there, Ariel was his. Bryce smiled despite the anger that stirred inside him. "I'll join you in a moment, darling." His words were sweet, but they held no warmth, and neither did his movements when he pushed Ariel toward her family.

"Bryce, old friend"—Dylan used the term loosely, intercepting and stopping Ariel—"I had hoped to have this dance with Miss Lockwood. You wouldn't mind, would you?"

Bryce ground his teeth in vexation. The smile he still wore belied his answer. "Not at all."

"Would you do me the honor?" Dylan asked, offering her his arm.

She gave Dylan a smile that left Bryce chilled.

"I would love to," she said and gently laid her hand upon the sleeve of his jacket.

They whirled out onto the dance floor. Bryce wondered why she had never given him such a smile. His hand clenched into a fist while he continued to stand and watch them. It was as if he wished to torture himself, to remind himself of what he wanted from her. Until now, it had not mattered that the woman acted as cold as a fish, never granting him even the smallest bit of warmth or feeling. But now it did.

No matter. You will be my wife, and you will soon beg for my touch, for my mercy. You will learn what I like, and I will be your teacher.

The thought brought a smile back to his face, but inside the coldness and anger remained in his heart.

Dylan gracefully moved her across the dance floor. He drew her into another world, a world where Bryce Harrington didn't exist, nor the tangled mess she found herself bound to. She wanted to escape to this place forever.

When Dylan had kissed her hand, it had set her on fire. This made her lift her gaze to face the man who created the feelings she liked and craved more of.

Instantly, Ariel knew it to be a mistake. Her breath grew short. She felt her knees grow weak, leaving her to depend on the strength of his arms for support. What was happening to her? She hadn't been prepared for what she had known would happen.

"Are you all right, Ariel?"

The words, whispered so close to her ear, robbed Ariel of her remaining composure.

Dylan held her up, helping her out to the veranda for some fresh air. Ariel tried to clear her mind by drawing in deep breaths of the crisp night air. "Please let me go, Mr. Christianson. I'm fine."

He dropped his hands and stood staring at her. She steadied herself and stood on her own, feeling very silly. "I assure you, I *am* all right."

"You grew so pale. It frightened me."

Their eyes met. All became still about them. The music, the gay chatter, the shuffling feet of the dancers all melted, and their world tightened, leaving them alone.

Ariel turned away from his stirring look and took another breath to quiet her trembling. "I must go back inside," she said, looking beyond his shoulder.

"Go back to Harrington, you mean?"

"I . . . He . . ." she began, then stopped. Frustrated, she tried again. "I don't think that's any of your business, Mr. Christianson."

Dylan looked contrite. "You're quite right. It is none of my business." He threw up his hands, seeming to give up.

"Yes," she agreed softly, "it isn't." Somehow, his words cut deep. In the last weeks her own frustrated anger had retreated, leaving a cold numbness. Now she felt disappointment seeping through it. It was easier to feel nothing at all. She turned to leave.

Dylan put a hand on her shoulder and stopped her. "Do you love him?"

Ariel's lower lip trembled slightly, but she bit it to keep it still. She pulled her head up and met his curiosity straight on. "That is also none of your business."

This time, she did step past him and, as much as she dreaded it, went back inside. To her dismay, Bryce was nearby.

"Ariel, darling," called Bryce, spotting her across the room. "I have a gift for you, and it's time for me to give it to you."

He didn't wait for an answer but walked to the center of the room. Having no choice, she followed him.

Bryce signaled for everyone's attention. "Family, friends. This, as you know, is a very special occasion. In celebration, I have a present for my bride-to-be."

He picked up a very large box and handed it to Ariel. "It took me almost two years to collect. I hope every time you wear it, you will think of me."

A strange feeling crept through her, warning her before she really knew what was wrong. It fell like a deadweight to her stomach, and she wished the floor would just open up and swallow her. She wanted to flee from all the eyes watching her, but she wanted to flee from Bryce Harrington even more. Then she saw her uncle and her aunt standing by his side. With renewed determination, she pasted a smile on her face.

Her hands trembled as she pulled on the bright, red ribbon adorning the box. When she looked up, Bryce was watching her, his raised brow telling her he had noticed. She returned her attention to the bow, but impatient, Bryce helped and pulled it free. Dread tugged at her heart when she lifted the lid, then horror froze her smile in place.

Bryce pulled the fur out and placed it with great ceremony around her shoulders. "I must admit, these Bengals certainly gave me a run for my money."

Men joined him in a round of hearty congratulations, each seeming to imagine with envy the thrill of such a hunt. The noise echoed off the walls, distorting into a sinister sound. Ariel felt the blood drain from her face as she touched the soft striped fur of the tiger.

Without further warning, blackness slid over her. "Kala Bagh," she whimpered.

To Bryce's dismay, Dylan was the one to catch Ariel when she wilted into a dead faint. Then, without a glance in his direction, Dylan carried her off, leaving Bryce to follow.

"Now what on earth is wrong with her?" Bryce spouted in anger, reluctantly following Dylan past the crowd of people and out into the hallway.

"You're a damn fool, Harrington."

Bryce stopped in midstep. "You're walking on dangerous grounds, old friend. So you'd best explain what the devil you're talking about."

Dylan turned, fury sparking his eyes into liquid fire. "You gave her a gift of tiger skins. You were there, you saw her pet."

"I saw a tiger I wanted displayed on my trophy wall. It's not like I killed her pet." Bryce reached out and took Ariel from Dylan. "This time, I'm going to ignore your insulting behavior."

"Ignore what you want, Harrington. Just remember"—Dylan's finger punctuated his point on Bryce's lapel—"I've always been ready for you. It's your choice."

Bryce nearly choked.

Dylan guessed had Bryce not been holding Ariel he might have chosen differently.

Since they were children, they had hated one another. Dylan knew Bryce wanted to take up his challenge—he could see it in his eyes—but caution had always kept Bryce at bay. And wisely so, Dylan thought, watching him disappear through the library doorway with Ariel in his arms.

Kicking open the door to his den, Bryce took Ariel to the couch and deposited her onto it. She was coming to, so he brought her some brandy. Holding it to her lips, he forced her to drink.

"It will help," he snapped.

The liquid burned, quickly clearing away all the fogginess that lingered in her head. "Enough," she coughed and pulled away from his touch.

"Damn nice reaction, love. You certainly know how to make an impression."

She felt a rush of anger warm her cheeks, but she tried to remain distant, aloof. "You could always break off our engagement."

She felt pleased by his reaction, the already dark hue of his face darkening further.

"Over my dead body, Ariel."

The venom in her eyes told him exactly what she was thinking. It was the look of a wildcat. He had seen that look before. Bryce struck her across the face. She fell back onto the couch.

"I warned you I always get what I want." He smiled, feeling the pleasure at the pain he inflicted and the desire it aroused.

Before Ariel had a chance to move, his hand pulled her into the prison of his arms. She struggled, but he held her firmly. His lips came down hard upon hers, demanding and bruising.

Repulsion writhed inside. She began to shake and thought she would be ill.

When he pulled back, his cold, gray eyes stared into her own. "You are mine, Ariel Lockwood. Nothing you can do will keep me from having you."

Fear struck a nerve in the back of her mind and, slowly, moved forward to full consciousness. She understood his meaning.

Then, he let her go. "But not tonight, love. I am a patient man." His hand came up to touch the softness of her cheek. "On our wedding night, you will be mine in all ways."

"Never," she hissed. She looked about for the door, her only thought to leave, to get as far from this man as possible. Then she saw them—all the trophies of the hunter, wall after wall, head after head. She met the blank eyes of the dead, stuffed mountings, a tribute to his dedication to killing.

Ariel stepped back in horror, stumbling to her knees over an object that lay on the floor. Skins of all kinds covered the oak hardwood. She had fallen over the head of a great Bengal, his mouth open in a silent growl. Her belly twisted violently, and she swallowed back threatening bile.

Pain and anger crowded inside her. She turned to the man she hated more with each passing second. "You . . ." She tried to think, but no words ugly enough came to mind. Tears blinded her, and a surge of emotion clamped about her throat. Unable to bear the sight of him any longer, she crawled to her feet and fled the room.

*   *   *

The carriage rolled through the streets, breaking the quietness as wooden wheels struck cobbled stone. The horses hooves keeping time calmed Dylan's anger.

When he had seen Ariel, standing next to Harrington, he had experienced a strange kaleidoscope of emotion. He stood, for the longest time, just watching them, unable to trust himself to go near.

How could she be so foolish?

The anger returned.

Bryce Harrington!

Dylan was still stunned. Of all the men Ariel Lockwood might have ended up engaged to, why Bryce Harrington? A long list of reasons why she shouldn't marry him rattled through his mind, the first being that he could be a cold-blooded killer, the very man who killed Ariel's father.

She didn't love Bryce. Dylan had determined that much. Then why the hell marry him? As far as Dylan could see, there was no good reason.

"I should leave the little minx to her own doings," Dylan muttered in frustration. But he knew he wouldn't. He would find out what had happened in India and what was happening here. It was the last thing his father had asked him to do.

Hell, it was the only thing he ever asked me to do.

Chapter Three

"Dylan . . . Lord Christy," the older man amended, coming out from behind his desk to greet Dylan. "It's good to see you."

Dylan took the hand his solicitor offered and shook it wholeheartedly. "Franklin, you've been a friend too long for that sort of thing."

Franklin Browning smiled. "I suppose you're right, Dylan. It's a real shame about your father. I can truly say there were few men better."

A strange feeling touched Dylan, and he wished he could say the same. Not that he thought his father not to be a good man, only that he wished he could have really known him. Now, it was too late.

"It was quite a shock when I received word from Evelyn."

Dylan sat in the seat offered him and made himself comfortable. It was true, it had been a shock to

47

find out about his father's death. It was something he had never contemplated, as if his father would live forever. Maybe he had done too good a job of blocking that part of his life from his mind, never allowing room for such thoughts. "Her letter caught up with me in the same packet of mail with a letter from my father. I read my father's letter first. It was particularly strange then to read the letter from my stepmother saying he had a heart attack only minutes later."

"Yes." Franklin nodded. "Your father's death was so unexpected. Nathaniel was always so damned healthy. How's Evelyn?"

"She seems to be doing fine."

"At least she has family around her to ease her sorrow."

Another new sensation took hold of Dylan. Guilt squeezed about his heart painfully.

"I'm sorry it took so long for me to come home and see to things. You've taken good care of the business affairs, Franklin."

The solicitor settled into his leather chair behind his piles of paperwork. "Your father has let Charles manage the estate since he and Francine were married. I've merely acted as his advisor."

"Charles is doing a fine job of it, then. My idea is to let him continue as is."

Franklin couldn't keep the surprise from his face. "I see no problem with that, though I guess I had hoped you would settle down now. Perhaps marry and start a family."

"Well," Dylan drawled, a knowing smile curling his lips up, "I don't think I am ready to give up my freedom. Every day I spend here a little part of me dies. I'm afraid if I stayed I'd wither away."

"The right woman would give you reason to live, Dylan. Not the sea. She's fickle, unfaithful at best."

"Yes, but she's wild and untamed. There isn't a woman who can make me feel as alive as the sea can." A vision popped into Dylan's mind, as if to challenge his own words.

"No, Franklin," he rushed on, putting the picture of Ariel from his mind, "there is no choice for me. The sea will have my heart. There can be no other."

"I was afraid not." Franklin smiled, his round, balding head bobbing up and down.

"I also have a few other things I'm anxious to settle concerning my sisters and Robert Junior."

"What would that be, Dylan?"

"First, I want trust funds set up for each of the girls. Of course, Evelyn, Francine, Robert Junior and Charles will live at Crestwood, and they will be sufficiently provided for. When Robert Junior is of age, I want the estate to be his."

"But Dylan, my boy, Crestwood is yours now," the lawyer argued, rubbing the afternoon stubble on his chin.

Dylan laughed. "I have no need of the estate or the money."

Franklin chuckled, too, his expanding stomach threatening the tight buttons of his satin vest. "You're certain you want to do this?"

"I'm certain."

"Then," the lawyer declared with the same enthusiasm as he would in court, "consider it done."

"Now that the family business is taken care

of . . ." Dylan hesitated, uncertain how to approach the next subject.

"What is it, Dylan?" Franklin prodded, when he did not continue.

"I mentioned a letter from my father, and, as you know, we did not correspond often."

Franklin only nodded.

"He expressed concern about the death of Jason Lockwood."

This did prompt a response from Franklin. "Yes, he mentioned this to me. He had doubts about the accident, though I was not aware he had written to you about it."

"He asked that I look into the matter."

"And?" Franklin asked, his curiosity apparent when he leaned forward, his belly pressed against the desk.

"I have only suspicions, nothing concrete. Mostly, I'm going on gut feelings, Franklin. I need more before I start throwing about accusations, especially of murder."

Slowly, the barrister leaned back, the seriousness of what Dylan said echoing on Franklin's face. The lighthearted humor between friends disappeared. "What is it you intend to do, son?"

"I want to find the truth. I owe my father that much, Franklin. He never really asked anything else of me, and even though he's dead, I don't want to let him down."

Franklin shifted, then sniffed loudly, the look on his face matching his words. "He'd be proud of you, Dylan."

Dylan felt uncomfortable and changed the subject. "What do you know of Ariel Lockwood's engagement to Bryce Harrington?"

"Seemed quite odd actually, considering."

"Considering what?" Dylan asked.

"Well," Franklin answered, "considering the girl would have nothing to do with him. Needless to say, Ariel's arrival in London to live with her aunt caused a stir, and Bryce has been quite obvious in his pursuit."

"Why her sudden turnabout?"

"No one seems to know. I'll nose about if you'd like."

"Yes," Dylan said, his mind already working on this new information. "Find out what you can. It may have some bearing on her father's death."

"Consider it done."

"Good." Dylan stood. "It was good to see you, my friend."

The lawyer took his hand again and shook it. "Good to see you too, my boy. It will be even better should you decide to stay a bit."

"I just might do that."

Outside, Dylan pulled the brim of his hat down to shade his eyes from the sun and better observe the busy street. *I just might do that.* Then he started down the walkway, his thoughts straying to Ariel Lockwood.

"Ariel, darling," sniffled Margaret Witherspoon, "Mr. Harrington didn't mean to hurt you. He . . . he only . . ."

Ariel turned a soothing gaze up to her aunt and patted her hand to comfort her. "I know." She tried to smile, but the soreness of her chin prevented it. "It really doesn't hurt so badly."

Margaret moved off the edge of the bed. Her hand touched the throat of her lacy morning gown in a helpless gesture foreign to her character. "I thought you two had come to some sort of understanding."

"I suppose he was not pleased by my behavior last night." She dropped her eyes to hide the flash of anger that bolted through her, but her voice remained submissive. "It was all too apparent I didn't like his gift."

"Oh, dear me," Margaret moaned. "I do hope Henry doesn't hear about this. He's been so upset about this whole thing."

Ariel bit her lower lip to keep from replying, a searing heat scorching her mind. She closed her eyes against the disappointment showing so clearly on her aunt's face. Dear Aunt Margaret. Ariel knew her aunt to be helplessly, hopelessly, in love with Henry, his weaknesses coddled by her own overbearing strengths.

"Bryce wasn't so very angry, Aunt Margaret. You needn't worry over it. It certainly isn't anything you need to mention to Uncle Henry."

Margaret sighed, wanting to believe her. "He wasn't terribly angry?"

Ariel's hand went to her face, remembering the blow he had dealt her. "No. He's the most understanding of men."

A smile overcame the wrinkles of worry, and she laughed in relief. "That's so nice, my dear. Men can be hard to live with, you know."

This time Ariel smiled, too. "Yes, he can be difficult at times."

Margaret crossed the room towards her niece. "You will be good, won't you? I just hate to think of you two quarreling."

"I know," Ariel said. She stood and gave her aunt a reassuring hug. "I promise I'll be good."

"Oh, Ariel," Margaret whispered, her hand soothing back her niece's stray hair, tears filling her soft brown eyes. "I worry about you."

"You needn't. I can take care of myself."

"I know." She sniffed delicately. "I know."

She moved to leave the room but stopped and turned back. "I love you, Ariel. You do know that, don't you?"

"Yes, Aunt Margaret, I do."

"Mr. and Mrs. Witherspoon are not in this afternoon, sir."

"And Miss Lockwood?" Dylan inquired further.

"Miss Lockwood is not receiving visitors today."

Disappointed, Dylan turned and walked away. He heard the servant close the door. He started to walk further but then paused in front of a side gate leading into the gardens at the back of the house. Memories of a time long past trailed through his mind, pleasant remembrances of visits here. He opened the iron gate and followed the narrow path leading to the back.

When Dylan came around the corner he saw her sitting with a cat curled up in her lap. Ariel looked beautiful in the garden, blooms of soft pink and coral roses framing her silhouette perfectly.

The thorny vines clung to a white painted trellis arching above her. Dark green hedges, trimmed to perfection, stretched out behind her. Pots of red geraniums graced each end of the wrought-iron bench. Clumps of white petaled daisies with soft yellow centers grew up behind, and salmon colored moss roses sought the cool, damp shade to bloom. Dylan did not move, enjoying her loveliness. The white satin gown and robe clung to her in a most appealing way, and her hair fell like a shawl about her shoulders. The slightest of breezes stirred her dark, auburn tresses, the ends springing up into tantalizing curls brightened by the sun's fire. Dylan found himself wanting to touch her hair, to feel the soft texture between his fingertips, to smell the sweet scent of jasmine he knew mingled in its length.

She raised her head, and he found himself drowning in the gold of her eyes.

"Are you going to stand there all day?"

Dylan blinked, as if rousing himself from a deep sleep. "I didn't mean to intrude."

Ariel smiled, a smile that made him smile in return.

"I'm not really dressed to receive, but you are welcome to sit." Her hand went up to stop him. "But only if you promise not to tell my aunt of my indiscretion."

A broad grin broke across his face, and he bowed elegantly in childish play. "I shall never breathe a word to a soul, my lady."

She couldn't contain a giggle. "I am forever in your debt, kind sir."

Dylan took the seat by her side and scratched the cat's head. A deep rumbling reached his ears almost immediately. "What's his name?"

"Oh, I don't know. I just call him Cat."

"Cat," Dylan laughed. "Surely we can do better than that."

Ariel kept her attention on the cat. "What would you suggest?"

He gave it some thought, then replied. "How about Tom?" This made her laugh a warm, pleasant sound, a sound Dylan liked.

"That's not much better."

"Then I guess he will have to be Cat."

"In truth," Ariel whispered close to the animal's soft head, bringing another quick response from him, "I don't think he minds."

"No, I don't think he does," Dylan agreed, his eyes glued to her delicately curved neck. "I remember this garden."

This took her interest from the animal, and Cat jumped down and scampered off. "That's why I came back here. I wanted to see if it had changed."

"When were you here?" Ariel asked.

Dylan thought back, drawing on his childhood memories. "I must have been about five or six. My parents, Robert and I came to say goodbye to your mother and father. They were moving to India."

Silence seemed to rule the next moments, leaving each to their own thoughts before Dylan finally spoke. "I think my father wanted to go with them. He envied their adventure."

Ariel considered this. "Your father had greater responsibilities to keep him from pursuing such dreams. His title and estates were here in England. My father had only this house. The money and title passed on long ago."

"Your father did very well for himself in India."

"Yes, he did." Ariel tilted her head up, studying the top of the trees to quiet the pain she felt. The words difficult to say, her throat clamped about them. "It never occurred to me when I left India he would not be there when I returned home. I never got a chance to say goodbye."

Dylan fought the urge to tell her the truth about her father's accident. But what would it accomplish? He had no proof with which to press charges. He didn't want to upset her. He rather wanted to see the smile return to her face.

Her head was bent down, her face hidden from him by her thick hair. Reaching out, Dylan pulled the long tresses back. His touch brought her face around, and, for the first time, he could see the bruise on her chin.

Ariel quickly moved away, embarrassed she had let him see, embarrassed by the look on his face. "I . . . I really must go in."

She tried to leave, but his hand moved to stop her. When he spoke, his voice was rock hard. "Did Harrington do this?"

The look in his eyes made her reply before giving it thought. "It's nothing."

Dylan pulled her to him, his grip on her wrists gentle but unrelenting. "He did this?"

"I don't know it is any of your concern. You're all but a stranger, Captain Christianson. I have been far too bold as it is in allowing you to stay."

It was the truth. He was a stranger. She knew nothing of him. She knew Bryce better than she did Dylan Christianson. She understood who Bryce was and what he was. But of this man who made her tremble at his nearness, she knew only that their fathers had been lifelong friends.

"Stranger?" Dylan stepped back, a look of hurt quickly replacing his look of anger. "I've never felt us to be strangers."

"I'm afraid you must leave now." Her voice shook slightly, and she was unable to bring her gaze to meet his.

"Ariel." Dylan corrected himself. "Miss Lockwood, I don't think your father would walk away knowing someone had mistreated you. I don't know that I can either."

Ariel felt touched, her heart skipping beats at his softly spoken words. "Please, I beg you to let it go."

Dylan didn't let go. "Why would he do this to you? For what reason?"

Ariel's eyes grew wide as panic struck home. Visions of her uncle being hauled away to prison filled her mind. The ugliness of it made her heart beat faster. "I embarrassed him with my foolish—"

"Embarrassed him!" Fury darkened his eyes.

"It was his right," she cried, afraid her own blundering would make things worse. She pleaded with Dylan. "You mustn't say anything. It will only make things worse."

Something in her tone checked his anger. "Are you so afraid of him?"

Her pride leaped forward in sudden defense. "I don't fear him. I merely seek ways to appease him. Angering Bryce will accomplish nothing. Don't you see? I have no choice."

"I *am* sorry, but I don't feel a man, any man, should strike a woman. And you should not allow it. And . . ." He paused, struggling with himself. "You have a choice. Just say no to Bryce Harrington."

Ariel felt foolish; then anger flooded in. "You have no right to judge me or my life."

He stepped forward, closing the distance between them. "Ariel, I'm not judging you. I want to help."

"I don't remember asking for your help," she snapped, his nearness creating havoc inside her.

"No," he said, pulling her even closer, "you didn't."

She tried to step away, but again he prevented it. Reaching up, he turned her face to his and looked clearly in her eyes. "Tell me, Ariel, where is the wild creature I saw walking out of the jungle?"

Ariel's breath came in fast, short gasps. "She no longer exists. Forget about her."

"I can't forget her." His hand moved to her cheek, his fingers tracing the line of her jaw. He traveled on to the contour of her throat, sliding down to the curve of her neck. "Somewhere inside you, I know the tiger sleeps."

"No," she whispered, her eyes still held by his. "No, Dylan, there is no tiger. India is a distant memory. Leave it be."

Dylan lowered his head, his mouth only a breath from hers. "I don't believe you." His lips claimed hers, his tongue seeking Ariel's sweet, inner warmth. He kissed her deeply, tasting of her, enjoying the sensation of the woman in his arms. His hands slid down the satin robe on her back, feeling the sensuous muscles along her spine, then the roundness of her bottom. He held her tighter, then lifted her to mold his hard body even closer to her generously soft one.

"Dylan," she whispered, his lips trailing down her neck where his fingers had explored. "Oh, Dylan."

He heard the slight plea through his haze of desire. Determinedly, the well-bred gentleman in him struggled to take control of his mutinous body. With great effort, he let her go.

"I don't know what games you are playing or why. I only know I don't believe your aunt has tamed you. And I don't believe India is only a distant memory. And," he stressed for the third time, "I won't leave it be."

Chapter Four

Dylan sat in his room brooding, a drink in his hand, a half-empty bottle of brandy at his side.

"Foolish woman," he grumbled to himself.

He took another drink, emptying the crystal snifter of its contents. The potent liquid seemed to subdue the burning passion that had lingered after he left Ariel. Yet he couldn't rid himself of her image—the soft, silken beauty he wanted so terribly. No . . . more than terribly.

"Oh, my tigress," he rambled on, "what has happened to you? What has taken the wildness from your eyes?"

Finding no answers, Dylan put his drink aside and stood. He moved over to his bed and plopped down on it. Slow and shaky, he yanked off his boots, his shirt and his pants. He carelessly tossed them on the floor.

"Foolish woman," he cursed Ariel again and fell back against the soft pile of pillows. "I'll not let you disturb me again."

Before his last word was fully spoken, Dylan felt sleep taking him, heavy breathing turning into a hushed snore before his eyes fully closed.

"Ariel."

"Papa," she called back. "Are you there?"

"Ariel."

His cry was weak, almost lost on the wind, but she heard it. "Papa, I'm coming. Wait for me. I'm coming."

Ariel ran, as hard as she could, but she couldn't catch up with him. He was too far away.

"Wait," she yelled, reaching out to him, but he came no closer.

"Wait."

She could no longer see. Tears blinded her. Ariel sank down to the ground, broken in spirit, her soul shattered.

"Papa," she whispered in sorrow. "I never got to say goodbye."

"Ariel."

Ariel moved away from the disturbance.

"Ariel," whispered a soft voice, a gentle hand smoothing back her tangled hair.

This time she forced blurry eyes open at the call of her name. "Aunt Margaret?"

"Are you still having bad dreams, dear?"

"I'm all right," she lied. "I just need to sleep." Ariel attempted to turn away.

Margaret Witherspoon only laughed in response to Ariel's grumblings. "Have you forgotten you and I are supposed to meet Mr. Harrington to pick out silver and crystal patterns? You've got to get up. Look at you," she scolded and pulled on a limp arm. "You're a mess."

"Oh, noooo," Ariel moaned, thinking of the dreadful day ahead. "I don't want to go."

"You've no choice." Margaret offered to help Ariel from bed. "You'll feel much better after a hot bath. I've sent Betsy to the kitchen to get lots and lots of water."

Slowly, with her aunt's persistent encouragement, Ariel got up. "You're too good to me, Aunt Margaret. What would I do without you?" There was a touch of irony in her words, but the tone of her words was warm.

"Oh, I'm sure you'd manage," her aunt replied, then brushed back the hair from Ariel's face. "Somehow. Some way."

This prompted a nod from Ariel.

"Come and sit, Ariel. I'll try to brush the tangles from your hair."

"It may be a lost cause." Ariel grinned, remembering her night spent in the park. She already felt a bit brighter and more awake.

"I'd better get started. It'll take a month of Sundays to get all of those tangles brushed out."

Margaret began brushing her long hair. Ariel closed her eyes, enjoying the gentle ministrations of her aunt.

A soft knock sounded; then the door opened and

the servants entered. Within minutes, her copper tub sat full of hot, steaming water. A delicate scent of jasmine tinged the morning air, and the small fire Betsy built in the fireplace took the chill from it. When the clatter of pails disappeared down the hall, Ariel discarded her gown and stepped into the bath.

"Does it still hurt?"

Ariel met her aunt's gaze, then glanced away. "You worry too much."

Margaret saw she had made Ariel uncomfortable and turned away. "I'll see you downstairs, dear. Wear something pretty."

"I will be perfect," Ariel agreed readily, her mind on other matters. Margaret quietly left the room. Ariel's thoughts lingered on the happenings of the day before.

Dylan Christianson had come back into her life. Only yesterday she had known exactly what she wanted, but now something else lingered in her heart—something new and disturbing, something wonderful. Still, the power of it frightened her. Had he popped into her life yesterday just to pop out again today?

Ariel wondered about him, her thoughts settling into a confused jumble, leaving a funny feeling deep in the pit of her stomach.

The heat that surged through Ariel was a combination of budding desire and the warm water. She recalled easily the tender look on his face, the bright blue color of his eyes, the strong set of his jaw. Just the memory of him brought forth a dizzy thrill inside her; it left her feeling weak and distraught.

This was ridiculous. She had more important things to worry about, like getting through this day.

Lordy, what am I going to wear?

Ariel rose from the tub and wrapped a soft towel around her. She walked over to her wardrobe and opened the wide doors.

"Something pretty," she mumbled, fingering the fine satins and smooth silks lining the closet. Ariel sighed and closed her eyes against the array of colors that confused her. Slowly, she opened her eyes, then closed the doors. She'd leave the dress for later. First she would have to do something decent with her hair.

She moved to her dressing table, the large round mirror reflecting the seriousness of her task at hand. Picking up her silver brush she untangled the wet strands.

Firelight reflected off the polished wood of the cherry furniture, its richness brought out by the dark hues of forest green and burgundy. Ariel found comfort in her room, even though her aunt had been horrified by her choice of decor. Margaret would have preferred soft pastels, even bright colors if they were feminine. But Ariel's choice was dark and soothing, like the jungle she longed for. Rich tapestries lined the darkly paneled walls, and thick, wool rugs covered the teak floors.

With another sigh, Ariel placed the brush down and began working the long lengths of hair the way her aunt had shown her. Only it seemed easier when Margaret did it, her own fingers clumsy and stiff. She kept her frustration at bay, determined to accomplish her task. For some reason, her aunt had felt it important for her to master styling her hair—something every young lady should know. Carefully, Ariel curled and pinned, twisted and pinned again. Slowly, she maneuvered each hair into place.

The mirrored image she studied was honest and unyielding, her hairstyle causing her to laugh. The clock on the mantel chimed the hour, immediately replacing her smile with a serious look.

I'm going to be late!

Quickly, Ariel pulled the pins from her head and let her hair fall back down around her shoulders. With a few fast brush strokes, she tucked the sides into a roll and tied it with a bow, allowing the full length to hang loose down her back. Wasting no more time, Ariel returned to her wardrobe and, without taking time to look at her dresses, grabbed one.

As she fumbled with the tiny pearl buttons, Ariel wondered at her aunt's fortitude. Didn't she know what a hopeless cause she was about? She wanted Ariel to fit in with London society, but all Ariel wanted was to run barefoot in the jungles of India, not struggle into uncomfortable shoes.

Ariel stood and walked over to the full-length mirror to examine the results of her labor. She doubted her aunt would be satisfied, but her worry was soon replaced with a smile when it occurred to her Bryce might not be happy with her either.

It would be worth Aunt Margaret's disappointment to irritate Bryce. Perhaps it was a bit childish, even foolish, to continue to anger him, but it brought her some satisfaction in a situation that seemed hopeless.

Giving it no more thought, Ariel braced herself for the long afternoon ahead and left the comfort of her room.

"Bryce," Diedra cooed in an overly sweet manner. "And Ariel, dearest. What are you two about today?"

Diedra's cool, gray eyes assessed Ariel and returned to Bryce, dismissing Ariel. She patted her blonde hair and smoothed the skirt of her gown. She looked bothered at having run into her brother, and even more so Ariel and her aunt.

Bryce gave his sister a quick kiss upon her cheek, careful not to get too close. "We have been to the silver and goldsmith to pick out our service patterns." It was impossible to miss Diedra's look of aggravation.

"Not to be nosy or such," she prodded, smiling again, the movement obviously forced, "but isn't that something for the bride to do? Haven't you more important matters to attend to than the picking of patterns?"

Bryce scowled, his gray eyes more steely than usual. "Ariel insisted I help her today. I'm afraid my intended does not care for such things."

"How odd," Diedra mused, a long, tapered finger carefully placed upon her full lower lip, before she turned her gaze back to Ariel. "Yet you've never seemed to do the normal things, have you, dear?"

Ariel felt warmth come to her face, not from embarrassment but from anger. She had a definite distaste for all the Harrington family. They were so much alike. "I suppose you are right, Diedra. I've never had much patience with frivolous things."

A perfect eyebrow shot up. "Frivolous? My dear, you are so simple. It amazes me still that Bryce finds you so attractive. But then, he has always been drawn to odd things."

Ariel could tell Bryce was growing impatient with his sister.

"Diedra, would you care to have tea with us?" His hand indicated the small, cozy café they had been about to enter. "I haven't had the pleasure of your company in so long."

It was a lie. Ariel knew that tone of voice, but Diedra seemed to accept it.

"Well," she preened, "since you put it that way, how can I refuse?"

"Excellent," Bryce said, overly anxious. Then his brows wrinkled together as a thought occurred to him. "Oh, my, I just remembered. I have another appointment to keep. Would you mind terribly if I leave the care of my bride in your capable hands, Sister?"

Diedra had been set up, and she knew it. Through gritted teeth, she mewed, "Of course, Brother. I would be delighted."

"You are too good to me," he countered sarcastically. "If you will excuse me, I really must hurry.

I believe I am late." Bryce turned to Ariel. "You do forgive me, don't you, my sweet?"

Ariel felt the prickle on the back of her neck at his endearment, but she smiled demure acquiescence nonetheless. "Of course. I am certain you have more important matters to attend to."

He kissed the back of her hand and bowed to her aunt. "Now, Mrs. Witherspoon, you'll see that these two lovely young ladies do not grow too wild on their outing."

"I shall do my best," Aunt Margaret offered.

Ariel knew her aunt was uncomfortable. In Bryce's company, Margaret became quiet, even melancholy. Ariel understood how difficult the whole situation was for her. And now they must endure Diedra, a woman who was beautiful, wealthy and titled, who used her assets like an expert craftsman used his tools.

Bryce left the three women standing in awkward silence. Finally, Diedra spoke. "Well, shall we sit, or shall we stand here all day?"

"I think sitting would be better," Ariel replied more evenly than she felt.

Diedra narrowed her silver eyes in anger and marched off after the waiter, deliberately leaving Ariel and her aunt behind.

Careful to pick the chair that would provide her with the best view of the café, Diedra seated herself. Quickly, she scanned the crowded room, giving no thought to Ariel and her aunt as they joined her. She had hoped there would be someone she knew here, someone to save her from sheer boredom.

Then she saw Dylan Christianson. Initial surprise turned into a calculated pleasure, and Diedra waved a gloved hand to catch his attention.

At first he seemed not to pay her any mind; then Dylan stood and crossed to them.

"Ladies." He bowed dramatically. "What a pleasant surprise."

Diedra felt his eyes skip over her impatiently and, to her utmost dismay, linger on Ariel.

"Captain . . . or should I say Lord Christy?"

"Miss Lockwood," Dylan murmured.

"Captain Christianson," Ariel whispered. Her heart raced out of control, leaving her breathless and shaken.

"Christy Manor and all of Crestwood Estates are yours now as Earl, aren't they, Dylan?" Diedra asked.

Diedra's use of his first name did not escape Ariel, and when she finally pulled her gaze from Dylan, she read the possessive look of Diedra quite well. Then, slowly, she realized what had been said. Dylan was the Earl of Christy; this fact never occurred to her. In her mind, he was the captain of his ship. She was awed by this discovery of his social position, then embarrassed at her slip of protocol.

"Yes, they are." He lifted his shoulders casually. "But I do prefer Captain over Lord. It seems less formal, don't you agree?"

His question was directed to Ariel, his look telling her it was all right. She tried to pull herself together. "It does suit you better."

"Yes," he agreed.

Dylan's look made her feel their conversation more intimate than it was.

"And it would please me more if you called me Dylan. I'm certain Bryce wouldn't mind."

He turned his gaze to Diedra. "Would he, Diedra?"

Ariel realized he intentionally used Diedra's game to his own advantage. Diedra knew better than to say differently.

"I'm sure my brother wouldn't mind, Ariel. We are all such good friends. Dylan and I . . . well, we go way back, don't we, Dylan?"

"Yes, we do go *way* back."

His insinuation apparently touched a tender spot. Diedra quickly refuted his meaning. "Well, perhaps not so far back."

Dylan grinned. "However far back you wish," he agreed too willingly. "As much as I would love to stay," his words were once again directed to Ariel, "I really must go."

"Must you?" Diedra pouted. "It's been so long since we had a chance to visit, Dylan."

"I do have an appointment to keep," Dylan explained, certain Diedra didn't even remember the last time they had spoken. It was a moment he most certainly had worked hard to forget.

"Men and their business," Diedra complained prettily. "You must promise to come by and see me. We have some catching up to do."

Her meaning was so clear that Ariel blushed for her.

"I shall do that," he replied, then turned back to Ariel. "I do hope to see you again, Ariel."

70

Ariel warmed under his heated gaze of blue fire, her heart skipping a few beats in its rush. "I hope so too, Dylan."

She said his name like a gentle caress, and this made Dylan deliriously happy. He did not care to examine the reasons why. He was happy. The reason was not important.

Diedra studied Ariel closely. She thought the younger woman uncouth and wondered what on earth these men saw in her. Ariel was an uncivilized witch, oblivious to genteel protocol and manners. Diedra didn't like her looks. Ariel reminded her of a wildcat. She wasn't even attractive. She was too . . . too natural.

As Diedra simmered, Dylan took Ariel's hand and kissed it. Diedra offered her own, but he merely bowed and left.

This did nothing for her foul mood. "He has the manners of a buffoon," Diedra mumbled, then turned her attention back to Ariel and her aunt. "Shall we order?"

Dylan settled back into the seat of the carriage, content for the moment to enjoy the effects of his brief encounter with Ariel. Her beauty remained imprinted in his memory, every detail vivid in his mind. The sweet scent of jasmine, the softness of her hand, the caress of her voice all came to life within him. Dylan would have preferred to stay and visit with Ariel, but two things kept him from it. One, Diedra. Two, he did have business to tend to.

So, regretfully, though not easily, Dylan set his

thoughts on business. The sound of the carriage wheels changed from the higher pitched tone of wood rolling over cobblestone to a deeper tone of planked wood. Dylan knew they had entered the docks. The air was heavy with the pungent odors of salt water and wood. The more sophisticated noises of the city gave way to the intensified sounds of workers, sailors, vendors and a menagerie of animals, all culminating to create a sound familiar to Dylan. It all surrounded him with a mood he welcomed, even craved.

The carriage stopped, and Dylan stepped out into the crowd. The smell of fish was strong, spiced with the odor of unwashed bodies. Dylan smiled and took it all in.

He moved in and out of the throng of people with ease, his steps taking him to the pier where one of his ships, *The Sea Hawk*, was docked. A sense of pride struck Dylan when he walked aboard. Everything meeting his critical gaze was satisfactory.

"Captain."

Dylan turned toward the voice. "You're the captain this time around, John. I just came by to see if the repairs were going all right."

"I hoped you'd changed your mind about shipping out with us."

It was a great temptation, but something even greater kept Dylan in London. "Not this time."

John did not press Dylan further. "We'll be ready in seven or eight days."

"Good. Who knows? Maybe I'll be finished with my business by then."

"Must be pretty important to keep you on land, Dylan."

"Yes, it is." Dylan slapped John on the back and grinned. "I'll buy you a drink, Captain."

John returned the smile. "That's an offer I would never turn down, mate."

Chapter Five

Ariel closed the door to her room and kicked off her shoes. The immediate relief to her sore feet brought a sigh from her. How could one day be so long and so boring? She plopped down in a chair and stretched her feet out in front of her, her head falling onto the puffy back of the chair. She closed her eyes.

"How could two people be so difficult and annoying?" she mumbled to herself.

Flashes of Bryce and Diedra played in her mind. Two pairs of cold, gray eyes, twin frowns of disapproval, like some permanent disfigurement, a family birthmark. Ariel moaned and massaged her temples, the pain in her head excruciating. Diedra Langley was a widow with claws. Diedra had married money—lots of money—and a title. Within the first year of wedded bliss, her husband had died in an accident. Inconvenient for him, convenient for her.

A frown puckered Ariel's forehead, this time from vexation instead of pain. She was aware of Diedra's interest in Dylan, and this irritated her. Carefully, she considered this unwanted emotion. Was she jealous?

"No," rushed out the denial before Ariel even really considered the question. "I barely know the man." But he made her feel things she had never felt before, a certain warmth just from seeing him. And when he spoke, she trembled from the tone of his voice, always so intimate to her. To touch him brought pleasure. Then again, Dylan Christianson also brought a lot of confusion and distress.

"I don't need you making my life even more complicated than it already is," she whispered, words spoken out loud seeming to be more definite in their meaning. "I have no time to bother with this, this . . ." she carefully chose the right word. "Attraction." She nodded her head in agreement with her own decision. "I have no time."

Dylan read the note from Franklin Browning again. He folded the paper back, then placed it on the desk in front of him. He leaned back in the leather chair and let this new information sink in. It made sense now, Ariel's engagement to Harrington. The bastard was blackmailing her.

Franklin had discovered the large gambling debt Henry Witherspoon owed to Harrington. That explained why she was willing to marry him, but it didn't explain why her father was killed. Dylan still had no evidence to support what he thought, what his instincts told him.

And pressing on his mind was a golden-eyed lady, one he was finding irresistible.

"Oh, Ariel," Dylan sighed, marking the words with uncertainty. "What am I going to do with you?"

His brow wrinkled as he considered interfering. He knew it would be best if he stopped this marriage, even if Ariel didn't understand the reasons. How could she? She didn't know all that had happened, and he didn't have the proof he needed to explain. Another thought plagued Dylan, one he didn't wish to consider. *Would I be doing this for her sake or for mine?*

He was not so naive to think no one would think he wanted Ariel for himself. Dylan did want her for himself, but to what end? Marriage?

Objections bombarded his mind and his conscience. If he stopped her marriage to Bryce, propriety demanded he ask for her hand in turn.

"Bloody hell," Dylan mumbled, pushing his fingers back through his hair.

Marriage loomed over him, a great monster on his shoulders. This was not to his liking. That he knew for certain, even if all else remained unclear.

Dylan recalled a scene, ten years past, one that brought him disgust at his own youthful foolishness.

"Diedra."

The name fell off his tongue in a sneer, his memory one of humiliation. At 19, he had thought his feelings for Diedra to be love. He foolishly begged for her hand in marriage. It was this remembrance that nagged at him—her high-pitched laughter mocking him, her look of incredulity that he would even think of such a thing. She had her sights set on a title and wealth, not a second son who would never be entitled to his family inheritance.

It was because of Diedra's disdainful rebuff Dylan went to sea and, in turn, found his freedom and happiness. How things had changed in ten years. Now, Dylan was wealthy, his shipping empire built from those years of hard work, work he loved, work he lived for. Was he willing to give up everything for a woman he barely knew?

Dylan leaned forward and stared at the note as if it would give him the answer. It did not. He pushed away from the desk and stood. The answer was in finding the truth and letting the matter with Ariel ride for the moment.

It couldn't hurt to wait for a while.

Diedra carefully penned Dylan Christianson's name onto the envelope and handed it to a waiting servant.

"Here," she snapped. "Let's be quick about it, shall we?"

The man nodded his head in answer, then without further delay left the room to do her bidding. A slow smile curled Diedra's lips. The masquerade ball she had planned might turn out to be even more fun than she had originally anticipated. Though the actual invitations had gone out weeks ago, Dylan should receive his in time to put the ball on his calendar.

"And that," she almost purred, "will make it perfect."

Actually, she had given little thought to Dylan over the past few years. He was always at sea somewhere, doing something. What, she wasn't quite sure. Tending to business most likely, but then he was certainly rich enough now to let others do that. And that would leave more time for her.

After seeing him today, she realized what fate had brought back to her. Who would ever have dreamed it would end up this way. The timing was perfect. Since the death of Lord Langley, her wealth seemed to have dwindled terribly.

Where could it have gone?

Perhaps it was only her accountant who told her she had so little money left. Maybe he was the real reason behind this money problem.

Distrust of the wiry, little man bubbled up inside her. Certainly, *she* hadn't spent it all. Whatever the cause, she must deal with the situation immediately.

Diedra knew she couldn't go to Bryce for money. Actually, she wouldn't go to Bryce. He'd never let her have money without continuously gloating over her. How she hated that. Being the firstborn son, the only son, Bryce had everything. It wasn't fair. Her inheritance hadn't lasted nearly long enough, while Bryce had more than he needed. She had to marry an old withered man to keep her life-style, and now she needed another.

Diedra drummed her fingers on her small writing desk, then stood, impatience causing her to pace. That was where Dylan came in. How simple it would be. How convenient. "And how pleasant," she whispered, her smile returning. Dylan no longer had the look of a youth but of a man toughened by the sea. Just the thought of being held in his arms made her shiver with anticipation. Then, just as quickly, her satisfied grin relaxed, and her eyes narrowed when she remembered the way he had looked at Ariel—and only at Ariel.

"Witch!" Diedra's voice rose. "I'll not let you ruin my plans." Ariel already had Bryce acting the fool over her. She had best keep her distance from Dylan. "Dylan's mine. He always has been." It was time they saw the chit for what she was, and Diedra would be more than pleased to show them.

Diedra smoothed back her hair, giving her reflection a sideways glance in a nearby mirror. She sat down again. Ariel should be no problem at all. Again, her fingers drummed on the surface of the small desk top, her manicured nails clicking on the hard veneer. Quickly, her mind scurried over all the possibilities open to her; then she formed one distinct thought.

She stood, and this time she turned her full silhouette to the gilded mirror and openly admired what she saw. "You are so good, Diedra," she cooed. "So very good."

Dylan entered the room, a haze of cigar smoke clogging the air. He slowly searched the club until he found the person he sought. It had been a long time since he had been in this place; long nights of drink and cards didn't appeal to him much. The aristocratic patronage made the atmosphere too stuffy for his taste. A pub on the docks would prove more fun than what he was about, but his purpose remained clear. He made his way to the table where Bryce Harrington gambled.

"Do you gentlemen mind if I sit in?"

Cold, gray eyes lifted to meet Dylan's gaze, his own look giving away as little feeling as Bryce's.

"Certainly. It would be a pleasure to take your money, Christianson."

Dylan accepted the offered seat across the table. He lit a cheroot and took a long, slow drag. He studied Bryce, watching his every move. It would be a long night.

The clock chimed the hour, the night nearly gone. It no longer mattered. Dylan had discovered what he had come for. This made him smile.

"You seem terribly happy for a man that's losing."

This made Dylan's grin widen even further. "There's always this hand, Harrington."

Bryce gave Dylan a lopsided grin, yet no humor was evident in the hardness etched on his face. "I hate to be the one to dash such confidence." He paused. "But I shall."

Bryce turned his cards over, his grin becoming an open smirk. Dylan knew how much he was enjoying himself. This fact made it even better when he revealed his own cards.

The smirk disappeared, but Bryce covered his surprise with his traditional stony look. Only the small spasm of his jaw muscle told Dylan of his inner emotion.

Dylan stood and gathered his money up. This last hand won back what he had lost during the night. Even more gratifying was the knowledge he had gained—Harrington had cheated Ariel's uncle. Just as he had tried tonight. Only this time, Harrington cheated the wrong man.

"My thanks, Harrington. It's been interesting."

When Dylan walked away from the table he saw the brief flash of anger in Bryce's cold eyes. Dylan wondered if he suspected he had been outmaneuvered at his own game.

As Bryce watched Dylan Christianson turn and walk away, indignant anger stirred inside him, the heat rising inch by inch up his face. What Dylan was about eluded Bryce, yet he felt suspicion mingle with the anger. Whatever it was, he didn't like it. Dylan's sudden appearance in London was beginning to annoy him greatly.

Chapter Six

Ariel rode along behind Bryce and Diedra, curiosity keeping her mind busy and less preoccupied with staying atop the trotting horse. Bryce hid a wide yawn behind his gloved hand. Ariel couldn't help but smile at the grouchy look he cast his sister. It was a beautiful morning, but neither of the other riders seemed to notice. Neither was a morning person. Ariel wondered what had gotten into Diedra to get her out of bed so early, especially for a ride in the park.

So, in silence, she bounced along on the ungainly sidesaddle. She longed for the simplicity of riding astride as she had in India, to feel the animal move beneath her and the wind tear at her hair and cool her face. When would it not hurt to remember?

Immersed in her memories, Ariel wasn't paying attention to what Diedra was about. Ariel caught a flash of Diedra's riding crop out of the corner of her eye, then heard it slap her own horse's rump. The beast shot forward in panic, and, unprepared, the sudden bolt nearly tossed Ariel from the saddle. She managed to grab on and somehow hold on, her mount running wild and out of control.

Ariel felt her hands slip and gritted her teeth. She was about to provide great amusement for her fiancé and his sister when she bounced along the ground. The skittish horse took a quick turn, almost leaving her midair. But instead of the hard earth coming up to meet her, she felt strong arms wrap about her waist and pull her against a broad, muscled chest, smelling pleasantly of musk.

A strong sense of security settled in Ariel. She was disappointed when rider and mount came to a halt. She pulled her head away and came face-to-face with Dylan Christianson. Her heart moved at such a pace it left her almost breathless and quite speechless.

"You came close to taking a nasty spill, Ariel. You should be more careful."

She swallowed, wishing she would stop reacting so strongly to this man. Her mouth opened, but she seemed unable to manage a single syllable.

Concern shadowed his face, and he continued to stare at her. "Did I hurt you?"

This ended her daze. "No, just the opposite." She could not help the grin that bloomed when she considered what might have been. "You saved me from an embarrassing situation. I think our audience would have gotten a chuckle from me landing unceremoniously on my backside."

Dylan's warm laughter drifted on the morning breeze. Bryce and Diedra rode up, a scowl on the culprit's face. Ariel was certain Diedra had not intended for it to turn out this way. This gave Ariel some satisfaction.

Ariel looked up just in time to catch the scathing look Diedra gave her, but this only made Ariel smile. And that certainly did not improve Diedra's mood.

Diedra gasped, then turned her horse and galloped off, retaining as much dignity as her stiff back would afford.

Bryce watched his sister's retreat, realizing why she had wanted to come riding at this hour of the morning. He turned back to the others. It was too bad Diedra was taken by Christianson; Bryce really found him unbearable. He would have to speak with her soon.

"Come, Ariel." Bryce decided to ignore Dylan altogether. "We must not let Diedra get too far ahead."

Reluctantly, Dylan set Ariel upon the ground. Bryce noticed his hold linger just a moment longer than necessary.

Bryce's voice lowered in irritation. "You'd best get mounted, my sweet." He intentionally used the endearment, but it came out forced, and Ariel winced in irritation. "I shall get your horse."

"I would prefer to walk for a while, Bryce. I have had enough of the sidesaddle for one day."

Her words were honeyed with innocence, but her eyes held a mischievous glint he did not trust.

"I couldn't possibly allow you to walk about unescorted. It isn't proper." He paused, but only for a second, then plunged on. "You really should master the sidesaddle, Ariel. It's just beyond my comprehension why you have so much difficulty with it. No, what's beyond me is that you were permitted to ride astride while growing up. India is truly an uncivilized place."

He looked at Ariel, ready to go on, but Dylan interrupted him. "I shall be happy to stay with the lady, and I promise nothing improper will occur."

Bryce halted his lecture, uncertainty crossing his foul expression. "I don't know . . ."

"We shall remain in your view at all times, Bryce. And when you are ready to return home, just come and get me." Ariel yearned for at least that much freedom from Bryce and Diedra, and she wanted to stay with Dylan.

Bryce really didn't care to have Diedra and Ariel bickering, especially since the horse's skittish flight was his sister's doing. She did not hesitate in showing her dislike for Ariel, and he was not in the mood for either of them. All this early morning fussing was bloody annoying. "I'll see if I can calm Diedra down somewhat before we come back for you." Then, as an afterthought, he snapped, "You really shouldn't bait her so. She's hard enough to live with without your making matters worse, Ariel. She will be your sister soon, so it's best you learn to curb your tongue now."

"I shall try my best," Ariel replied smoothly, though her inner turmoil belied her even tone.

Bryce nodded and rode off.

"I admire your tolerance, Ariel. I'm afraid I have none when it comes to those two."

Ariel turned to Dylan. He stood directly behind her, and his closeness unnerved her. "I . . ." She took a deep breath to steady the quivering tone of her voice. "I try to ignore them as much as possible, but I must admit at times it's very hard. Sometimes, I wonder how much more I can stand."

"If you marry him," Dylan stated, "you will need the patience of Job."

"Yes, I suppose I will." She turned away from his ardent gaze.

"Don't," he said.

This brought her gaze back to meet his. "Don't what?"

"Don't marry him."

She seemed to consider this, then replied more calmly than she was feeling. "Dylan, there is so much you don't understand, so much I can't explain, things I have no control over at this time." Ariel started walking, her mind whirling. Too many emotions plagued her to think straight.

"It would be a pity if you married such a man."

She paused and let him catch up to her. They continued on in silence for a while before she finally spoke again. "Diedra seems to be taken with you."

Dylan shrugged his shoulders indifferently, so Ariel went on. "I think that was what this whole early morning ride was about. Do you come here often?"

"Nearly every morning."

A giggle tickled through her. "How predictable."

He laughed; the sound was warm, like a caress. "I guess I am, at least for Diedra."

She joined him. "But now I know. And I might not discourage her from another outing when we might *accidentally* bump into you."

"Perhaps you can have another runaway horse." The twinkle in his eyes turned serious. "I wouldn't mind saving you again."

Not ready to give up the humor, Ariel continued. "I don't think I would mind either, but I believe Bryce and Diedra would."

"They're fools!" His smile disappeared altogether. "And you don't belong in the company of fools."

Their playfulness replaced by uncertain tension, Ariel directed their talk to other things. "I love the park. Though I prefer night to day."

Surprise, if not a bit of worry, widened his eyes. "You don't come here after dark, do you? It's much too dangerous."

Realizing her slip, Ariel corrected herself. "No, just in my mind. I visualize this place in the silence of the night. If you were to try, you could hear it."

"Hear what?" Dylan asked curiously.

"The music of the jungle. Well, not quite the jungle, but this is as close to it as London has to offer."

She walked on, her head tilted, listening. "In the light of day, you hear the songs of the civilized. It's all around us. The talk of people, the cries of children, the snorting of the horses. It all mingles with the background of birds singing, dogs yelping, and carriage wheels turning as animal hooves plod in even time."

Ariel stopped and whirled about slowly, as if looking for her next words. "Underneath, though, you can smell the sweetness of the flowers and even hear the soft buzzing of the bees as they work. The trees are calling to the gentle breeze, their massive limbs stretched in the warm air. Dust stirs into small musty clouds on the ground mingling with the scent of the grasses. It's all very pleasant."

Dylan seemed impatient for her to go on. "And the night?"

"The night holds a special magic. Something not seen, felt or heard in the light of day. It is what I miss most about India—the black jungle and its mystery. But even here, the park turns into a special place at night—a place for the wild."

A great sadness came with remembering the jungle, and it robbed some of her pleasure. But it was not strong enough to dim the warmth that lingered in her heart when she recalled her nights with Kala Bagh. "The noises are not as defined, more subtle and soft. When all is hushed, you can hear the water flowing in the streams, their melodies accented by the distant howl of a hound, quickly mimicked by others. The sound is woeful and sad. Perhaps they, too, wish to run free in the night."

Neither of them spoke then, afraid words would break the enchanted spell woven about them. Finally, in a hushed voice, she went on. "In the darkness the wind whistles its song, its mournful wail stronger in the silence of night. You can hear the snap of a twig, the step of a foe. Even the ragged breathing of an intruder is loud in the night. You can smell the tangy scent of the dampness that clings to the earth and the sharp odor of black thunderheads."

Ariel had stopped, her eyes closed, imagining all she spoke of. Suddenly, she became aware of all the talking she had been doing. She opened her eyes, almost shyly. "I'm sorry to chatter on so. I must be boring you."

Her apology brought Dylan from his own reverie, her softly spoken love of the night bringing a strange reaction of his own. She made him want to see it and feel it, as she did. But mostly, he wanted to share it with Ariel. "Don't you know there isn't anything you say or do that bores me?"

A muted blush colored the high bones of her face. "No, I didn't."

Dylan longed to take her delicate hand into his, but he knew Bryce was not far off. Dylan restrained the urge and started walking again. "You are so different, Ariel."

"So I have been told," Ariel mumbled.

Dylan saw her change in mood and added, "I did not mean it as taken, Ariel." He stopped walking again and looked directly into her hurt-filled eyes. "You are a true delight, like a breath of fresh air."

Ariel felt a tremor rise from deep in her belly, immediately followed by a heated flush of pleasure.

"Would you meet me here in the morning?" Dylan cast a sidelong glance toward Bryce, who still remained out of hearing. "Without those two."

"Why?" she asked before thinking. Then she blushed profusely. "I meant to say . . . I don't think I should."

Dylan grinned in a devilish way. "I promise to behave myself. I won't take advantage of you."

"I didn't think you would," Ariel rushed on, finding his teasing even more flustering than his heated looks. "I'm sure you are always the gentleman, Dylan. I didn't mean to infer—"

He put up his finger to stop her. "I am not always the gentleman, my tigress, and I would like nothing more than to take advantage of your generous nature. I like your company, and I like seeing you smile. And . . ." He paused, uncertain of what it was he wanted to say. "I would like to hold your hand without Bryce standing guard over you."

"I don't think that would be proper," Ariel answered in a breathless whisper.

Dylan looked up to the sky a moment, then back down at her. "Somehow, I don't believe it truly matters to you what is proper and what is not."

Taking a deep, settling breath to gather her courage, Ariel replied honestly. "You're right. I don't care what they think or anyone else. I merely try to do what is expected of me."

"Why is that?"

"It makes life easier, Dylan. And, for the time being, that is what I want. No, it is what I *need*." She turned pleading eyes to him. "Please, don't complicate my life."

Dylan felt his heart twist. He wanted to do as she asked, but he couldn't. "I want to be a part of your life, not to complicate it."

"Why is that?"

"I don't know," he said, leaving them in silence once more.

They walked on; then he said quietly, "I only know the need, Ariel. I don't know the answer."

Ariel saw Bryce and Diedra returning. She turned to Dylan to say goodbye. Surprising herself, she said, "I will see you in the morning."

Chapter Seven

Dylan stood in the drizzling rain, watching daylight finger through clouds hanging low, casting the new day in damp darkness.

Why was he here in the rain waiting for someone who most likely wouldn't come? Why was he doing this? The last thing he needed was to get involved with Ariel Lockwood. He was here to find a murderer. Nothing more.

"You're a fool," Dylan mumbled, aggravated with himself in the most awful way. He pulled the collar of his coat up around his neck. The wind chilled him, but he continued to wait.

Leave. His mind continued to do battle with his heart. *Just leave now and be done with her. Let her marry Bryce. Let her uncle take the responsibility of the whole matter.* As he rolled these thoughts about a clear image came to his mind—Ariel bending to

Bryce's verbal abuse, the fiery flash of her eyes masked behind blushed indifference.

It bothered him that she did this, that she allowed her fiancé to bully her. But what did he really expect her to do? Obviously, she knew better than he. She said she had her reasons. It was best he did not interfere. This brought him back to the beginning. He should just keep his nose out of her business. He should not pull Ariel into his life.

Still, his feet would not move. What his mind wanted was in direct conflict with what his heart demanded. His heart told him to see her, to get to know her better, to . . .

"I didn't think you would be here."

Her lilting voice drove through him like a herd of horses, trampling all logical thought and decision. Dylan turned to her, his eyes searching for the light of her golden ones. He found them and was lost.

"I practically bullied you into coming. I dared not stay away." He held out his hand. She hesitated, and he held his breath, waiting, fearing she would reject his small gesture. Somehow, to hold her hand meant everything.

Ariel saw his doubt, the reflection of it clear upon his face. She gave him her hand. At the contact of his flesh upon her flesh, she felt the warmth rush through her. His long fingers threaded through her smaller ones, work-roughened skin beneath her touch. His hands were masculine and reassuring, unlike Bryce's soft ones.

Dylan asked, "Are you cold?"

She looked away and whispered, "No, I'm fine."

"I'm a cad to make you come out in the rain," Dylan said.

"No." Ariel turned her face back to his, a bit of delight touching the softened lines. "I love the rain. It does not bother me to get wet."

A vision of Dylan came to mind, standing at the wheel of his ship, wind and rain pelting him. Vicious, yet wonderful. "If it weren't quite so cold, I would let it fall on my face. I have always liked the feel of it."

"The first time I saw you, you were walking in the rain."

"Yes, I had been in the jungle with Kala Bagh."

"You must miss Kala Bagh terribly."

A sadness overwhelmed Ariel, and her eyes filled with tears. "Yes. I feel . . ." She paused, searching for the right word. "Incomplete." She knew it was a strange thing to say, yet Dylan seemed to understand what she meant.

Dylan recalled the big cat touching her cheek with affection—no, reverence. Something yanked at Dylan's heart, bringing pain. *How strange. I can almost feel her unhappiness.* "Perhaps, someday, you can go back to him."

A single tear overflowed onto her rose-tinted cheek. It rolled down to her chin, then disappeared into the raindrops that clung to her hooded cloak. "Not perhaps, Dylan. I *will* return to him. I must."

He heard urgency in her words, strong will and determination to do as she must. Something kept him from asking what would happen if she did not.

Instead he asked her another question. "How did you two come to be together? It is a rather strange friendship."

"My mother was in labor with me. It was warm, and her bedroom doors were left open to let the breeze into the room."

Ariel paused, remembering the tale her father had told her many times while growing up. "A wounded tiger came into her room, carrying her newborn cub. At first my mother was frightened; then she realized there was no threat. The tigress gave the kitten to my mother, then died. At that moment, my mother felt me coming and called for Mrs. Applegate and my father. She made my father promise to care for the orphaned animal."

The sadness of what came next was always there, the years having not eased the pain of loss. "My mother died only minutes after giving birth to me. My father kept his promise to her. Of course, Kala Bagh grew much faster than I. By the time I was walking, he was nearly full-grown. The first time I followed him into the jungle I was only two. My father nearly went crazy looking for me, but he soon learned Kala Bagh was the best of baby-sitters. He also learned I could not be kept from going with my Kala Bagh."

"Kala Bagh," Dylan repeated. "What does it mean?"

"It means black tiger." Ariel felt a comforting warmth at his interest. "When the mother tiger gave him to my mother, he was still covered in blood. He looked black, and the servants called him the *kala bagh*, the black tiger. It stuck as his name." She felt for the chain around her neck, for the small object hanging from it.

"What is that?" he asked, his intense gaze drawn to her delicate hand.

"My father had one of Kala Bagh's baby canines made into a necklace for me. I feel Kala Bagh close to me when I wear it, so I never take it off."

"You must not like England," he said.

"Why do you think that?"

He wasn't certain why, until he gave it more thought. "I guess I just assumed after living such a free life in India with Kala Bagh in the jungles, this would be very stifling. All this . . ."

"Civilization," Ariel finished.

"Yes." The vivid image of her walking from the jungle in the rain was clear in his mind. "You were like a wild tigress yourself in India."

Ariel turned away, her longing for those simpler days so strong it nearly destroyed her. How she wanted to roam the night darkened jungles with Kala Bagh. How she wanted to feel that freedom once again. But, it was not to be—not yet.

Dylan pulled her chin around so he could look into her eyes once again. "They have tamed you, my tigress. They have taken the flame from your eyes."

Ariel's lips were parted, and her lower one trembled at his gently spoken words. Her tongue darted out and licked dryness away.

The simple action was Dylan's undoing. He leaned closer and tasted the softness of her, molding his mouth over her moist lips. A sweet warmth flooded through his veins; then as the kiss deepened, so did the heat within him, turning from sweet to savage.

He pulled away, suddenly aware of what he was doing. "I'm sorry," he mumbled, feeling too close to being out of control. "I promised to behave, didn't I?"

Disappointment surged, its strength taking Ariel by surprise. "Yes," she whispered weakly, "you did promise."

Looking sincerely rebuffed, Dylan nodded. "That I did." He hung his head in mock shame. "Though I must confess it was worth going back on my word for the brief moment of pleasure."

Awkwardness made her look away. "I should go."

"Must you?"

"Yes, I must."

As Ariel made her way home, her mind whirled in total disarray. How could she let him do that? How could she enjoy it so much? Over and over she replayed the scene, and over and over she came to the same conclusion. She was a fool, a complete and utter fool. Her life was already complicated, too complicated for her to fall in love. In love!

She hadn't thought about that. "What a mess," she mumbled to herself. She didn't want to marry Bryce Harrington. She didn't want Dylan Christianson in her life. All she wanted was to go home to India and to Kala Bagh.

"But he is," she told herself, uncertain why Dylan was now a part of her life.

Ariel walked around to the back entrance of the house and slipped inside. She stopped and removed her cloak, shaking the rain from it before moving into the back stairway. She went upstairs, pleased to find the house still quiet. She moved down the hall to her room.

"Where have you been, Ariel?"

Her uncle's voice stopped her. She turned to face him. "I went for a walk, Uncle."

A frown creased his tall forehead. His extremely large lower lip pushed out. "Alone?"

She nodded.

"Hasn't Margaret told you before a lady doesn't venture out alone?" Light hazel eyes studied her.

"Yes, but I forgot." Ariel really didn't need her aunt's displeasure right now. "I guess it's all the things I have on my mind to prepare for the wedding. I just wanted a bit of fresh air."

The mere mention of the wedding softened Henry. "I do understand the adjustment you've had to make, Ariel. Margaret doesn't need to know about this."

"Yes, I believe it best for everyone if we keep this to ourselves, Uncle Henry." She gave him a quick kiss on the cheek. "I won't forget again. I promise."

Henry went on his way, and Ariel breathed a deep sigh of relief. She ducked into her room and found she was trembling from the emotion running through her. If her aunt and uncle found out about Dylan . . . if Bryce found out. She shouldn't chance Bryce's anger for this man—not any man. Shame washed over Ariel at her foolishness.

"What a mess," she repeated. She was playing a selfish game. No, she was playing a dangerous game. If Bryce Harrington found out, he would go mad, and, somehow, she did not think she would survive such a catastrophe. It would be devastating for her aunt and uncle as well. It definitely would be best if no one found out about Dylan Christianson.

Chapter Eight

The grass was wet between Ariel's toes. A slight chill brought bumps to her skin. It had rained all day, leaving the night damp and cold, but Ariel didn't mind. She merely pulled the cloak she wore tighter about her shoulders. At least she had taken the time to grab it.

Intensely, she studied the darkness that surrounded her, the shadows that moved in the muted light like old friends. A certain warmth always permeated her soul when she was out at night, out in the park where she felt free.

Ariel knew she needed to sleep, but she preferred the weariness she felt when awake to the torture her dreams brought. It was a vicious circle; the less rest she got, the worse the nightmares became.

Reaching her favorite tree, Ariel climbed into its wide, comforting limbs. She sought solace and settled against the broad trunk. Then she stretched out on a limb face down, clasped her hands beneath her face and let her legs dangle free on each side of the branch. Her cape covered her, and if someone had looked up into the leafy branches, they would have thought she was a black animal of some sort.

Disturbing thoughts eased from her as the silence settled in, broken now and then by the howl of a dog or the cry of an owl. The leaves quaked in the gentle wind, their shuffling a soft hum on the night air. Slowly, her eyes closed.

"Leave me be."

Ariel came awake, instantly tense and alert.

"Come now, old man. Give it o'er."

She saw a giant towering over an aged man, his back bent from years of hard work. The fickle clouds skidded past the moon, and its yellowed light revealed his whitened hair and gnarled hands, reflections of a difficult life.

"I seen what was given t' ye, and I want it."

The giant's voice was gravelly and rough, his speech slurred from too much drink. A large hand reached out and grabbed the collar of the old man's worn coat. "I've a mighty thirst, and the coin in yer pocket will see t' it."

"I have no coin."

A snort reached Ariel's ears. She could not believe her eyes when the big man lifted the other into the air. "I don't want t' hurt ye none, but I will if ye don't stop yer lyin' ways. I saw the gent give o'er the coin.

101

and from the sound of it, it were plenty."

"No," stuttered his victim, fear clear in the single word.

"Yer lyin' and I do not take kindly t' it." The snorting sound turned into a wicked laugh, and he easily hefted the old man higher. "I'll be takin' the coin and leavin' yer dead bones behind."

Just as his huge fist raised to strike, Ariel jumped from the tree and landed on his broad back. She was furious he threatened the old man, her own safety secondary to her anger. She dug her fingernails into the flesh of the big man's face at the same moment he flung her from him. His yell of pain was followed by her cry of fury. She rose from the ground and lunged at him again, aware but unheedful of his size and strength.

His surprise took some of the power from his blow, but all the same it sent her flying back onto the ground again. Common sense would have kept her down, but in her red haze she pushed it aside in her mind. Primal instinct surged through Ariel's blood. Her hand clamped onto a large piece of wood, broken off the tree that branched out above them. She came up swinging, her makeshift weapon serving a smart blow to his head.

He just stood there, stunned, not only from the injury but from pure shock. She watched him closely and became keenly aware of his great height and superior strength. He took a wobbling step forward. She braced herself, her stick poised to swing again.

His brow wrinkled, as if confused; then his

mouth opened to speak. Nothing came out. He started to sway back and forth, reminding her of a large willow bending to the wind. When he fell to his knees, the look of surprise remained on his face, and when he toppled, his fall was slow and easy.

Ariel grimaced at the sound of him hitting the ground, his full weight landing hard as an anvil dropped from a second story window. Once the threat was gone, she experienced the fear that should have forewarned her. She threw her club aside and turned to see if the old man was all right. He was gone.

Thinking it a good idea, she gave the giant one last quick glance and started to leave. But something kept her there. She turned back to the silent form. He was so quiet.

Was he dead?

A new terror overwhelmed her. *I've killed him!*

Ariel began to shake all over, and a sudden weakness made her knees give way. Taking a deep breath, she reached out to see if her greatest fear was true. Her fingers trembled when she poked at him, and her eyes closed in reflex, expecting him to jump up and pound her into the earth.

He did nothing. Panic climbed from deep within her, making her heart pound viciously.

He is dead. What am I going to do?

Visions of her aunt and uncle flashed in her troubled mind, followed by the clamoring of Bryce's angry voice. Ariel rested her head in her hands and rocked back and forth on her heels, her hair dragging on the ground.

A rough hand clamped around Ariel's wrist. Her heart jumped into her throat. She choked on a scream and fell back. She pushed out with her feet and hit his chest all in the same movement. Ariel twisted free and scrambled out of reach. Then she ran as fast as her feet could carry her.

At the edge of the park, Ariel stopped and listened. When she heard the giant's grumbling, relief flooded her mind and caution prompted her to seek cover to avoid another confrontation. She hid.

Her victim staggered out of the trees, nursing his aching head and bloodied nose. Ariel watched him walk off down the street cursing. Never had she felt more like crying. When she thought it safe, she ran home.

By the time she reached her room, she collapsed onto her bed and wept. Exactly for what she wasn't sure. Exhausted, physically and emotionally, her mind turned to Dylan in need.

Why? The only thing she was certain of was the knowledge that if he were to hold her hand, it would bring her comfort.

Ariel pulled her knees up under her chin and wrapped her arms about her legs. For the longest time, she sat upon her bed and stared at the walls of her room.

What am I to do, Dylan Christianson? I think I'm in love with you.

Ariel's sleep-riddled mind started to comprehend that Diedra, of all people, was in her room.

"Come on, you lazy little chit." Diedra slapped at the pile of covers with her riding crop.

Ariel bolted from under her covers and sat up. "Diedra?" was all she managed.

"Ariel, even I am up at this time in the afternoon."

A scowl marked Diedra's forehead. Ariel finally voiced the question fumbling about her garbled head. "What are you doing here?"

"I'm here to take you riding, my dear. Can't you tell?"

Her riding habit made that clear enough, but that wasn't what Ariel really needed to know. Certain she wouldn't ever know the truth, she dragged herself out of bed.

A silky eyebrow shot up at Ariel's appearance. "You look positively horrid. Why, by the looks of you, I'd think you had been out all night."

Astute gray eyes checked out her grass-stained feet, and honest shock registered in them. Her brows raised. "You didn't . . ." she started. Ariel glared at her. For possibly the first time in her life, Diedra did not venture further.

"If you don't feel like riding, I understand." Now she was searching for a way out. "We can do it another day. After all, we will be family soon."

It was all a bunch of nonsense, and Ariel knew it. And that was the second time someone had reminded her they would be family soon. It did nothing to brighten her mood. "Yes," she drawled, "we will be family soon. Isn't that a pleasant thought?"

Diedra seemed to experience what Ariel thought might be another first. Diedra didn't know what to say. So she left, closing the door behind her a bit harder than necessary.

"Good riddance," Ariel growled, determination renewed inside her. Never, not ever in her lifetime, would she become that woman's family. Never!

Stomping over to the bell cord, she yanked it angrily. Her head ached, and her jaw was sore. Moving to the mirror, she examined her face. No discoloration showed where the giant had cuffed her. She opened her mouth wide, then shut it, making certain all worked well. It did.

Moving to the window, she pulled the drape aside just enough to look down upon the street. Bryce stood on the walk, apparently waiting for Diedra to return with her. Ariel watched his displeasure when Diedra appeared alone.

Diedra allowed Bryce to help her back onto her mare, his face scrunched up in a scowl. He mounted his own horse. "Isn't Ariel coming down?"

"No," she snapped, her irritation rising. "She didn't seem to be feeling well."

"Oh." Bryce's mouth opened, then snapped shut. He looked like a small boy being denied candy.

"Don't pout so, Bryce. It doesn't become you." She slapped her riding crop on her mount's backside, prompting the sleek mare into a trot. "You can see her later."

Bryce cast one last sultry glance at the upper windows of the house, knowing which one Ariel hid behind. He kicked his stallion into a trot. His day was ruined. It was Ariel's fault. She rarely spoke to him and only curtly when asked a direct question. This made him wonder why he sought her company so often. He did get great pleasure from looking at her. Ariel was a rare beauty. He also enjoyed parading her around, much like the feeling he experienced when showing off his trophies. He could see the envy and desire in other men's eyes.

She would be a good wife, an obedient wife. He had no doubt of that. The fiery side of her nature would give way soon enough, and the taming of her spirit certainly would be entertaining. He was looking forward to it.

Bryce smiled, and he considered how good life would be. He was filthy rich, extremely handsome, and his political plans were in play. Soon he would be appointed Governor of the Bombay Province, and he would have the power he longed for. Money and power over life, death—and Ariel. He would have it all.

"My, my," Diedra crooned. "What has you so happy, dear brother? One minute ago you were brooding over your true love."

He turned to her, never giving up the good feeling. "I just realized what a lucky man I am."

"Lucky? You've never struck me as a man to think of luck."

This made him laugh outright, something he rarely did. "Now, don't get me wrong, Dedi." He noticed the slight twinge on her face at the use of his pet name. Every once in a while, it slipped out, a leftover from their childhood days. "I believe I am deserving of such luck."

"You think you're lucky to get a woman like Ariel?"

"Yes." He knew this was leading to disaster, but he went on. "She's perfect. In every way."

"She's perfect in every way," Diedra mimicked. "Bryce, are you blind? She's a witch, an uncivilized witch."

"Now, Diedra, I realize you don't like her, but then you don't like any female who detracts from you. She's beautiful, and you can't bear it."

"You wouldn't have thought her beautiful this morning. She was a fright. I certainly don't know what she did last night, but she looked horrid. Positively horrid."

This brought Bryce's full attention back to her. "What do you mean?"

A look of pure satisfaction lit her eyes. "I mean she was up to something last night. It was apparent. And she was hostile toward me."

"It's a natural reaction to be hostile with you," he started, no longer happy and carefree. "Your personality brings that out in people, Diedra dear."

Diedra puffed up. "If I were you, I'd be finding out who Ariel really is. What you see will not be what you get. I'd bet on it."

"You'd bet on anything. As much as you lose at the gaming tables, I don't think I'll get too worried."

"Do as you wish, Bryce, but don't be angry when I turn out to be right. Mark my word, Ariel's hiding something, brother dear. I know about these things."

* * *

"Are you feeling better, Ariel?"

Bryce's question brought Ariel's shadowed eyes up, the slightest flash of uncertainty making him alert to her answer. "I'm feeling fine."

It told him nothing. "Diedra mentioned you weren't feeling well when we came by earlier this afternoon. I'm glad to see you are better."

Ariel remained silent, leaving the burden of small talk to Bryce.

"You seem quiet."

"I have nothing to say."

A muscle in his jaw twitched, and he rubbed it until it relaxed. "What did you do last night?" A direct question he hoped she could not avoid.

"Nothing. I slept, as most people do."

It was a lie, and he knew it. "You did not go out?"

She met his hard look, and she did not bat an eye. Neither did she back down. "No. Why do you ask?"

Bryce forced a shrug.

"I don't know. It must have been something Diedra said." Bryce ground his teeth together in vexation.

"What did she say?" Ariel asked.

Bryce considered using force, grabbing her and shaking the truth from her. She seemed too calm, too collected. "She said you looked a mess." He looked away, his neck stiff with anger. "Like you had been outside, or something like that."

"I was outside."

He turned back to her, shock registering on his face. "Whatever for?"

"I woke up from a bad dream and needed some fresh air. I came out here." Her hand waved through the air indicating the garden they now stood in. "I spent some time weeding the flower beds. It seemed to help. I was a lot dirtier than I thought when I returned to bed. And that is how Diedra found me. Quite grimy and wild-looking, I'm sure."

Relief came to his face before he could hide it. Instantly, his cool veneer returned. "Well, I knew there was a logical explanation, but you know Diedra, always suspicious and looking to cause trouble."

"Yes," Ariel mumbled.

Another thought came to his mind. "I do hope you don't weed the flowers very often, Ariel. It isn't proper. There are servants to do that sort of thing."

Ariel could almost see his nose rising into the air. She wondered what he did in the rain. He could drown. "I do it only at night, in secret." Just then, Cat jumped up on the bench between them. Ariel tried to intercept him before he irritated Bryce—or before Bryce irritated the cat—but to her surprise, Bryce reached out and scratched the cat's head.

"Still, you'd best not do it at all. I don't want your delicate hands roughened by manual labor." He drew in a deep breath, puffing his chest out like a cock. Bored with his display of affection, he brushed the cat aside. "You have a position to maintain, my dear. You will be my wife soon. That is a serious undertaking and one you should consider more than you do. For your own sake, as well as mine."

"I will try." Ariel hurried inside, leaving Bryce to follow.

Chapter Nine

The ballroom was ablaze with light, hundreds of candles flickering their golden glow on the happy people. Unimaginable costumes met Ariel's curious gaze, but the exuberance of the others did not warm her.

Ariel didn't feel prepared for Diedra's party. Bryce's visit the evening before still weighed heavily on her mind. Had his suspicions been put to rest? Ariel decided she must be more careful. Worry mingled with the new and tender emotions she had discovered, the thrill dampened by the risk of it. She couldn't be in love. Not now. The turmoil drained her.

"Who is he?" she heard a breathy woman ask.

She turned to see who the woman found so interesting. Her gaze met blue fire, and it took her breath away.

Dylan was dressed in a pirate's costume. No other could have suited him so well. Ariel turned away, unable to deal with the havoc his presence created inside her.

Ariel felt Dylan's closeness even before he touched her elbow. The glass of champagne she held threatened to reveal her trembling hand, but she quickly steadied it with her other hand.

"Miss Lockwood."

Dylan's voice was lazy and soft. It created a warmth in her belly, but when she turned and their gazes met the warmth became heat rushing through her entire body.

"Captain Christianson, what a pleasure to see you again."

"Yes, it is."

Three simple words—*yes, it is*—and she was nearly swooning like a schoolgirl. She hated being so foolish.

"Where's Bryce?"

The mention of Bryce's name shattered the heat and the excitement. She shrugged. "I don't know. He disappeared with his friends."

"He doesn't seem very attentive."

If Dylan was merely providing polite conversation, Ariel would just as soon he said nothing. "Sometimes I'm not very good company." Ariel did not like thinking of the possibility of Bryce's company.

"I would think it's more the company you keep, Ariel."

Dylan's gaze was like a flame scorching Ariel to the bone. He reached out and took her empty glass. She jumped away at his touch.

113

"I thought I might get you some more wine."

"Yes, that would be nice." Ariel felt a fool. "Thank you."

A delightful twinkle lit his eyes, sending her further into emotional tumult, but it was his smile that made her weak in the knees.

"I'll be right back. Don't go anywhere."

"Of course not," she mumbled, looking away. Why on earth would she go anywhere? Then again, maybe she should run away. It would be best to get away from his unmanageable effect on her, to get away from her own . . .

Dylan returned before she decided. She took the glass of wine he offered her.

"You looked like you were about to flee."

"I was," she confessed. She couldn't pretend with him, but everything else she did or thought was uncertain where Dylan was concerned. The warmth, the noise, the strain of his presence . . .

"Do you want me to go away, Ariel?"

It was a simple question. No, it was an impossibly complex question. "Yes," she blurted out. "No . . ." she countered immediately.

Dylan smiled. "Which is it? Go or stay?"

Ariel didn't know, and Dylan seemed pleased by this. "Are you going to ask me to dance or not?"

This widened his smile even further. "I would love to dance."

Before she had time to reconsider, Dylan had placed their glasses aside and whisked her out onto the dance floor. Her feet barely touched the glossy wood. He seemed to carry her in time to the music.

"What is wrong, Ariel? You don't seem yourself."

Ariel lifted her head and met his steamy look. "You're making me nervous, Dylan Christianson," she answered honestly.

"Me?" he responded, humor lighting the dark blue depths of his eyes again. "Why would I make you nervous?"

Unable to pull her gaze away from his mouth, Ariel found herself watching him form the words. His lips seemed to caress the word *why*, and she wanted to touch them. She had to concentrate hard on his question.

"Because I find myself powerfully attracted to you."

Had she really said that out loud? His look told her she had.

"Is that bad?"

Another question. So many questions! "Yes. I shouldn't be. I'm engaged . . ." The word nearly choked her. "To another man."

The eyes that studied her so closely darkened. "And why is that?"

Her head was buzzing. The room was a blur as he continued to swing her around. A kaleidoscope of color and noise closed in on her. "I can't breathe."

Dylan danced her past the crowd of people and out the patio doors. When Dylan came to an abrupt halt, she pressed against him so closely she smelled his wonderful muskiness.

He held her still but pulled back so he could look into her face. Worry marked his handsome forehead. "Are you all right, Ariel?"

"It all seems to crowd in on me, and I can't

breathe. The people, the noise . . ." Ariel took a deep breath of the fresh air to dispel the lightness in her head and rid her senses of his scent. "I'm not very good at parties." Noticing Dylan's frown, she reached out and smoothed the wrinkles out. "There, that's better."

"You haven't answered my question."

"I'm sorry. I don't even remember what you asked."

"I asked," Dylan stressed for a second time, "why is it you are engaged to Harrington? You obviously don't like him."

Ariel found herself agreeing quite readily with his assumption. "Yes, I obviously don't like him."

"Why are you going to marry him, Ariel?"

"At the moment," she mumbled, "I don't know."

Ariel found herself wanting something she couldn't have. She wanted Dylan to pull her into his strong arms and take her lips to his. She wanted . . .

Ariel stood on her tiptoes and slid her arms around Dylan's neck. Almost lip to lip, she whispered, "What I do know is that I want you, Dylan. And I shouldn't."

She kissed Dylan. Ariel felt his arms wrap tightly about her. The need within her deepened, abruptly, almost violently. She gave herself over to the feel of his lips smothering hers, drawing the passion from her, stirring her need into desire.

Suddenly, Dylan was pulling away, undraping her arms from his neck. Ariel opened her eyes.

"Ariel, you don't realize what you're doing or what you're saying. I think we'd better go back inside."

As if she were an errant child, Dylan turned her about and marched her back into the crowded ballroom. It wasn't until she was standing alone that Ariel realized what had happened. Anger was the first feeling to push through her confusion, then the most terrible hurt she had experienced in a very long time.

"There she is." Diedra pointed at Ariel. "Really, Bryce, I told you she was still here."

"I've been looking for you, Ariel."

Bryce's scowl told Ariel he was not happy with her. "I've been right here," she lied, blinking back the tears that filled her eyes.

Bryce seemed to know it was a lie, but let it be. "You look a bit flushed. Are you not feeling well?"

"Yes, dear," Diedra added with a coy smile, "you are a bit rosy in the cheeks."

"I think this should help," Dylan offered, coming up from behind. He handed a cool drink to Ariel.

Ariel was unable to look at him.

"How very sweet of you, Dylan." Diedra's voice took on a calculated sweetness. "You make a dashing pirate, Lord Christy."

Bryce seemed impatient with the polite chitchat. "I should have known you'd be here, Dylan." The accusing look he cast his sister filled in the blanks.

"Bryce, it *is* my party, and I can invite whom I want. And it gives me pleasure to have Dylan here." She placed a possessive hand on his forearm.

"I can see that," Bryce growled through clenched teeth.

Ariel wanted to scream. "Did you want something, Bryce?"

"Just your company, Ariel."

Ariel wanted to leave.

"How very sweet," Diedra cooed.

"If you will excuse me," Ariel said. She all but fled to the ladies' room, seeking the small comfort it provided. Tears she had forced back earlier now fell onto her face. Ariel slapped them away. Anger, hurt, humiliation and exasperation all worked inside of her. Finally, she gave in to it all and lay her head into her hands.

"Ariel."

Hearing Diedra's sharp voice, Ariel wiped her face and steeled herself for the encounter.

"I've been sent in to see if you're all right."

The tone, the look, even her jerky movements signaled Diedra's mood. "You needn't have bothered yourself. As I said earlier, I'm just fine."

"Personally . . ." Diedra paused and examined her nails. "I don't care one way or the other, but my brother feels differently than I do, even after you publicly embarrassed him at your engagement party. You just can't account for some men's taste. I think his lust has blinded him."

"If you can convince him the error of his ways, please do. I would be forever grateful."

It was blunt, straight to the point, honest. Diedra was stunned. "You don't want to marry Bryce?"

"No, Diedra. I'd sooner fall into a pit of snakes."

Diedra's eyes narrowed. "You want to marry Dylan!"

It was an accusation fired with jealousy. "I don't want to marry anyone, but especially not your brother."

This did not appease Diedra. "You're lying, you little witch! I've seen the way you look at him, the way you go all soft when he's near."

Silence hung in the air until Ariel was able to muster up a denial. "You're imagining it, Diedra."

"Am I?" Diedra's eyes narrowed into hard little slits. "Has Dylan told you why he's staying in London instead of returning to sea?"

"Of course not. It's none of my business."

This made Diedra perk up, an irritating smile curling up her red lips. "Well, I know. He's come back to claim his inheritance and title."

"So?"

"You see . . ." She paused for effect, then Diedra's voice took on the tone of an adult speaking to a slow-witted child. "Ariel, dear, ten years ago, before Dylan went to sea, he asked me to marry him."

Ariel knew little about Dylan, but she couldn't help but be surprised. As much as she wanted to call Diedra a liar, Ariel couldn't.

Diedra was gloating openly now. "I couldn't marry him then. He wasn't heir to his father's title or wealth. His older brother Robert was. So I married someone else. But now, it's perfect! I'm a widow, and Dylan is Lord Christy. It just couldn't have worked out better."

"Dylan has asked you to marry him?" The question came out a strangled whisper as pain grappled with her other emotions.

"Not yet. But I've never been more certain of anything in all my life. So you see, Ariel, you might as well marry my brother. Dylan's mine. Always has been. He's waited all these years for us to be together."

It was such a definite statement that Ariel felt ill. Whether she really believed Diedra or not, overwhelming hurt attacked her. Regardless of the emotional war going on inside of her, Ariel maintained a calm, collected manner. She would not allow Diedra to know it mattered dearly to her. If Bryce were to find out how she felt . . .

"As I said, I don't wish to marry anyone." She had to take a deep breath to finish her statement. "Dylan's all yours, Diedra."

Before Diedra could say more, Ariel turned and left the room. It was time to go home.

Bryce had apparently been watching, and before Ariel got close to the front door he had her by the elbow. The voices, clinking of glasses, laughter and swishing movement around them were an unsettling blur.

"Ariel, are you going somewhere?"

"I'm going home, Bryce."

He stopped, forcing her to stop beside him. "It's not time to go yet, my dear. The party's just started."

"I don't care. I'm leaving."

Bryce tightened his grip, finding pleasure in the pain he caused. "But I have some news I'd like to share with my bride-to-be."

How Ariel hated that term.

Forcibly, Bryce guided her to a less crowded corner of the room.

Ariel pulled away, her anger quite apparent. "All right, what is it?" She wanted to get this over with and go home.

"I thought you might be interested in knowing my plans for us after we are married."

"Actually, that is the last thing I want to know."

Anger flooded Bryce. "Regardless, I will tell you anyway."

Gritting his teeth at her uncaring look, as honest as her words, he continued. "After we are married, we will live in India. I have been appointed Governor of the Bombay Province."

Ariel remained still, saying nothing. Finally, Bryce took her hand in an odd show of tenderness, his temper retreating for the moment. "I'll be taking you home, Ariel. We can even live at your father's plantation part of the year. Wouldn't you like that?"

Bryce found himself wanting her approval. At some time during the evening he began to yearn for the looks she gave Christianson instead of the hate he always saw in her golden eyes. He wanted something he had not expected, something Ariel wasn't giving him. "Doesn't that please you, darling?"

The color drained from Ariel's face, leaving her ashen. She licked the dryness from her lips, then spoke. "No, it doesn't please me."

Genuine confusion overwhelmed Bryce. He had never tried pleasing anyone other than himself, and he was already regretting trying now. "And why not?"

"Why not?" Ariel's tone made it clear he should know the answer. "You steal away all my money and my home. Then you dare to suggest the possibility of living on the plantation you took from me—and you expect me to be happy, even grateful?"

"I didn't make your uncle gamble away your inheritance." He didn't like her manner. Not at all.

Ariel's face shone with her fury and hatred. "You are despicable. You probably cheated."

Bryce's hand itched to slap her, but he knew he couldn't. Not here, not now. Later. Yes, later he would teach her to curb her tongue. "You are lucky to be where you are, Ariel. Otherwise I would teach you not to speak to me that way."

It was a clear enough threat, but it seemed to have no effect on Ariel. She shrugged. "It must be my lucky day."

It was an ironic statement meant more for herself than Bryce. Ariel was thinking just the opposite. Bitterness from the last hour left her finally numb. She knew the danger of pushing Bryce too far, but indifference led her down its rocky road.

Bryce, on the other hand, was livid, the look in his eyes murderous. His hand clamped about her arm for a second time, and he all but dragged her from the house. Ariel should have been afraid, but she wasn't. Instead, she laughed. An even deeper color came to his face, an even harder look to his cold eyes.

"Bryce, are you going to take me into the gardens and murder me?"

It was a likely possibility, but still she provoked him further. Ariel was saying things she knew she shouldn't.

When they were outside, Bryce flung her against a brick wall then planted his arms on either side of her, pinning her in. "At this moment, I could very easily do something I might regret later, my sweet. Your tongue is vicious, and I feel the need to silence it."

Ariel tried to turn away, but his hand pulled her face back toward his. Still, she felt no fear. "Perhaps you should reconsider our marriage. Can you stand my tongue for the rest of your life?"

A smile played on his lips, relieving the ugliness of his anger. "I assure you, Ariel, you will learn to curb it soon enough."

"I don't know." Ariel again made light of the situation. "I can be stubborn, obstinate, willful—"

Bryce yanked back her head with a handful of hair. "You will learn," he demanded in a harsh whisper, just before his lips claimed the mouth that defied him.

"Ariel, are you out here?"

Pulling back, Bryce swore beneath his breath, then let her go. Diedra and Dylan came into sight.

"There you are." Diedra smiled at having found them.

"Are you feeling better?" Dylan asked.

Ariel took her chance. "No, I'm not. I wish to go home."

Bryce stepped forward from the shadows. "I will take you home, Ariel."

Almost too quickly, Ariel objected. "No. There

123

is no reason for your evening to be ruined. As you said, the party is just starting. I will hire a carriage."

Dylan never said a word. His look remained dark and unreadable.

"It's not proper to let you go home alone."

"I will, proper or not." Before anyone said anything more on the matter, Ariel turned and left the garden patio. When she looked back, she saw Dylan keep Bryce from following.

Bryce felt nearly out of control, and Dylan's interference pushed him further.

"I've been meaning to ask if you've been hunting in India lately?" Dylan asked, so casually you would think they were sitting around a fire with a drink in hand.

The air whooshed out of Bryce's chest in a hiss, his amazement at Dylan so complete he didn't have time to mask it. "What?" He was stupefied.

Dylan's smile merely played on Bryce's nerves, bringing suspicion to the front of his mind. "I asked if you've done any hunting in India lately?"

"No." Bryce cleared his throat. "I've become a bit bored with it of late."

"I guess the last hunt you were on must have been last year?"

It was said in a manner of indifference, only Bryce wondered at its intent. "Yes, I suppose that would be the last time."

"I understand that Jason Lockwood finally let you hunt on his plantation."

Bryce did not answer.

"I was surprised. I thought Lockwood was quite

determined that no one hunt on his land. That's the impression I got."

"He changed his mind." Bryce disliked the look in Dylan's eyes.

"Was that before or after his accident?"

Dylan saw the fury play out on Bryce's face before he turned and went inside. Directing his attention to Diedra who still stood nearby, he tipped his hat to her.

"I think it's time to say good night."

Even Diedra was dumbfounded and only nodded in return.

Chapter Ten

"Ariel." Margaret tapped lightly on her door. "Are you still awake?"

Still awake? Ariel feared she would never sleep again. "Yes, Aunt Margaret. Come in."

Margaret came into the darkened room and crossed to the chair where Ariel was sitting. "Dear, is everything all right?"

Ariel placed her hand on her aunt's, resting on the high back of the chair. "Everything is fine, Aunt Margaret."

Her aunt stepped around in front of her. "You came home very early." She smiled, but her eyes gave away her concern.

"I wasn't feeling well."

Margaret bowed her head and looked away. Slowly, she sat in the chair next to Ariel. "I'm

126

so sorry, Ariel. I wish I were strong enough to say you needn't marry Bryce, but I can't."

Looking at Margaret, Ariel was reminded of her father, the resemblance tugging at her heart.

"I'm scared, Ariel."

Never had Ariel seen her aunt show vulnerability. "Don't worry, Aunt Margaret. It will work out. I promise."

Margaret's hazel eyes filled with tears. "Henry hasn't slept well. He . . ."

She didn't finish. Her words choked off.

Ariel watched her aunt bring all her features back under control and dab a lacy handkerchief at the corners of her eyes before it disappeared back into its hiding place in the sleeve of her sitting gown.

"I thought you would love it here, Ariel. The parties, the beautiful gowns, dances and balls. I even had dreams you would fall in love and get married."

This time, it was Ariel who teared up. "Sometimes . . ." Ariel cleared her throat, then continued. "Life doesn't turn out the way we dream it will."

Margaret stood and leaned down to kiss her on the cheek. "Good night, dear."

Margaret shut the door quietly behind her, leaving Ariel to her misery. Tears came to her eyes. Heat scorched her face. Flashes of the evening haunted Ariel with resounding clarity, and with them came a new onslaught of emotions.

Unwilling to live it again, Ariel stood and crossed

to her window. Sleep would not be a comfort tonight.

Dylan watched the upstairs window. He knew from the shadow that moved within Ariel was awake. Somehow, instead of going home, he had ended up here, standing across the street, staring up at her room.

Had he lost all control?

The first raindrops fell on him, but he made no move to leave. He hadn't just lost control; he had lost his mind!

Definitely. Positively. Absolutely!

When Ariel swung open her window, Dylan's heart raced. He couldn't take his eyes from her dark silhouette, certain if he even blinked, she would disappear. He was concentrating so hard he didn't comprehend she had crawled out onto the wide limb of the giant oak, then dropped gracefully onto the dewy grass. When this finally caught hold in his mind, Ariel had already started across the street.

Excitement surged through Dylan when he thought she was coming to him. Ariel had never looked more beautiful. She still had on the costume she wore to the dance—a sari, the same as the first time he had seen her. Her dark auburn hair was loose, hanging free about her shoulders, as it had that night.

The rain came down harder, rousing Dylan from his reverie. Slowly, he came to his senses. And slowly, it dawned on him she was not running to him, but past him. He turned and watched her disappear into the darkness of the park that stood like a wall behind him.

"Ariel," he called out. She did not hear him.

The moment Ariel's feet felt the damp grass cool against their bareness, the burdens eased from her. Like a magic elixir it freed her. Anticipation surged through Ariel, making her all but fly to her special place where the trappings of a civilized world fell away, like the winter fur of an animal shed in late spring.

The doom of her impending marriage no longer weighed heavily on her mind. Even the ache in her heart melted away. Nothing and no one mattered, only the freedom of the night.

"Ariel."

She heard her name called, but it did not find a place in her whirling mind.

"Ariel."

This time she stopped.

Dylan closed the distance between them in seconds. "What on earth are you doing out here in the dark?"

She made no move and did not answer. He stepped closer. "You're soaking wet. Let's go back."

He reached out to take her arm, but she moved away. Concern filled his voice. "What's wrong?"

Still, she did not answer. She heard his words but did not comprehend his question. Only the harried beating of her heart sounded in her ears, driving her further into the wild world. She saw his lips move, forming the words, but she only understood the sensuous movement, the soft lines she ached to touch.

Rain dripped down the squareness of his jaw and onto the sinewy muscle of his neck and under the white collar of his shirt. She knew the look in his eyes, felt the passion ignited within their darkness. The flame he lit inside her became a consuming fire.

Dylan sensed something different about Ariel, like *déjà vu*. The rain had soaked her costume, and it clung to every womanly curve. It was cool, but a warming heat spread through him as his desire rose. His memory whirled back in time to the very first moment he had seen Ariel walking from the jungle with Kala Bagh. It was the same, the aura of wildness about her. A tightness came to his throat, and his heart skipped a beat.

He reached out and touched her cheek. "The tiger sleeps no more."

Dylan's touch made her tremble. Their warmth melted together, building intensity between them. No logical thoughts came to mind. She only knew a great need, so demanding and forceful it could not be denied.

She placed her hand over his, keeping him from pulling away. Ariel kissed his palm, then ran her lips down his finger, her tongue licking the rain from it. Dylan gasped, and when she raised her gaze back to his, the pleasure she'd evoked was clear in his eyes. She smiled.

Her smile held neither innocence nor guilt. Dylan saw only passion, a burning vitality in her eyes. "Ariel, you are a sweet temptation. You'd best stop now. I'll not push you away a second time."

Still, no words of reply came. Ariel stood on tiptoes and kissed him. Dylan drew in a long breath of air. As she sucked the fullness of his lower lip into her mouth he held it. Only when Ariel playfully bit the fleshy softness did he exhale.

"You little minx!"

Dylan grabbed for Ariel as she made to flee, but his hands caught only air.

"Ariel," he called after her just before she disappeared among the shadows. He ran after her.

Ariel watched Dylan as he hunted for her, the lofty perch she had found in a tree giving her a clear view.

"This is not the time to play games."

Before he moved off in another direction, Ariel lowered herself and locked her legs about his lean waist. She felt, more than heard, his deep chuckle as she slid her full weight onto his broad back, wrapping her arms about his neck. She nibbled on his ears, nuzzling in the hair curled about his neck. She smelled the earthy dampness of the park mixed with the musk that was so much a part of the man. It was intoxicating, as was the taste of Dylan's flesh, the feel of it beneath her tongue, each wet caress.

Finally, Ariel allowed Dylan to twist her about until she was nestled comfortably in his arms. The temptation of his lips drew her again. Ariel sought their softness with her own, a gentle uniting of flesh. The warm wetness of his mouth gave her gooseflesh, and a lightness filled her head. Darkness whirled about her.

Dylan's kiss deepened, becoming more demanding, first matching then leading her fervor. She shifted and curled her legs tightly about his waist, freeing his hands to explore. Slowly, his fingers inched beneath the wet sari and up her long legs, over the curve of her hips, finally caressing the indentation of her waist.

Love guided Ariel, its song only passion, its melody strong and sensual. Her hips rocked to the silent music. Dylan's tantalizing hands slid back down her legs, tingling her skin. He moved to the muscles of her buttocks, exploring, reading every inch wrapped about him. He slowly stroked the tip of her feet, twisted securely behind his back, then up to the delicate inner flesh of her thighs that he teased with his thumb.

Ariel reveled in the sensations he aroused. Despite the cool rain still falling on them, she was hot. The heat raced through her blood. She was aflame. But even stronger, building its unbreakable hold on Ariel, was the need—a need that would not be denied.

Dylan raised her and pulled her closer, his mouth seeking the roundness of her breast, the hardened nipple pushed against the see-through dampness of her dress. The warmth of his mouth caused a tightness clear down to the center of her being. Impatient with the fabric covering her, Ariel pulled free of it and let the wrap drop to the ground. She wanted only to feel his lips on her, to feel his flesh against her flesh. The need within her was overwhelming.

A low moan came from Dylan as he whisked away tiny droplets of rain with the tip of his tongue, pulling from her a sound much like a purr. Again he suckled her breast, drawing the need from the pit of her belly to settle lower within her womanhood. Slowly, she began to comprehend what it was she wanted, what it was that would ease this.

Ariel wanted Dylan. She wanted to feel him inside of her, his hardness filling her completely. She pressed harder against him, but it was not enough. Ariel pulled Dylan's lips away from her breast. Gently, she bit his chin, then soothed the playful nip with the tip of her tongue. She licked his waiting lips, then kissed him again.

Dylan lowered her to the grass, a spongy bed that smelled of dampness. Ariel's skin was like silk beneath his fingers, and he could not get close enough. When she attempted to pull his shirt off him, the fabric ripped. Dylan shucked his trousers.

Never before had Dylan known an innocent to react with such abandon, and it fed his own desire. She lay beneath him trembling, her expression telling him all. Dylan's heart tightened, and a strange feeling invaded his being.

"Ariel, I . . ." He wanted to say something, but the words stuck in his throat. She didn't give him a chance to try again.

She needed something more than words, much more. She pulled him closer with her legs. She wanted him to take her to him, to satisfy their needs. Ariel felt his weight along the length of her body. His desire sought her warmth. The silent rhythm still moved Ariel, slow and easy, and she lovingly accepted him within her. The barrier o. her maidenhead gave way to their building urgency, the momentary pain only taking her to a deeper sensuality and surrender.

Dylan made no further attempt to speak. There was no need as he carried her to the ultimate release, fulfilling the demanding need that ruled them both.

Tears stung Ariel's eyes as she clung to Dylan the strong beat of his heart loud in her ears. Only one thought was clear in her head. She loved him Ariel Lockwood loved Dylan Christianson.

Dylan didn't understand what the tears were for He pulled her closer and comforted her. He didn' ask, not wanting to break the silent spell. Soon Ariel's crying gave way to sleep. As the heat of their lovemaking left her, the chill of the night crept in When Dylan felt her shivering, he laid her gently aside and dressed. Gathering her up, he carried her home.

"Hold on, my sweet," he whispered into her ear rousing her just enough for her to do as he asked Years in his ship's riggings made the tree climb with his small burden easy. Within minutes he had her tucked into her bed.

Leaning down, he kissed the pink blush tha remained on her cheek. "Sleep tight, Ariel." Dylar stood with every intention of leaving, but sudder regret at having to separate from her attacked him. He yearned to lie beside her still, her head snuggled into the crook of his arm. He wanted to listen to her soft, even breathing as she slept

feel her next to him, her curves fitted tightly
to him.

Dylan closed his eyes a moment, needing to gather his thoughts. He found only confusion and complication.

Saddened, he left.

Chapter Eleven

Ariel drifted, slow and lazy, half-asleep. Warm and comfortable, she wanted to stay asleep. She snuggled deeper into the covers.

"Dylan," she mumbled. She stretched and yawned, euphoria still clinging to her. Suddenly, she stilled, and reality snuck in on her dreams. Ariel sat up and looked about in momentary confusion. Dylan wasn't here. She was in her room, alone.

Images flooded back, and Ariel felt the blush clear down to her toes. Looking about, she saw her costume on a chair by the window, reminding her she was naked beneath the sheet that now covered her.

"Dear God," she whispered out loud. "What have I done?"

Tears stung her eyes. Ariel hated feeling sorry for

herself and stubbornly blinked them back, but the hurt was not so easy to dispel. Throwing back the covers, she swung her legs over the bed's edge. Sore muscles were a nagging reminder of their night of lovemaking.

"Never . . . never again." Ariel pulled her robe on, taking each movement with care.

A soft knock drew her attention. "Yes?"

Her aunt looked in. "Ariel, dear, Bryce is here to see you." She stepped inside when she saw Ariel. "You're not even dressed, Ariel. Is something wrong?"

Not wishing to concern her aunt, Ariel tried to smile. "I'm just a bit under the weather is all."

"Oh, but what of Bryce? He—"

"Tell him I'm not well and get rid of him," Ariel snapped. Immediately ashamed, she added, "Please, Aunt Margaret. Couldn't you send him away?"

"I will take care of it, dear. You do look quite pale this morning. I'll send someone up with water for a bath. That should make you feel better."

This time Ariel did smile. "Thank you. A hot bath will work wonders, I'm sure."

Margaret turned the doorknob but paused before leaving. "Would you like me to send up a tray for you?"

"Yes. Thank you."

As her aunt left the room she called back, "Just let me know if you need anything, Ariel."

"I will."

Ariel watched the door shut, and a terrible sense of sadness assaulted her. Lately, lines of age had appeared on her aunt's face. Ariel decided she must control her ill feelings toward Bryce around her. The poor woman carried enough guilt without it being added to.

She had little time to dwell on this. A servant appeared with an overladen tray. Promptly, others arrived with buckets of water for her bath. Within minutes Ariel was soaking in the scented water. Never had it felt so good.

She willed thoughts from her, allowing them to drift away like the steam rising from the water. Purposely, Ariel kept everyone and everything from her mind and her heart. The heat eased the soreness and tension from her body. Slowly, her eyes closed.

"Ariel."

Dylan's lips were hot against her throat, trailing down to the place where her neck curved into her shoulder. She felt the tip of his tongue trace wet lines along the ridge of her collarbone before dropping lower to claim a taut nipple.

"Ariel."

Ariel jerked awake, causing the water to splash over the edge of the large, copper tub.

"Aunt Margaret, I'm sorry I didn't hear you."

"Mr. Harrington's gone dear. Is there anything else I can do for you?"

"No, I'll be fine. I just couldn't face him so soon. Thank you."

Margaret nodded then walked back to the door. "Perhaps you should take a nice walk to the zoo. I know how you like to visit the tiger there."

Ariel was surprised. She didn't know her aunt

even knew about her trips to the zoo, walks Ariel took alone without proper escort or chaperon.

"I'm sure it would perk you up, dear."

Her aunt's attempts to make an intolerable situation bearable touched Ariel. "Maybe I will take a walk."

A hot bath, a little food and some sunshine did make Ariel feel better—at least physically. She wished her mental state were so easy to heal.

Ariel walked along the well-tended paths through the zoo, the cages of each animal like a map telling her the way. As she passed a long row of cages, monkeys chattered at her. She paused a moment and smiled at their acrobatics and play. A mixture of scents, as varied as the noises, filled her senses. To some they might have been offensive, too strong and earthy, but to Ariel they were natural and welcome after the smells of the city. The rain had cleansed the air of the smoke and soot, the air still damp. She moved on.

Ariel sat down on a bench near the tiger's cage, her shoulders sagging from the tiredness that still plagued her. Unwilling emotions collided with remembrance, the clarity of each straining her reserve.

"And how are you, my friend?"

The great bengal tiger let out a soft growl in answer. An understanding of sorts existed between them, and Ariel had spent many hours in his company. To see such a magnificent animal caged made her sad, but she couldn't stay away. At times, she could even close her eyes and imagine the rumbling purr belonged to her Kala Bagh. Ariel also felt her presence meant something to the wildcat. They were each alone in a world not of their choosing, far from home.

The bars of his cage loomed before Ariel, and she contemplated them seriously. At least she wasn't in a cage, never to run free again. Even her unwanted engagement to Harrington was not so grim. Or was it?

Doubt snuck into her weak reserve, stealing away her confidence. If the marriage was unpreventable, what would she do?

"No," Ariel whispered. "Never."

But visions of what still might be attacked her. Panic grabbed her, choking the breath from her. It would be worse than being caged. Fear built.

Ariel swallowed it back, trying to gain control. She could no longer see the tiger. Tears blinded her.

"Never," she reaffirmed. "I can't marry him."

The comfort of saying the words was overridden by the lie. She *had* to marry him. If she didn't, her family would suffer. Uncle Henry couldn't survive in prison, and Aunt Margaret couldn't survive without Henry to take care of. What would happen to her?

"I *have* to marry him."

It was hopeless. Ariel's thoughts turned to Dylan. Even if he had honorable intentions, could she respond with honest love, or were her feelings born of desperation and despair?

Ariel no longer trusted her own judgment. What if it wasn't love in her heart? Was she merely seeking a way out? Was she being fair to Dylan, or was she merely using him? Awful feelings of uncertainty crashed in, and she cried.

For several minutes Dylan just stood and watched Ariel. Should he speak to her or not? Caution made him stay back at first, but when he saw her wiping the tears from her face, he walked up to stand before her.

"Hello, Ariel."

Ariel looked away. "Hello."

Dylan cleared his throat, discomfort making him awkward, unsure.

"It's a beautiful day." Dylan tried polite chatter; nothing else came to mind. "The rain cleared the air."

"Yes, it did."

Again, silence.

"Do you come here often?"

"Yes, I do."

This wasn't going to be an easy conversation. Ariel's short, blunt answers were making him work at it. Still, Dylan ventured on. "Does the tiger remind you of Kala Bagh?"

"I suppose so."

"Ariel, you're making this very difficult."

Sad eyes finally turned to look at him. "Am I? I don't mean to."

"I know you don't." Getting up his nerve, Dylan plunged into the one thing they were avoiding. "I'm sorry about last night, Ariel. It shouldn't have happened."

Immediately, Ariel was swamped with pain. Her worst fears were becoming reality. He regretted last night. "You needn't worry yourself over it, Dylan. I certainly didn't make it easy on you."

A sad sort of nervous laugh sounded; then Dylan said, "You were persistent."

Ariel's lower lip trembled as she fought back tears. "I did what I yearned for in my heart. It's the only way I know. But what happened between us doesn't change anything. You have no obligation to me, and I none to you."

The words were what Ariel thought Dylan needed to hear. Her own pain kept her from seeing his.

"You're still planning to marry Harrington?"

"Of course I am."

The anger on Dylan's face confused Ariel. What had he expected? He said their lovemaking should never have happened.

"Why? Why would you marry him?"

The question confused Ariel more. "And why shouldn't I?"

"After last night, I thought . . ."

He didn't finish, leaving Ariel to assume the wrong thing. "You thought what, Dylan? Are you proposing marriage?"

It was so direct, so stunning, Dylan could not speak. A deep-seated memory crept into his muddled thoughts and mixed with his instinct to protect his freedom. Without realizing it, Dylan stepped back. It wasn't until he saw the expression on Ariel's face he realized what his reaction looked like.

"Ariel, I . . ." For the second time, he was unable to finish.

As if paralyzed, Dylan merely stood there and

watched Ariel stand and walk away. His heart told him to follow her, to catch her and tell her.

Tell her what? He loved her? This thought created further anxiety, disabling him altogether. In the end, his mind won out and kept him there until he could no longer see her.

Chapter Twelve

Bryce felt the whiskey burn all the way down to his stomach, the dizzy aftermath of the potent drink welcome. He intended to finish the entire bottle, then perhaps start on another. Brooding thoughts bubbled into dangerous ones.

"Ariel, my sweet witch, how is it you've cast your spell on me? I have no heart, yet you make me suffer."

In one fierce swipe of his arm, Bryce cleared a nearby table, the sound of breaking glass bringing a smile to his lips.

"Witch!"

Visions of Ariel continued to plague Bryce, sending him deeper into his seething cauldron of desire and hatred.

That morning Ariel had pleaded ill to keep

from seeing him, yet, only an hour later, had met Christianson.

"Witch."

But why did it matter? Ariel was and would be his. She dared not marry another. He had her backed into a corner with no way out. He had made sure of it. Then what was going on between her and Christianson? Their encounter could have been by chance. They spoke for only a short while and never touched. Even this he had been unable to stand, and he had left, running away from Ariel and from the emotion he was experiencing. But mostly, running from himself.

Suddenly, the room was too small, closing in on him, tightening the air he breathed. He needed to find his friends—and some more whiskey.

Ariel wriggled her toes deeper into the green softness, the feel of the grass cool and soothing. She drew in a long breath of crisp night air, easing the dullness that had descended on her. The pace of her heart quickened as she ran across the lawn to the dense trees that stood like giant sentinels of the dark.

Another sleepless night had driven Ariel to her refuge. It was her salvation, her restoration. The gentle sound of water greeted Ariel, then the music of a light breeze rustling through the trees, the deep hoot of an owl. It brought a smile to her lips, but she could not completely shake an underlying sadness. Too many emotions wrestled in her heart.

Over and over she relived the scene at the zoo.

How could she be so foolish? She had allowed her feelings to conjure fantasies that would never be. The look on Dylan's face had made his own feelings clear. They had no future. He was right; last night should never have happened.

That thought brought her back in full force. Ariel looked up and concentrated on the clouds that scurried across the sky like puppies nipping each other's heels. Every once in a while, a great gray billow would run across the full moon, blocking its blue-white light.

Homesickness grasped her fiercely. She thought of the many nights she had run free with Kala Bagh, a full moon guiding them. Old pain twisted with new.

"Oh, Papa. So much has changed. If only you were here."

But he wasn't. And everything had changed.

Too much pain assaulted Ariel. She gave in to it and cried. She sank slowly to the bank that bordered the twisting stream, a shimmering snake between the grassy knolls. Defeated, she hugged her knees to her chest and rested her forehead upon them. Eventually, the tears stopped.

How long she sat there, Ariel didn't know. She allowed the night again to work its magic on her. It lulled her and eased the stress from her, taking her away from her pain.

An unfamiliar sound pulled Ariel from her special world. She raised her head to listen. She heard nothing out of the ordinary, yet the hair on the back of her neck bristled.

Standing, Ariel moved further into the trees, the

thick growth of underbrush picking and tearing at her. She kept on, uncertain what guided her. Her bare feet carried her swiftly across the park.

The first thing she heard was his laugh. More noises. Her heart beat faster. Instinct warned her of the danger of his presence. But again, she moved on.

Ariel knew it was Bryce. Still, she could not find any reason for his being here. Men's laughter and talk echoed in the quiet night, their voices distorted and strange.

Ariel scaled a tree, disappearing into the leafy foliage just as the four intruders appeared.

"Where the hell did he go?"

From her perch above them Ariel watched as Bryce looked about, seeing the pleasure on his face, the delight. "Seems he's got a lot more life in him than we thought. It's time to get serious."

The smile that widened Bryce's face sent a tremor through Ariel.

"There he is," cried out another, and they all instantly gave chase.

With the stealth of a jungle cat, Ariel jumped down and followed. Like shifting light in the darkness, she shadowed them. Her mind told her to leave, but an odd tenacity kept her in step behind them.

"Hurry, Bryce. He's getting away."

"Hell, Bryce has got him easy."

Their faces were dark masks, but Ariel recognized the voices of Bryce's friends. Even their laughter gave identification, their malicious hooting and hollering surrounding her.

She understood they were chasing someone, but the who and why of it was not clear. They stopped again, and Ariel moved closer.

One man stood only a few feet away, breathing heavily. It was obvious the foray had begun some time before. His breathing stilled, and he listened, his body turning while his eyes searched the area. Ariel didn't move a muscle when his gaze moved in her direction. He came closer. At that moment, the moon was swept free of the clouds blocking its misty glow. Ariel could see the expression on Bryce's face clearly. She was afraid to breathe. He took another step, his hand reaching out.

Out of the darkness came the man they chased, nearly running head-on into Bryce. He seemed to be a bum, some hapless derelict falling prey to their lark.

Ariel was angry they could be so cruel, grown adults playing at vicious games. But she could do nothing, and she certainly could not allow Bryce to see her here. All she could do was hope they would tire of their ugly entertainment and go away.

"You put up a good chase, but you could do better. After all, your life depends on it."

Bryce's tone was lecturing, as if he were explaining something complex to a child. "Now, run. And be quick about it."

Ariel remained still, her mind trying to clarify what she thought she had heard.

"Jeeezusss, Bryce. You let him go."

Bryce turned to his friend as he stumbled out of the brush. "He won't get far."

"Maybe we should just let him go. I'm beat."

148

The other two men skidded to a halt near Bryce. "Me, too. Let's go get another drink," one said.

"I'm for that," the last joined in enthusiastically.

The three of them started to walk away, but they stopped when Bryce did not move.

"Come on, Bryce. You caught him. You win."

A bizarre silence descended on them all, and one shifted uncomfortably at the look on Bryce's face. Ariel waited, as they did, for Bryce to speak.

"The hunt isn't over."

One of the men snorted. "Hunt? Hell, we were just having a little fun. That's all."

"Yeah, Bryce. Let's go."

Bryce stood his ground, a strange glint in his eyes. "Haven't you ever wondered what it would be like?"

The others looked at each other in total confusion. One lifted his shoulders. Another shook his head.

"Wondered about what?"

"About hunting the most challenging and cunning prey of all."

Bryce obviously put his friends ill-at-ease.

"I really can't say I have," mumbled one. The other two agreed readily with vigorous nodding of their heads.

"I have," Bryce said.

Ariel swallowed hard, a sick feeling in her stomach. He was mad!

"Come on, Bryce. That's crazy!"

"He's right. It's time to go."

The three again tried to leave, but Bryce remained where he was. "Are you afraid?"

"It's not a matter of being afraid," one argued, looking put off by his cutting remark. "It's a matter of being in your right mind."

"You're talking about murder," another added. "Plain and simple."

"Who's to know?"

"He's a man, for God's sake!"

"He's a beggar, a miscreant." Bryce's face twisted into an ugly mask. "He's better off dead."

A chill brushed over Ariel. She shivered. Bryce was talking calmly of killing a man, of hunting him down, like the animals he had hunted in the past. As the initial shock of it wore off, a tremendous fear crept in.

For the longest moment, no one seemed to move. Then Bryce took off in pursuit of his quarry. The others followed.

Ariel didn't move. What was she to do? What could she do? Surely, his friends wouldn't let him commit such a deed.

She followed.

She must find the man before Bryce did. Ariel ran faster.

The ground was rocky, biting at the bottom of her feet until they bled. Limbs scratched her face and tore at her hair as she cut through the thick undergrowth. Her cape and gown ripped.

She had to find him.

Out of breath, Ariel stopped. How could this be happening? How could Bryce even consider . . . ?

A twig snapped, and Ariel dove into the brush to hide, hugging the ground. The vagrant stumbled into view, and she started to stand, but Bryce appeared right on his heels. She pushed further back into the protective cover of the shrubs.

A tenseness hung in the air, closing about them like solid walls. Ariel squeezed her eyes shut and prayed, harder than she had ever prayed before. Tears streamed down her cheeks, and she bit her lower lip to still the trembling and to keep from screaming in horror.

"L . . . leave me alone!"

Bryce moved closer. Ariel dug her fingers into the cool, damp soil, wishing fervently it was the flesh of his face instead.

Yes, her mind cried out. *Leave him be.*

Ariel was mesmerized by the fear on the poor man's face. She felt his terror, his hopelessness. The full moon shook free its last cloud and spilled light down on the two men, revealing the long knife Bryce now held in his hand. Ariel tried to move, but she couldn't. Survival instincts overruled her emotions, keeping her frozen where she lay.

Bryce said nothing. His movements made his intent clear. He grabbed the man by the scruff of the neck and all but lifted him from the earth. He paused briefly when his friends called out to him.

Yes. They can still stop him.

Without further warning or hesitation, Bryce plunged the knife deep into the man's middle, then smiled as he pulled the bloody blade out. Slowly, his victim crumpled to the ground.

A moan slipped from Ariel. She clamped a hand over her mouth, aware Bryce had tensed. She swallowed her threatening cries.

He turned in her direction, staring intently at the

dark silhouette of trees. Cautiously, he moved closer, until he was only inches away. Bryce's breathing was labored and shallow, giving her the distinct impression of a near sexual pleasure.

She stared at his dirt-smudged boot. Then her gaze inched up past his spattered pant legs and came to rest on the knife still in his hand. A single drop of blood fell onto her own hand, dark against the white of her skin. Ariel feared she would be sick.

Just then, the others came upon the derelict, drawing Bryce's attention to them. He stepped away, and Ariel finally let her breath out.

"Oh, God," one choked.

Another reacted in anger. "You son-of-a-bitch! Have you gone mad?"

The other just stood dumbfounded, running his hand through his hair in disbelief.

"We've got to get out of here."

They all took off at a run. Only Bryce remained. He seemed to hesitate; then he walked from the forest.

When all their noise quieted, Ariel dared a peek from her hiding place. She crawled out. Fearfully, she moved toward the man who lay in a pool of his own blood.

Ariel was shaking so hard she thought she might fall apart. She took a deep breath, then wiped at her eyes with the back of her hand in renewed determination.

She must get help.

She turned to leave, but a low groan stopped her cold. Dropping to her knees, Ariel reached out and turned the stranger's face to her.

He was still alive!

Happiness caused the tears to start again.

"Sir," she whispered, "I'll go find help. Just hang on. Don't die. Please don't die."

His eyes opened, and she thought he understood. Then his hand snapped up and grabbed Ariel about the neck. She struggled against his strong grasp as he squeezed off her air.

"Nooo . . ." She wanted to tell him she was only helping him, but his choke-hold kept her from speaking. Fear gave him tremendous power, and Ariel sagged beneath his assault. Only death loosened his grip and allowed her to pull free.

Terrified, Ariel moved away, drawing in gulps of air to relieve the burning in her lungs. Shaken, she rolled onto her side, just in time to see Bryce returning. Still on her knees, Ariel eased back into the thick undergrowth. Then, stumbling to her feet, she fled with Bryce only a few steps behind.

Ariel ran like the wind. Years spent in the jungles of India gave her an edge even against his longer legs and greater strength. Yet his persistence kept him on her trail.

Finally, unable to go further, Ariel reached up, clamped hold of a low lying limb and flipped herself into the tree. Within seconds, Bryce ran beneath her. To her horror, he stopped.

Turning about, Bryce wildly searched the area. Just as she feared he would look up, a noise in the distance distracted him. Some animal had been awakened. She thanked God fervently when Bryce moved away.

153

It was several minutes before Ariel felt it safe enough to climb down. Confusing emotions clamored about inside her, but one distinct thought came clear. She must go to the police. She must tell them what happened.

Chapter Thirteen

By the time Ariel reached Whitehall she was near exhaustion. She stopped to catch her breath, her lungs near bursting from her efforts. Only a little farther and she would be at Scotland Yard.

Ariel stepped out into the street and ran right into a man. Startled, she pulled back from the arms that had kept her from falling.

"Hey now, lassie, what's yer big hurry?"

When Ariel looked up, she saw the uniform he was wearing and felt a rush of relief. She was still out of breath. Where would she start? It was so horrible. Images bombarded her mind, confusing her, adding to her stressed state of mind.

Her lower lip trembled. The bobby patiently watched her, his face blurred through the swarm of her tears. "I . . . he . . ."

"Yer lookin' a bit worse for wear, lassie. Perhaps ye'd best come with me."

"He . . . he killed him. I saw him." Ariel allowed the bobby to take her elbow and guide her down the street toward the station. "He killed him."

"There now, who killed who?"

"My fiancé. He killed him . . . he murdered him. I can't marry him. He's a cold-blooded killer. I just can't . . ."

The man nodded. "Yer fiancé?"

"Yes, yes. Bryce Harrington. He's making me marry him . . . he's . . ."

The elderly man kept nodding in understanding. "Calm down, lassie. Now ye say yer fiancé, this Bryce Harrington, killed someone?"

Ariel nodded her head vigorously. She tried to speak but instead could only sob.

"There now. I'll take care of ye. Ye've nothin' to worry 'bout now. I'll be takin' good care of ye."

Had Ariel not been so tired, she might have felt wary of him, but at that moment she wanted to be taken care of. She felt safe in the comfort of his protective arms.

"Sit here, and I'll be gettin' us a wagon."

"Yes," Ariel sniffed. "We need to get back to the park. That poor man . . . that poor man." The sobbing started again. She wrapped her arms about herself and rocked back and forth. How could he do such an evil thing? Horror, fear, pain—all ran their course inside Ariel.

Ariel pushed back the hair from her face, and her fingers caught in the tangled mass. She pulled a leaf from a loose curl. She realized what a fright she must look, noticing now the dirt beneath her broken fingernails. Then her gaze fell on the dark spot on her hand and the stains on her gown and cloak—the blood of Bryce's victim.

Her mouth opened in a silent scream as she pushed out the air from her lungs. Ariel wiped her hand on her dirtied clothes, then tried to rub the dark patches off the cloth.

"No . . ." she muttered, working harder to scrub them away. "No!"

"'Tis all right, lassie. I promised to take care of ye, didn't I now?"

She saw him step toward her.

"Come now," he coaxed in a soft, singsong tone.

"Are we going back to the park?"

"Maybe tomorrow."

Ariel felt weak, confused. She couldn't think straight. "We've got to go back. Tonight."

"Not tonight, lassie." The bobby's voice took on an even more gentle cooing. "Tonight I'm goin' to take ye to a place where ye can rest. Ye look plum worn out."

Ariel *was* tired. No, she was exhausted. But they needed to go back to the park. "You don't understand." She needed to explain better. "He killed a man. He hunted him down, like an animal, and killed him!" She was near hysterics.

"Like an animal, ye say?" asked the policeman as he moved even closer.

"Yes. Bryce Harrington's a trophy hunter."

"And he's yer fiancé?"

She didn't comprehend what he was wanting from her. They should be going back to the park! "Yes."

"And yer unhappy 'bout this, are ye, lassie?"

"I hate the man," she answered without thinking. "He's vile." Her head was pounding so fiercely she couldn't make sense of anything anymore. "But that isn't the point."

"Isn't it now?"

"No, it isn't. Don't you understand? He killed a man. He murdered him!"

"And ye saw this, did ye?"

More questions. Ariel wanted to scream and shout; instead she answered him. "Yes, I did. I saw everything."

A cross look came to the man's face. "Now what would ye be doin' in the park so late at night? And alone?"

Ariel swallowed hard. Something wasn't right. "You don't believe me." It came out a hoarse whisper.

"Ye need a good rest's all. Then everythin' will be better. I promise that."

"I know what I saw," she replied through clenched teeth. How could she make him believe her?

"Aye, lassie."

He was patronizing her. "Blast you," Ariel cried. She turned to leave and found her way blocked by two other men.

"Get out of my way," she demanded with as much authority as she could muster. They didn't move.

"Now, we're not goin' t' hurt ye."

Ariel whirled back around just as the bobby reached out for her, grabbing her arm. She screamed out in anger, but another of the men stuffed a rag into her mouth to silence her protests. The third man had a blanket snugly wrapped about her before she could react. She was hefted onto a shoulder and dumped into a waiting wagon.

It took a full moment for Ariel to realize what had happened.

Her body became rigid with a new and paralyzing fear. They thought she was crazy!

As the wagon bounced over the cobblestone roads, helplessness sapped the small amount of strength Ariel had left. She couldn't even raise her head to see where she was being taken. To the sanitarium, most likely. She was wrapped up so tightly in the blanket, she didn't even try to get free. To waste her energy now would be futile. She must rest so she could get away later.

Later, she concluded as her eyes fluttered shut. *Later, after I sleep.*

"Go away," mumbled Ariel, unwilling to let go of sleep just yet. But the nuisance was persistent, a poking and prodding with bony fingers.

She pulled the blanket tighter about her body. It was cold, but the little warmth it provided disappeared when it was yanked from her, bringing her awake.

Ariel rolled over. She came nose to nose with a crowd of faces peering curiously at her. Hands reached out to touch and pry, causing her to pull back. A wall stopped her from further retreat. One odd looking man grabbed her hair, and

Ariel screamed in horror as others reached out, stroked and felt her. She slapped at their hands, terrified. A woman screeched; another laughed in a grunting, snorting way; another moaned eerily. They all moved closer.

The room whirled about her precariously.

"Off wi' ye!" The crowd surrounding her scattered.

The order had been barked out by a stocky man who now wobbled up to where she sat huddled in the corner. The man, almost as wide as he was tall, stood in front of her, his arms folded, a chewed-up cigar hanging from his mouth. Dirty underwear covered his chest and arms and stretched over his bulging stomach. A hole here and there revealed hair and skin beneath. Perspiration stains marked the shirt, which like his red trousers was splashed with unidentifiable spots of food. What little hair he still had hung around his face, stringy and gray. Dark salt and pepper stubble marked his face. Glaring intently at her, his eyes were bloodshot, pale blue. He licked his fat lips, revealing yellowed teeth sparingly spaced within his gaping mouth. Ariel shuddered.

"Yer causin' them t' get riled up."

He rubbed his jaw, the sound of callused fingers running over stiff whiskers reaching her above the noise.

"Ain't got much t' say?"

If he expected an answer, he didn't wait for one. When he reached out and clamped a large mitt over her arm, Ariel pulled away. His smell was worse than the sight of him.

"I'd best be puttin' ye alone fer a bit. They'll not let ye be. New ones always rile 'em up."

Ariel started to object, to state firmly she did not belong here. Something kept her silent, and she allowed the grubby man to pull her along beside him.

A great sadness overwhelmed her at the sights and sounds around her. Young and old, men and women, all crammed into cages unsuitable for animals, let alone human beings who suffered sickness of the mind.

The noise deafened her. Moans, screams and cries of terror mixed with the jabbering of the insane. The potency of too many unclean bodies living too closely burned Ariel's nostrils and choked her with its heavy stench. Distorted faces mocked. She cringed as hands reached out, touching, pinching and grabbing.

"Off wi' ye," her jailer bellowed, then jerked her along behind him.

His gruff command sent the curious ones back from the bars in their doors, their shrill screams adding to the uproar.

Suddenly, they stopped. The jailer all but tossed her into a dark, damp cell. When the door slammed shut and locked, Ariel felt raw fear creep in past her shock and horror.

No one believed her. She wouldn't be here if they had. They thought she was crazy, that her story was a wild fabrication of a sick mind.

Why had she blubbered on so, giving credit to the bobby's first impression? And why did she even mention their engagement? It was stupid; she knew that now. Now no one would believe her. Why would they?

Ariel backed against the cold, stone wall, a sense of utter hopelessness descending on her. Exhaustion played cruel tricks on her dulled mind. Perhaps it was all a bad dream, a horrible nightmare that would be gone when she awoke. Yes—a nightmare.

Her eyes drooped. Slowly, she slid to the floor. When she woke up, everything would be right.

When something ran across Ariel's bare feet she jerked awake, uncertain what had startled her. The rat scurried back for a closer look, and Ariel realized what was living in the shadows. She kicked out at the vile creature. It squealed when her foot sent it rolling across the floor.

She listened closely but did not hear it return. She let her breath out. It ended in a sob. One followed another.

Ariel's head shook back and forth, denying all she was seeing, hearing, smelling. It was beyond comprehension.

"Nooo," she cried out to the empty cell. She shivered in horror. She wrapped her arms tightly about her and tucked her feet beneath her cape out of reach of sharp teeth. She laid her head upon her knees and whimpered.

Time seemed to stand still. Ariel fought her weariness, struggling against sleep in fear of the rats she heard every now and then in the blackness around her. Horror grappled with fear, obscuring any logical thoughts she might have managed.

Visions of the tiger at the zoo haunted her, his giant form pacing back and forth, pushing against the bars of his cage.

Chapter Fourteen

Dylan sat on his mount, the morning sun warm against his face. His horse pranced beneath him, straining against the bit in its mouth, anxious to run again. Dylan gently rubbed the animal's long, muscled neck.

"Ease up, boy."

The big black horse calmed with his master's touch and soft voice. Dylan surveyed the vast expanse of park, his eyes taking in the beauty of it, yet his mind remained distant. Other thoughts disturbed him, taking away the tranquility the ride would have provided him. Over and over he relived his rejection of Ariel. Over and over he chided himself for being the biggest of fools.

He knew what triggered his hesitation about Ariel—Diedra. Her rebuke still carried weight inside him, dragging him down, making him do things he

164

shouldn't. It was uncanny how long it had remained within him. He thought he had rid himself of the mental baggage long ago. Still, in the face of Ariel's innocent question, he had backed off. Now he knew how foolish he had been. There was no comparison. He knew it. So why had he acted the way he had? Did he really fear losing his freedom by marrying? That too faded in the morning light.

One question led to another. Most distinct—did he love her? And, if he did, could he marry her? Would he lose or gain freedom if he did? Should he follow his heart or his safety-seeking mind?

"Blast it," he yelled out loud, making his horse quiver nervously. Unable to stand his self-inquisition, Dylan let the animal run, allowing the beast to take control. He preferred the exhilaration of a dangerous ride to the frustration of his own uncertainty, his own insistent yearning for a forbidden relationship.

Forbidden! The word clung to Dylan as if it were alive, wrapping about him and squeezing the air from his lungs. His father asked him to check into his friend's death, not look after his friend's daughter. He had no right to interfere in Ariel's life. As much as he knew this, understanding fully the dangers he courted, he had still walked forward, directly into the fray. And, he admitted, he still could not keep himself from doing so.

Breathless from his ride and his thoughts, Dylan pulled the horse to a halt. At first, he didn't see what he was looking at, his mind still whirling from the inner turmoil he was battling. Slowly, he came to the realization that a great number of people were milling about, each craning his neck to see over or around the others in the crowd.

Dylan dismounted and pushed forward into the mob. He stopped a gentleman and asked, "What happened here?"

"A man was stabbed to death last night."

Dylan followed the man's pointing finger and found the reason for the stir of curiosity. Turning away, he started back to his mount. Something more specifically someone, caught his eye.

Bryce Harrington stood across the way, but he did not seem to notice Dylan's presence. His eyes were set on the dead man. Many other people stared, curiosity and horror keeping them spellbound. But the look in Bryce's eyes was different. When he left, Dylan followed.

For the second time, Bryce wondered why he had come back here. Still, he could not shake the feeling someone else had been here last night.

There was no one, his mind confirmed. Still, when he saw the old man, he stopped.

The wiry little man was holding up a necklace, delighting in the sparkle of reflected sunlight it cast off as it dangled from his hand. Something struck a chord deep in Bryce's mind, and he moved closer.

"Govna'," the old man muttered, his faded brown eyes cast down.

"Any idea what this is all about?"

A gnarled hand wiped across his whiskered mouth; then he smiled, showing his missing teeth. "Maybe. I can't know fer sure."

Bryce believed he did. "Would this help you tell what you know for sure?"

"Aye," he agreed readily, taking the coin Bryce offered him. "Tis right good of ye, govna'."

Keeping his patience, Bryce once again asked, "Did you see anything strange last night?"

"Aye, I saw 'er again last night. 'Tis the second time."

"You saw her? You saw a woman, here in the park?"

The head nodded. "I seen 'er the other night. I was lookin' for a place t' sleep. Then this giant of a bloke stopped me and threatened t' take me coin some gent were kind enough t' give me."

Bryce acknowledged his story with a nod of his own, hiding his growing impatience behind a smile. "A giant of a man, was he?"

"Yes, he were a bloody giant. I was near me end when she jumped from a tree onto his backside."

"This woman jumped from a tree?" Bryce continued to question, instinct urging him on.

The man's nodding resumed with more force. "Sure as I'm 'ere. A woman came flyin' out of the tree. Like a wild creature, she was. Saved me life, she did."

"Like a wild creature?"

Another nod answered.

"Tell me," Bryce started. "If this all happened the other night, why didn't you tell the police?"

Blank eyes stared for a moment; then the old man answered. "I decided it were best t' invest me coin and not chance another giant takin' it."

"And you thought it best to invest it in?"

A lower lip puckered out, and he said, "In a pin of ale or two."

"Maybe this wild woman you saw was from too much ale, old man. The drink can cause you to see things, even women flying from trees."

The white head shook back and forth in dis agreement. "She were real. I know it. An' the gian knows she were real enough too. Left her mark on his face, she did."

For some reason, Bryce believed his wild tale "You saw this woman last night, the same woman that helped you the other night?"

"She came runnin' from the park lookin' scared The way she took after the giant I would no' have thought she would be afraid of nothin' or no one.

"What scared her, do you know?"

The old man pursed his lips and shook his head no.

"You were looking at something, a necklace Where did you get it?"

Frightened eyes darted up, then looked away. " found it. 'Tis mine."

"I know it's yours. Can I see it?"

Hesitantly, the old man pulled it out and gave i to Bryce. Anger seared his mind. His fist clenched about the necklace. His patience was gone, yet he remained in tight control.

"Where did you find this necklace?"

Again the old man hesitated.

"I'll buy the necklace," Bryce offered, and he saw the man's eyes light up. Slowly, he counter out more coin than it was worth, the clink of the money emphasizing his offer. "But I need to know where you found it."

Licking his lips, the old man reached for the money. "Found it in his hand." He pointed back to the place where the derelict was found.

Never before had Bryce felt such fury.

"Did you see where this woman went?"

"Aye." He shook his head sadly. "Poor lass. They took 'er off. Thought she were touched."

Bryce would have liked nothing better than to take his anger out on this dirty, old man, to crush him beneath the heel of his boot. Instead, he forced a smile again. The idiot seemed content with the coin and wandered off, most likely to drink up the money in his hand.

Dylan wasn't able to hear the conversation Bryce had with the old man, but he was suspicious from Bryce's unusual display of kindness. Bryce was not taken to conversations with people he considered beneath him. When Bryce left the park, Dylan followed.

Ariel's chin fell onto her chest, the jerking movement wrenching her awake. She blinked several times to chase off her drugged sleep. She couldn't sleep; she was afraid to. When her eyes closed and her head dropped again, Ariel stood. Cold seeped through her cloak and flimsy nightgown. She turned to face the wall that kept her imprisoned and placed her forehead against the dampness. It felt good, the chill working through the numbness that enveloped her.

She was past coherent thought. Only a grave terror remained, gnawing at her, keeping her aware of where she was and why.

"God, why is this happening?" Her fingers clawed at the hard stone. She wanted to cry, but there were no more tears. "Why?"

Distinct noises drifted past the haze clouding her mind—the usual screeches and howls—but there was another sound of movement, of feet shuffling and people scurrying. Someone was coming. For the second time, she experienced the hair on the back of her neck bristling. "It couldn't be," she whispered out loud.

In the few minutes that passed before the guard reached her cell, Ariel drew in her reserve and gathered her defenses. She was tired, so very tired. How could she face him now?

The lock clicked, the sound loud as it echoed off the bare walls, nagging her with its power to keep her caged within. The door squeaked. The brightness of the lantern blinded her, but she heard footsteps, then the closing of the massive portal, its dull thud sending Ariel's heart into a faster rhythm. Calmly, or as close to it as was possible, she faced her visitor.

The sight of Bryce Harrington sent a tremor through her. Why was he here? The same fear she had experienced in the park threatened to take away the strength in her legs. Determination made her lock her knees to keep her standing; then instinct drove forward to rescue her flailing emotions.

He said nothing. He just stood there, watching, waiting for a reaction. She gave none.

Bryce took a couple of steps forward. Ariel had to make herself stand her ground. Only the muscle in her jaw clenched. But as hard as she tried, she could not still a flinch when his hand reached out and pulled her chin up for him to see her better.

He let her go, then slowly pulled out a crisp, white handkerchief to wipe his fingers. With care, he tucked it back into his breast pocket. Bryce cleared his throat before devoting his full attention to Ariel. Never had his eyes been so cold, gray shards piercing into her. Still, she made no move.

"What am I to do with you, Ariel?"

It seemed an open-ended question. Did he mean, *what am I to do with you because you have embarrassed me by ending up in an asylum?* Or, *what am I to do with you because you saw me kill a man for the pure pleasure of it?* Not certain which game he was playing, Ariel said, as lightly as she could manage, "I would like to go home."

This seemed to amuse him. "I'm sure you would like that. Your accommodations are a bit grim."

Just at that moment, one of the inmates let out an unearthly scream.

"You're shivering, dear," Bryce said, stepping closer.

Ariel tried to still her trembling but lost the battle as her knees knocked together. She tried to find the right words, but they were out of reach. So she remained silent.

Bryce's breath was hot on her face. "Why are you here?"

She swallowed hard to ease the dryness of her raw throat. "I . . . it was a misunderstanding."

His brow arched, and she knew he did not believe

171

her. But she gave no other explanation and waited for him to respond.

"A misunderstanding?" he repeated.

She nodded, still not caring to speak.

"Let's see exactly what was not understood." Bryce raised his hand and brushed some dirt from her cape. "Was it that you were out at night alone . . . and in a state of . . . let's say, undress?"

He meticulously picked a twig from her hair, seemingly calm, yet the cold fire in his eyes showed Ariel he was not. Flicking the twig from his fingers, he continued.

"Or was it the wild stories you're telling?"

Again, Ariel said nothing.

"What have you been up to, my sweet?"

Words still didn't seem appropriate.

Bryce grabbed her wrists and pulled her hands up for him to examine. "You're filthy! Have you been out in your flower garden again?"

His words prompted no response, but his touch made her jerk away. "Don't touch me," she hissed.

"So . . ." He let out a slow, wicked smile. "You've found your tongue."

Bryce caught her chin between his thumb and forefinger. "Don't lie to me, Ariel."

Repulsion scorched her very soul, his touch unbearable. Ariel twisted away. "Don't touch me," she all but screamed at him. Visions plagued her, haunting her weakened mind with the horrors of what he had done. "Don't touch me. I know what you hunt in the night."

She hadn't meant to say that and immediately regretted her mistake.

172

"It *was* you," Bryce mumbled.

Ariel tried to move away from him, but she was not quick enough. He reached out and jerked her back to him. Despite the anger shining in his eyes, he grinned. It was the coldest, most evil smile Ariel had ever seen. He pulled her closer, his face only a hair's breadth from hers.

"Well," he drawled, slow and lazy, "what am I to do with you now?"

Ariel struggled against his cruel grip but stopped when she realized it was useless.

He chuckled, then went on, his words hot in her ear. "I could kill you, silence you forever."

Ariel's heart beat furiously. She felt it in her temples. Bryce brought one hand up and enclosed her throat with his long fingers. Bruises marked her neck from the murdered man's grip, and as his pressure increased, so did the pain to the already tender flesh.

"It would be so easy. Just one snap . . ."

He let his words trail off. "No one would know."

He was right. No one knew she was here. No one would ever know she was dead, what happened to her.

"Or," he went on, "I could just leave you here to rot in this stinking hellhole."

This was even more terrifying than death. She could not bear to spend the rest of her life in this cage.

"Never to see the light of day again."

Ariel was helpless to stop her rising panic. She knew Bryce could see the fear. He seemed to feed on it.

"The walls are a bit tight, don't you think? The air a bit stale." This time, his awful chuckle exploded into full laughter, echoing off the walls he spoke of. He tightened his hold on her. "Soon, you would be as crazy as they are, darling. Your mind turned away from reality."

Ariel renewed her struggle, fear taking control of her. She knew she could not survive such a place. Just one night had taken its toll, to even think . . .

"It's not a very pleasant thought, is it, Ariel?"

Bryce shoved her against the wall, stilling her sudden thrashing with his body. Then he forced her to look up at him, and she fully understood the threat as she locked onto the dark eyes. The blood pumped through her head, his choke-hold causing it to gather, the pressure on her throat allowing only a minimal amount of air.

"There is one other alternative."

His breath was warm on her face, sending chills of repulsion through her. The change in his tone told her of his abrupt mood swing.

"I can marry you."

In her state of mind it caught her off guard, and she managed to choke, "Never."

Bryce's chest moved with his laughter, only no sound came out. "It would solve my immediate problem and promise such pleasures to come."

"You're mad. I won't—"

His hand came up to cover her mouth, stopping her and thankfully relieving the pain he was inflicting on her neck. "Watch what you say, love. You aren't in a position to argue."

Ariel wanted to say she didn't care. She hated him and would never marry him. She would rather die! Or would she? Slowly, she forced herself to look at the choices before her, with as much indifference and common sense as she could manage. To remain here was beyond her thinking. Quickly, she narrowed it down. Death or marriage. Once she was out of here, she could . . .

"I see you're thinking."

She wished he would be quiet.

"I would consider a thing or two while you're at it. As my wife you cannot testify against me. Now . . ." Bryce paused, seeming to relish this whole thing. "You could tell your tale, but to be quite honest, dearest, no one will believe you. I think that point has already been made. Otherwise, you wouldn't be here."

Shock and anger twisted together inside Ariel so strongly it left her breathless.

"That's better," he murmured, his lips brushing her face. "Now, I've got some things I need to do before the wedding."

Ariel bit her lower lip to keep from saying what she longed to say.

Bryce turned away but twisted back around and grabbed her viciously by her face, his fingers digging deep into the soft flesh of her cheeks. Ariel gritted her teeth against the renewed pain.

"Remember, Ariel, my dear. Not only is your life in my very capable hands, so is the future of your aunt and uncle. I will be back in the morning for you. I want you to spend the night thinking on this."

A new and greater terror struck her heart, nearly stilling it within her chest. Ariel had already witnessed how easily he killed. She did not doubt his threat.

Ariel couldn't stop shaking, the chill Bryce left her with staying long after he was gone. Even her teeth were clattering, loud in the silence that once again permeated the dark room. She needed to think, yet she couldn't form coherent thoughts. Slowly, Ariel sank into a despondent state, awake yet unfeeling.

Dylan stood before the closed door, a marathon of emotions whirling through him. He maintained a calm veneer as the guard unlocked it. He managed to mumble his gratitude to the man. Accepting the lantern, Dylan watched him close and lock the door, leaving them alone. His heart lurched forward as he held up the light and searched the room; it nearly stopped when his gaze found Ariel huddled in the corner.

Closing his eyes, Dylan took a moment to overcome the pain assaulting him. His hand shook. Dylan placed the light down.

"Ariel," he whispered hoarsely.

Ariel lifted her head, but no recognition came to her eyes; only a dullness met his look. Dylan stepped closer and knelt down. He reached out to her. "Ariel, I've come to take you home."

This time, a single tear slipped out and rolled down her dirty cheek. Ariel still did not move.

Never had Dylan felt such anguish, anger, pain. The bastard left her here! Gently, Dylan pulled her up from the floor and gathered her into his arms. He could feel her shivering and held her even closer.

"Guard," he hollered. "Open the door."

If the guard had any thoughts of denying Dylan's request, his mind was changed by the edge of steel in Dylan's words. The lock clicked and the rusty hinge objected as it was forced open. The guard stood in the opening.

"I'll be taking the lady home."

The man did not move, his slack jaw showing his surprise.

Dylan stepped forward.

"Sir, I beg your pardon, but the other gent made it very clear tha' he would be back in the mornin'."

"And I'll make it very clear that I intend to leave this place with the lady. Stand in my way, and you'll regret it."

The guard stood aside. Dylan walked past him, then paused. "I think I'd make a point of not being here in the morning."

The man nodded vigorously. "Very good idea, sir."

Chapter Fifteen

The fire crackled and hissed, loud in the silence of the room. Dylan leaned against his hand on the marble mantel. He stared at the dancing flames. His gaze moved to the door, then back to the clock. Only a minute had passed since he last looked at it. When he had returned with Ariel, Dylan had left her in the care of his housekeeper. He was impatient to talk to Ariel, to learn what happened.

Again he felt a rush of anger strike him.

"Dylan."

Ariel's soft voice penetrated his being like a bolt of lightning, sending all emotions running, save one.

"Ariel." Dylan moved to her side and tenderly took her hand in his. It was so small and delicate compared to his larger one. "Come, sit." He guided her to a chair.

So many questions, yet he found it difficult to know where to start. Ariel remained silent, offering no explanation or answers.

Gently, Dylan reached out and nudged her to look up to him. Her eyes were dull, as if her spirit was broken, the dark smudges beneath showing the strain she'd been through.

"What has happened, Ariel? Why were you there?"

Dylan's touch was nearly Ariel's undoing. She wanted to collapse in his arms and let him make everything right, to tell him she loved him and she wanted only to be with him, but instead, she held these thoughts silent. "It is hopeless. I don't know what to do."

"Tell me, and we shall see."

"I have no right to involve you in my problems."

Ariel looked away, but Dylan pulled her gaze back to his again. "Did our night of love mean so little to you? Don't these feelings we share have some meaning in our lives?"

The tears were no longer controllable; they spilled over the rims of her eyes and down her cheeks. "It meant everything, Dylan. That's why I can't marry him. Not now. Not ever."

A joy unlike anything he had ever experienced came over Dylan, warming his heart and soul. He wanted to whoop with joy. Instead, he replied calmly, "Harrington is not for you, Ariel." It was hard for Dylan to say no more, but Ariel looked so fragile he held back his true, angry emotions.

"He'll be looking for me in the morning. We are to be married then. I can't go back home, Dylan.

My uncle is afraid of him. Henry will not stop this marriage. I cannot go back. I cannot . . . marry him."

The pleading in her voice caused great alarm within Dylan. There was more to this than she was telling. He wanted to know the whole story. "Why has Harrington decided to marry you sooner than planned?"

Blank eyes stared at him, looking even more confused and distraught. "I don't know."

It was a lie, he could tell. "Please, Ariel, I must know what is happening."

Fear crept onto her face as she considered his question. "As I said, I don't know why."

A great urge to shake her, to make her tell him the truth, almost overwhelmed Dylan, but he controlled it. "Regardless of his reasons, we do have a problem."

Ariel's lower lip trembled. "What am I to do?"

Dylan's mind whirled. He knew of only one solution. He reached out and took her hand into his again. "I think we should be married. Tonight."

Surprised, she looked to him, then focused her gaze back down on his hand and the long, callused fingers that held her so gently. "You what?"

"I think we should get married."

The vision of his face when she had mentioned marriage at the zoo hung in her mind's eye. "I don't think so."

"It's the only way, Ariel."

"No!" Ariel pulled her hand away and stood. "I wouldn't think of it. You made it very clear to me marriage was not to your liking. I don't need your pity."

"Pity!"

Ariel started for the door, anger giving her the energy she lacked. "I should not have let you bring me here."

Dylan jumped up and grabbed her, this time not as gently. "Well, you *are* here. And you *will* listen to me."

"Let me go." Ariel struggled to free herself, her self-control gone. She was sobbing openly now. "I don't want to marry anyone."

It was a lie. She knew it in her heart, but pride kept her from accepting what he offered. She loved him. How could she bear marriage to him knowing he could never return her love? That was worse than . . . than what? Marriage to Bryce? No . . . she was terribly confused. "Please let me go."

"Ariel." Dylan's grip softened as did his voice. "Please, listen to me. I can't let you go, not now." For the first time, Dylan knew he loved her. He *wanted* to marry her. But to say this now would be futile. It would take time for him to convince her of his true feelings. His reaction at the zoo had assured that.

He all but carried her back to her seat. "Listen to me," he demanded, his tone brooking no argument. "Marriage is the only way I can protect you from Bryce. Don't let your pride stand in the way, Ariel. At the moment, it's the only choice you have."

This was quite a sobering statement.

Seeing he had her attention Dylan went on. "Is marriage to me really so bad?"

The eyes that looked back were emotionless. "As you said, I really have no choice."

Bryce lifted his brandy, saluting an empty room and non-existent audience. "Ariel, my sweet, tomorrow you will be mine, then and always."

His laughter filled the room. He had a right to be pleased with himself. From the first moment he had seen Ariel, he had wanted her. He knew she was not like the other women he had been involved with. They were too easy to have. Ariel would not be so simple a conquest. In the beginning, she had actually scorned him!

You're not the kind of man Ariel could ever love. I know my daughter.

Jason Lockwood's words disturbed Bryce's memory. With remembrance came the heat of anger. Lockwood had thought his daughter too good for his proposal of marriage.

Slowly, fury drifted over Bryce, taking his mind back in time. Once again, he relived the hunt. Only this time, he claimed his greatest prize, Jason Lockwood. Oh, he hadn't meant to shoot him in the beginning, but as he had looked down on the wounded man, an idea formed, a brilliant idea.

Without Lockwood standing in his way, he could win Ariel's favor. Bryce was certain of it. Then he thought of his carefully planned political ambitions for India. Jason Lockwood was denying him what he wanted. No one ever denied Bryce Harrington.

It had been easy to pull the trigger, as easy as when he had an animal in his sights, as easy as . . . Bryce closed his eyes, the thrill as exhilarating as it had been in the jungle, as it had been in the park.

But Lockwood was right. Bryce opened his eyes to stare into nowhere. Even with her father dead, Ariel was beyond his reach. She still denied him what he wanted. So he'd found a way past her wall of defiance, and she would not dare refuse him again. He held the fate of her uncle and aunt in his hands—and her own. Even the latest turn of events had worked to his advantage. That, too, had been easy.

"I always get what I want, Ariel Lockwood."

Dylan closed the front door and turned to Ariel.

"I had my housekeeper get you some things you might need, and I sent word to your aunt and uncle you are with me and safe."

"Thank you," she whispered.

He pointed upstairs. "I've had a room made up for you, Ariel."

Ariel didn't even look up; it took too much effort. Instead she continued to stare at the gold band that circled her finger. "Thank you, I am tired."

It felt strange, looked strange, but it was now fact. She was Dylan Christianson's wife. The day had gone by in a whirl, but Dylan had tended to every detail. The small chapel was beautiful, the ceremony simple yet sweet. He had even purchased the creamy, satin gown she wore, complete with a fresh bouquet of flowers. Orchids with long stems of fern, much like she had picked in the jungles of India. Again, she touched the wedding band he had placed upon her finger. She *was* Dylan's wife.

A cold wind swept over her heart. Bryce Harrington's evil plagued Ariel, robbing her of any joy she might have felt. What would he do?

Dylan stood before her, offering his arm. "May I see you to your room?"

"Of course."

All the pretense was maddening. Still, she allowed him to escort her to her door, as if it were the most natural thing for him to do. Neither spoke. The silence gave Ariel time to think, to hope. Maybe with time, Dylan could learn to love her.

They arrived at her door. She longed to say something, to express her feelings, but she wasn't sure what they were.

Dylan was aware of her distress and feared pressing her too far. "Should you need anything, I'm just next door."

She only nodded then disappeared inside the room.

He stood, for the longest time, just staring at the door. He didn't hear any movement inside and finally knocked lightly. Ariel answered so quickly he realized she must have been standing just on the other side.

"Are you all right?" It seemed a feeble question, but the only one he could think of.

"I'm fine."

"I was worried," Dylan whispered. He reached out to touch her cheek. "Are you sure—"

Ariel pulled away and stopped him midsentence. "It's been a long day, Dylan. I'm tired."

"Then I'll say good night."

Ariel shut the door, and this time she heard

him walk away. She wanted to call him back. She wanted . . . the impossible.

Closing her eyes, she leaned against the door. Sleep, she needed sleep. Tomorrow she would sort everything out.

"I could kill you . . . just one snap."

Bryce's face distorted into a mask of pure evil. Black eyes pierced her soul, stealing her will. His mouth gaped open, enlarging until it could suck her into its blackness. She wanted to run, but her legs would not move. Even when she saw him pull the long knife from its hidden sheath, she was frozen in place.

He stood before her, wickedness lighting his eyes. He raised his arm, ready to strike, ready to kill. Her gaze locked onto the shining steel. Blood dripped from the tip and onto her face. When she wiped at it the spots became larger. Soon her hands were covered. She could no longer see. She could hear his breathing, coming closer, but she couldn't see anything but the scarlet haze that blinded her.

"I could just kill you."

"No!"

Ariel came awake screaming. "No!"

All the horror and fear returned, battering down her meek sleep-ridden defenses. "No," she continued to cry out, the nightmare too real.

Dylan came running into the room, a robe half on and half off. "Ariel," he called to her. In a second he was next to her, pulling her into his arms.

"No!" Ariel struggled against his hold.

"It's me, Ariel. It was just a dream. Just a dream."

Slowly, her night visions faded, and Ariel realized it was Dylan who held her, not Bryce.

Dylan smoothed back her hair, his words, his touch soothing her. "It's all right. I'm here."

She nodded, unable to speak. Dylan held her close, the comfort and security he provided stilling the great beating of her heart. She wanted to be held forever and ever.

"Ariel."

His voice broke into her thoughts, and she looked up.

"Do you want to tell me what is troubling you?"

She opened her mouth to speak, but no words came out.

"Please, Ariel, I can't help you unless I know."

His voice was soft, understanding. She wanted to tell him. Still, fear kept her silent, tears her only answer.

Dylan watched indecision play over her features, disappointed when she remained silent. He leaned over to kiss away her tears.

"My sweet tigress, what can I do when you keep it all inside?"

He could smell the musky scent that still lingered on her delicate hair. He became acutely aware that only a thin nightgown separated them. The warmth of her body fused with his, stirring a greater heat deep within. He could feel the roundness of her breasts and the hardness of her nipples.

"I'd better go," Dylan mumbled, his voice deep with emotion.

"Please, don't leave me."

Her cry was so soft he wasn't even certain she

had spoken, but the look in her eyes told him more than her words. More than anything, he wanted to stay with her, to hold her close. "I can't stay, Ariel."

Immediately, Dylan regretted saying that. "I want to, but God knows I'd better not. You're much too tempting."

The blush on her face told him she had not considered that. She seemed to think this new aspect over; then she calmly said, "Please stay, Dylan."

Never had he been so afraid—afraid that if he moved closer, she would send him away. "Are you sure?"

Instead of answering him, Ariel caressed his cheek, the night stubble of his beard bristling beneath her tender touch. Gently, she kissed him, offering what he longed for.

"Please stay," she whispered in his ear, then nibbled on the roundness of his earlobe.

Dylan needed no more assurance. He pulled her to him, his mouth seeking hers. He wrapped his arms around her to give the security she seemed to crave. Passion surged through him, fired his blood. The softness of her lips melted with his, her mouth open to him. Their tongues touched and danced, the sweet taste a delight. He hadn't realized how much he wanted this to happen, to share his newfound love, to explore and share with her the feelings that came with the discovery of it.

He felt the need to draw the very being from her and unite his soul with hers, making them one not only physically but in spirit as well. Never had he known such joy in just holding someone close.

The largeness of his hands discovered the delicateness of her small frame, the contours of her fragile back. He touched every silken inch of her. A sudden fear overwhelmed Dylan. What had happened to bring Ariel to him? What great fear had brought her to his arms? This thought created a nagging fear of his own. If something happened to her, he couldn't bear it.

Ariel was his wife now. He would see nothing happened to her. Dylan pulled her even closer, the feel of her in his arms dispelling his apprehension. Tenderly, he kissed the pinkness of her cheek, moving to the line of her jaw and on down to her long neck. The flesh of his lips memorized the gentle curve of her shoulder before moving lower to nuzzle the fullness of her breasts. Ariel pulled away slightly and opened the bodice of her nightgown. He took one rosy tip in his mouth.

The warmth within Dylan flamed into a great desire. Her hips moved beneath him, pressing against his growing passion, the insistent language of her body calling him to her. He slid his hand down the long length of her leg, then back up beneath the thin gown that still kept his body from hers.

Impatiently he pulled at the fabric until it fell away. He smiled. He reveled in the golden glory of her honeyed body, her eyes no longer filled with fear but with love. That look fed him.

With a newfound tenderness, Dylan took her to him, the trembling of her passion matched by his own.

Spent, Ariel lay with her head cradled in his

shoulder, safe and secure in his arms. Sleep fought hard to claim her, the lingering warmth of Dylan's lovemaking leaving her easy prey, the strong steady beat of his heart lulling her. Yet she resisted, fearing the dreams would return. But as hard as she tried, too many nights of too little rest ruled. Her eyes drooped. Tomorrow she would make sense of it all. Tomorrow.

Dylan could tell when Ariel finally drifted off, her breathing deep and even. Something quite strange clung to him. Something he couldn't define.

Unable to understand and not certain he wanted to, he pulled her closer. It felt good to hold her; this he did know. For the moment, it was all that mattered.

Chapter Sixteen

The sun streamed ribbons of light into the room across the flowered carpets. Dylan stretched, then turned onto his side. Ariel still slept. He studied the beauty of her flushed face. Her even breathing fell like a song on his ears, and happiness warmed him. He felt like a child, with childish expectations. Then again, the night they had shared was anything but childlike. This remembrance stirred something else in him, and he chuckled at how easily she aroused him.

The temptation to kiss her neck was too hard to resist. He gently brushed aside the scattering of tangled auburn curls to do just that. Ugly, dark bruises caused a sudden rise of heat, the blood rushing through his veins and ringing in his temples. Dylan tried to stop the rush of thoughts, but they cascaded forward.

"Ariel." He spoke quietly so as not to startle her. She stirred but did not awake.

"Ariel."

Noises from downstairs distracted Dylan. "What the—"

Dylan threw back the cover and swung his long legs over the side of the bed. The commotion grew louder. He went to the hallway, then realized he had no clothes on. Cursing beneath his breath, Dylan stepped back to his own room to grab his pants, yanking them on in haste.

"Dylan."

Hearing Ariel call his name, he stuck his head back in. "It's all right, Ariel. Go back to sleep."

She was sitting up in bed, a look of bewilderment on her sleepy face. Bright topaz eyes stared at him, the fear he had seen the day before again strong in their depths. Dylan was struck by her vulnerability. She clung to the blankets covering her. The strength, so much a part of her, was gone again. As he turned away, a strangeness clung to him, almost stifling the air he breathed.

"Where is she, Christianson?"

Coming face-to-face with Bryce was a surprise, not that Dylan had not expected a confrontation, but certainly not in his own home. "You've a lot of nerve, Harrington. I don't take kindly to people bursting into my home and disrupting my privacy."

Generally, Bryce was cautious around Dylan, but this morning he was beyond control. "I don't take kindly to you compromising my fiancée." He pushed his way past Dylan into the room.

191

When Bryce saw Ariel, he stopped cold; only the red shadow that slowly descended over his face told of his reaction. Then a long, low growl filled the room.

"You bitch!"

This prompted Dylan into action. "Back off. You've no right to barge in here. And I'll warn you only once not to call my wife such names again."

The word *wife* seemed to echo about, stilling everyone's movements. Henry, who had lagged well behind, finally moved to the side of the bed. His face was pale, blots of sweat marking his forehead and upper lip.

"Are you all right, dear?"

Blank eyes looked up, but nothing seemed to be reflected in them. She nodded, started to get up and succeeded in keeping her modesty only when her uncle helped her wrap the sheeting about her.

Bryce finally found his voice, but it was anything but calm. It was deadly. "You lie."

Dylan felt too calm. "We were married yesterday. I have the papers if you wish to see proof."

"You lie!" Bryce yelled. He lunged at Dylan, his full weight slamming into him, sending them both stumbling into the hallway. Bryce lashed out, his fists striking flesh. His fury drove him haphazardly. One blow split Dylan's lower lip, another pushed the air from his lungs.

It took only a second for Dylan to recover from his initial surprise. Never had he thought Bryce would challenge him. Even Bryce's fear of Dylan had been overpowered by his jealous rage. To strike from behind was more Bryce's style; this head-on attack was a real shock.

Facing him, Dylan studied the ugliness twisting Bryce's face into a sinister silhouette. An uneasy feeling pricked at Dylan's mind. The dark eyes that watched him were different, a strangeness in them he had never seen before.

"You will pay for this, Christianson."

This time Dylan was more prepared for Bryce's attack and easily fended off his wild swings. "It's over, Bryce. Go home."

If the words were meant to soothe Bryce's anger, they did just the opposite. With a bellow of rage, he rushed Dylan.

Ariel watched both men fall down the wide staircase. They grappled as they rolled and bumped, finally stopping two-thirds of the way down the stairs.

Ariel freed herself from her uncle's arms. She cried out, but her voice echoed in her ears like it came from someone else. An almost distant feeling overtook her as the fight played out before her. She felt slow, the buzzing in her head loud, almost drowning out the strangled yells of the battle.

She stood at the top of the staircase and watched, unable to move. She heard the beating of a drum. No, maybe it was her own heart struggling against the confines of her rib cage. Slowly, she became aware Bryce had pulled his knife, just as he had in the park. Flashes of memory garbled reality.

"No," she screamed, stepping forward. Her uncle's arms again stopped her, holding her back.

"No!"

Bryce brought his arm up in a dangerous arc, the knife grazing Dylan's bare chest. Blood squeezed from the cut, holding Ariel's gaze. She couldn't breathe. Dylan's body twisted, avoiding Bryce's second slashing attack. Dylan brought his fist up and slammed it into his attacker's chin. Bryce stumbled back, the rail of the stairway smashing him in the kidneys, knocking the breath from him. In two swift movements, Dylan had Bryce by the wrist, twisting it viciously until he dropped the knife.

Bryce's head came up and slammed into Dylan's, the crack loud. Ariel's knees threatened to buckle beneath her. Dylan fell back, then stumbled, tumbling down the remaining stairs. Bryce jumped on top of Dylan before he could gain his balance, landing square on Dylan's back. Dylan stood, carrying Bryce's full weight on his shoulders, then threw him off. Bryce hit the floor, rolled and smashed into the entry door.

In three long-legged strides Dylan had Bryce by the scruff of the neck. "You've always been a bad loser, Harrington. But I warn you, stay away from Ariel, or I'll be tempted to kill you the next time."

Before Bryce had a chance to say anything, Dylan hustled him out the door, giving him a final shove down the front stoop.

The front door slammed shut. Ariel felt her uncle's grip relax. She ran down the steps. She stood only a few feet from Dylan. Her breathing was labored, rattling in her chest with each movement. Sweat glistened off his naked torso, mixing with the blood that still dripped from his wound. His nose was bleeding, as was a split in his lower lip.

She wanted to ask him if he was all right, but no words came out of her dry mouth. Instead, her tears questioned him. Dylan reached out and tenderly wiped the tears away.

"It's over, Ariel."

She attempted a smile, though it was weak and trembling. Dylan became alarmed at the unnatural glaze in Ariel's eyes and laid the back of his hand against her forehead. "You're burning up."

Dylan swept Ariel into his arms and carried her back up the stairs and into her room. "Send for the doctor, Henry."

Gently, Dylan laid her down and lovingly tucked the covers around her. "The doctor will be here directly."

When Dylan looked into her fevered face, fear snaked into his thoughts, drying his words of encouragement and comfort. Then, just as suddenly, anger took control.

"You sleep. I'll wait for the doctor."

Ariel's eyes dropped shut. Quietly, he left the room, pulling the door closed behind him. With a new purpose, Dylan strode downstairs and found Henry Witherspoon helping himself to a glass of sherry.

"It's a bit early, don't you think?" Dylan jerked a shirt on, his movements betraying his pent-up anger.

"Considering everything, I didn't think it would hurt."

"I would like to know what you were thinking of when you agreed to let Harrington marry Ariel?"

Henry finished his drink, then shrank into a nearby chair, his shoulders sagging from shame. "I'm a weak man. I can't stay away from the gaming tables. I need them too much. Bryce, he's a smart one. He used my weakness to get at Ariel."

Dylan understood, but not totally. "Yes, that's Bryce's way."

Henry bobbed his head up and down. "He sucked me dry. Then to pay off my debts, I started to steal money from Ariel's inheritance. At first I didn't think she would ever miss it since she had so much, but I kept losing." Henry was wringing his hands, choking back the tears of apparent despair. "So I kept forging her name. It became easy—easier than staying away from the tables. Even when I had taken everything, it wasn't enough, so I signed over her estate in India. Still, I lost more."

Dylan couldn't say anything, overwhelmed by his anger at Henry's betrayal.

"Bryce was willing to forget my debts to him if Ariel would marry him. She had no choice, Dylan. The girl was only trying to keep me from going to prison. It's hard to believe she could possibly love such a pathetic excuse of a man, isn't it?"

All of Dylan's rage left him like an exhaled breath of air. "You're her family, Henry, and Ariel has a big heart."

Henry wiped at his face. "I prayed for a miracle, but I never dreamed you would be it." Then, as if an afterthought, Henry asked, "You do love her, don't you, my boy?"

As awful a thing as Henry Witherspoon had done, Dylan felt his heart go out to him. "I've loved her from the first moment I saw her."

Tears filled Henry's eyes. "That's a comfort."

For the first time, Dylan understood Ariel's devotion to her uncle. He had a kind heart, but it was hard to see when his weaknesses were so great. Ariel saw this goodness in spite of everything he had done.

"However much you owe Harrington, I'll see he's paid. You go home now. I'm sure Margaret's worried."

"What do you mean my brother isn't home? Where on earth would he be at this hour?" Diedra didn't wait to be asked to come in. She just pushed past the stuffy butler Bryce employed.

Spotting the stacks of luggage and trunks, Diedra questioned the servant. "Is Bryce planning another hunting foray? Strange, he never mentioned it to me."

The sour-faced butler drew up to his full five-foot-six height and faced Diedra as best he could. "Your brother has gone to get Miss Ariel. Arrangements have been made for their marriage this afternoon. They will leave for an extended honeymoon tonight."

If ever Diedra had been taken by surprise, she was now. "Why, he said nothing to me about this . . . this sudden change in plans. They hadn't even set a date. I don't believe you."

The pinched look never flinched at all. "I've no
been privy to the reasons, madame. Only tha
this is the plan. I am not one to question my
employer."

Diedra conceded, her mind already on othe
matters. "Of course not. You've always been mos
adequate. Now, have my carriage brought bacl
around. I'm in a hurry."

"Yes. Right away, madame."

Diedra's narrowed eyes watched the butler's stiff
retreating back. As much as she hated Ariel, i
would get her out of the way. If anyone could
destroy that chit's goody-goody ways, it was Bryce
He could be so . . . terrible.

This thought prompted a smile. "Well, I'd bette
be off to wish the bride-to-be my best."

"My brother is not here?"

No, madame. He left with Mister Witherspoon.

Diedra was losing all patience, short of it to
begin with. "Is Miss Lockwood in?"

"Madame, she is not."

"Is anyone here?" Diedra snapped.

"Only Mrs. Witherspoon."

"Heavens," she mumbled. "Could you at least tel
me where my brother was going?"

"He's gone to find Miss Lockwood."

Diedra peeked behind the butler to Mrs. Wither
spoon who stood only a few feet away. "To find
Ariel?"

Margaret Witherspoon's gaunt face told Diedr:
more than her words. "Poor child. We've taker
advantage of her good nature."

Mrs. Witherspoon made no sense to Diedra. "Where is Ariel?"

A confused look pushed Margaret's features into a frown. "It seems that she is with Dylan Christianson. I certainly don't know why. Ariel doesn't even know him."

Jealously and anger came alive. So the little witch was with Dylan. Well, Bryce should have her in tow by now, and that left Dylan to her. This brought her smile back.

Don't you worry. Everything will be fine. Her eyes narrowed with renewed determination. *I'm sure of it.*

Chapter Seventeen

The doctor snapped his black bag shut, having finished dressing Dylan's wound.

"Are you sure Ariel's going to be all right, Doctor?" Dylan's words were laced with uncertainty and worry as was the expression on his face.

"She's exhausted, mentally and physically. She' caught a bad chill and has a high fever. I've lef you some medicine so she will sleep well."

"Is there anything else I can do?"

"Just see she gets plenty of rest." The doctor started to leave. "Don't forget to rub some salve into your wound."

"I'll do that, Doctor. Thanks for coming sc promptly."

"Call me if you need anything."

Dylan walked the doctor to the door and, just a:

he was shutting it, saw Franklin Browning coming up the walk.

"Franklin," he called out. "I'm glad you could come."

"I hope I've not come at a bad time." His eyes followed the doctor as he drove off in his carriage.

"No, come on in."

Just as the door closed, the bell rang. Dylan answered it. Diedra stood on his stoop in a cloud of perfume and bright yellow silk. Dylan looked back at Franklin and drawled, "I certainly seem to be popular this morning."

"Oh dear, have I come at a bad time?"

Dylan made a sweeping gesture with his arm. "No, not at all. Do come in."

Franklin made an attempt to cover his laughter with a cough, then cleared his throat loudly. Diedra's mind must have been on other things for she did not notice.

"What do you think of this news, Dylan?"

Diedra's voice held a note Dylan knew meant trouble. Patience, Dylan reminded himself sternly. "What news is that?"

A smile turned up the corners of her red lips. "Don't play innocent with me. You know my brother has become impatient, and they are to be married today."

Diedra watched Dylan closely, his reaction to her announcement suddenly of great importance to her.

"Really?" Dylan asked, revealing nothing.

"Yes . . . really." Diedra felt smug. If Dylan had indeed been interested in Ariel, it had come to no

end. And this made her exceptionally happy. Whatever he had seen in that wild chit was beyond her.
Quickly, she scurried over her options in making
Dylan suffer for being such a fool and for neglect-
ing her.

Franklin broke into her private reverie. "Is this
going to be a private thing, or are we invited?"

"Well, to be honest, I don't know the details. I
was just on my way to see my brother. Actually, I
had hoped to catch him here."

A dark cloud fell across Dylan's face, but he still
said nothing. This was irresistible to Diedra.

"Did Bryce take his errant bride-to-be home?"

"Actually, he didn't."

An immediate fear intruded on her delight,
stealing away her joy. "He didn't?" she choked.

"No, he didn't."

Dylan didn't offer more, and Diedra felt the
anger tingle inside her. "Oh, wasn't Ariel with
you?"

"Yes, she is."

"She's still here?"

"Yes, she is."

Diedra wanted to scream at him, to slap his
straight, calm face. She wanted to do anything to
get some sort of reaction from him. "Why didn't
Bryce take her back with him? I didn't think he
would tolerate such a thing."

"He didn't have much choice."

She swallowed hard. "Why not?"

A wry smile touched the hardness of his lips,
softening them a bit. "You ask a lot of questions,
questions about things that are really no concern
of yours."

Gray eyes narrowed into piercing slits. "And what exactly is of no concern to me? Spell it out, Dylan."

"Ariel is my wife."

"Your wife?" Diedra's voice came out a squeak.

"Yes," he repeated. "My wife."

Diedra could hear her own gasp, but it was the flood of heat that made her wonder if she might swoon. Sheer determination kept her afoot. She would not embarrass herself further.

"Is that clear enough?" he asked softly.

Dylan was enjoying this, she could tell. That galled her and brought her chin up, pushing her nose up in the air. "Yes, I believe you've been quite clear."

"Good," Dylan finished with a happy smile. "I wouldn't want us to have any misunderstandings. After all, we've been friends for, oh, so long."

She was aware Dylan was making fun of her, but some odd persistence kept her from fleeing in tears. "You are a fool, Dylan Christianson. An even bigger fool than my brother."

The anger inside her repaired any damage her dignity had suffered. Diedra turned and stomped off, her feet slamming against the polished floor. Fools! They were all fools!

Dylan flinched at the sharp sound of the door slamming, then felt simple relief she was gone— and hopefully out of his life for good. It was hard to imagine he had ever felt pain from her rejection. But then, he reflected, wisdom and youth were not always compatible companions.

Turning his attention to his remaining guest,

Dylan brought his mind to the solicitor's visit. "Shall we go into the office, Franklin?"

Franklin stepped forward and offered his hand to Dylan, his face showing shock. "I am happy for you, Dylan."

Dylan accepted his hand and smiled warmly. "It was sudden, but I have no regrets."

Franklin returned the smile, but it didn't touch his normally jovial eyes. "What's going on, Dylan?"

"I don't really know everything, but we have much to discuss."

Ariel watched the two men disappear into the library, the door closing.

"Mrs. Christianson."

The young voice brought her gaze to the servant, who stood with an envelope in her hands. "Yes." Ariel couldn't remember her name.

"This was delivered a few moments ago. I didn't want to disturb you, but since you're up, I thought I'd best give it to you."

Taking it, Ariel smiled weakly. "Thank you." Still, she couldn't recall a name.

The girl disappeared down the hall. Ariel opened the note.

You think you have won, but remember, dearest Ariel, I get what I want. I have your necklace—the one you always wear. It was found in the dead man's hand. Quite incriminating, wouldn't you say, Ariel? Especially coupled with an eyewitness who saw you leaving the park that night, the same man who has seen you attack another in the park on another night.

And then there is the very man you tried to kill. Another witness to your violent nature.

Ariel gripped the rail for the strength she did not have. Her gaze was glued to the letter, her hand moving to her throat to verify the necklace was missing. A great fear crawled into her fevered mind, overpowering all logical thought.

She read on.

The game has changed, my sweet. If you don't leave Dylan and come to me, I will see that you hang for murder. Your uncle will go to prison, and your aunt will be left destitute. It would all be so easy to do. Do not push me further. If I can't have you, no one will.

Ariel stepped back in horror. Terror closed in, robbing the air from her lungs, her trembling legs refusing to give support. She crumpled to the floor.

She wanted to cry, but there were no tears left. "Think," she mumbled, but it was too difficult. Pain and heat filled her mind, not thought. She didn't want to believe what her mind was conceiving. It was all too much. She was ill, but she had no time to be. Struggling to her feet, Ariel leaned against the dark paneled wall until the room stopped spinning. She licked her dry lips.

She must go. Far away. She must get away from Bryce.

Ariel struggled down the hall to her door and paused as her hand turned the brass knob. This time tears did find her, and her heart felt as if it were being ripped apart. She loved Dylan, but she could not stay. Even he could not protect her now.

A strong survival instinct took control, and Arie
stepped inside her room.

She must go home.

Dylan stared at the clock, listening to each sec
ond tick off. Franklin was right. He and Arie
needed to talk. Plain and simple. Tonight, when
she awakened. For now he let her sleep. The doctor
said lots of rest. Later would be soon enough.

Deep down, Dylan was terrified she would rejec
him. No, he argued with himself, time and time
again. He was certain she felt something for him
There was a great attraction between them—and
definitely passion. That had been obvious from the
first moment their eyes met. Her lovemaking held
a certain tenderness. Was that love?

Just thinking of Ariel loving him made his heart
pound and blood warm. Then doubt swooped in
and bombarded his small trickle of confidence.

Don't be a fool, he reminded himself. *Ariel isn't*
anything like Diedra. Besides, what he felt for Ari
el was love. Whatever he had known with Diedra
paled in comparison. He had allowed himself to
dwell on something insignificant.

He loved Ariel. And no matter what, he always
would. Even rejection could not destroy his love
Ariel gave him the very thing he feared she would
take away—freedom.

This revelation made Dylan feel better. She was
his wife, and he took comfort in that. Time would
take care of the problems that seemed to stand
between them. He would be honest with her, and
in turn, she would learn to trust him. Whatever

created the fear in her eyes, they would take care of together. Together they could face anything.

Ariel shoved the few things she had into a tapestry bag. She had very little money. Unable to concentrate long on any one thought, Ariel's harried mind let it be and went on to another worry. She could leave the back way so Dylan wouldn't see her. Then, once out on the street, she could hire a carriage to the docks. Would there be a ship leaving for India tonight?

Again, she gave it only a moment's thought, then darted to another concern. First she must get there; then she would consider her next step.

Gathering her meager belongings, Ariel moved to the door and listened a moment before opening it. All was quiet, so she peeked outside. No one was about. "So far, so good," she mumbled, even her hushed words seeming too loud. She nervously glanced behind her to make certain she had not alerted anyone to her presence.

She knew she was being paranoid, but she was helpless to stop it. Even her ragged breathing seemed extremely loud. She was certain someone would hear the fierce beat of her heart. Ariel was trembling, and she worried her weak legs wouldn't get her out to the street. Using the wall as support, she moved to the back stairs. They loomed before her, an impossible obstacle. Her head spun at the abrupt drop. Carefully, she guided herself down the steep stairs, then breathed a deep sigh of relief when the last step was conquered.

The door was only a few feet away, so close yet

seeming so far away. Her breath came in short raspy gasps. Her lungs felt as if she had run for miles. Ariel rested for a moment, then stepped to the door. Daylight streamed in as she inched it open, the brightness blinding her with spots of color. She shaded her eyes, then carefully moved outside.

No one was about. Even the streets seemed to be empty. Success brought her energy, and she made her way down the street, relieved when she spotted a carriage for hire. She hailed it, then crawled inside.

"The docks, please."

Her voice sounded shaky and frail. It echoed in her dulled mind. She turned to look one last time at Dylan's home as the taxi pulled away. The horse's clopping hooves resonated with the terrible pounding in her head. Leaning back in the seat, she pushed doubt away and concentrated on staying in a sitting position. That took everything she had.

"Lord," she whispered, her eyes turning upward. "Just get me aboard a ship to take me home."

Chapter Eighteen

"Stop!"

Diedra braced herself with an extended arm as her driver did her bidding. She narrowed her eyes as she watched the carriage stop and let Ariel out, then drive on.

"And where is the blushing bride off to?" she mumbled. "And without her new husband?"

Her own choice of words cruelly reminded her of her pain. She wallowed in self-pity, working it into a rage. The blame didn't lay with her, but with Ariel.

Unable to still her curiosity, Diedra called out to her driver. "Stay with her, Donald. Don't lose her."

The sleek barouche jerked into motion. Diedra sat quietly, her mind churning, fast and furious.

What she hoped to gain, Diedra didn't know. She

wanted to slap Ariel's silly little face and tell her exactly what she thought of her wily ways.

She was so intent on her fantasies, Diedra wasn't even aware of where they were until a distinct smell penetrated her senses.

The docks. Its sounds, sights and odors were like no other place. Diedra paid only a moment's notice to her new surroundings. Only Ariel's destination mattered. She was so intent on what Ariel was doing and where she was going that when the carriage could go no further, Diedra got out without hesitation. As much as she hated the docks, she dogged Ariel until she reached the shipping office.

Afraid to be seen, Diedra dared not go inside. She drew a few unwanted stares. She was thankful she had thought to bring Donald along. He stood rigid and faithful, always a few feet behind her. His intense black look seemed to be enough to discourage those who looked from speaking to her.

Diedra couldn't imagine what was taking Ariel so long.

"Go in and see what she's doing," she snapped, irritated to the limit.

Donald turned to her with hooded eyes and nodded, then without saying a word ducked inside. It was several minutes before he emerged from the dark, dingy building to stand beside her. His look never wavered, always something between bored and cold.

"Well?" Diedra demanded.

"She is purchasing a ticket, madame."

"A ticket? For ship's passage?"

Almost a flash of emotion, the slightest look of impatience crossed Donald's face. "Of course, madame."

Diedra was so intent on learning about Ariel, she spent no time on his lack of manners. "And where is she off to?"

"She has booked passage for India on a ship called *The Indian Princess*. It sails tonight."

She was pleased. She felt a smile curve her mouth. "How interesting." Her mind churned. The only thing that was certain was her brother should be told.

"Let's go. We need to stop by Bryce's on the way home. Oh, dear, I've so much to do."

The prospect of Dylan's bride running away left her ecstatic. Of course, his marriage had only been a temporary setback. Diedra certainly had never let that stop her before. Now, it would be even easier for her. She certainly intended to be there tomorrow to comfort Dylan.

Bryce slammed down the decanter, amber liquid sloshing about in the crystal bottle. He started to walk away but decided to take the brandy with him.

He needed more than a stiff drink; he needed many of them. The decision made, he emptied the snifter in one gulp and poured more in its place.

The burn of the liquor seemed to relieve Bryce of some of the anger that coursed through him. Again and again his mind recalled the humiliation he suffered at being literally cast out of Dylan's house.

He looked at the gun he had grabbed from its case moments before, a surge of violence returning. He took another drink.

How he had wanted to go back and call Dylan out, to kill him on his own front steps. The thought was so tempting Bryce took another step forward, then shaking his head, turned away.

No! There were better ways. Slow, cold revenge was better.

"Yes," he shouted out loud, his anticipation building.

To kill him fast was too easy. Dylan must suffer for what he had done. Then, when Dylan was out of the way, Ariel would be his.

"Bitch," he mumbled, tipping the glass up once more. "I'll not let you get away." Bryce threw the fine crystal snifter across the room. As always, the sound of it made him smile. He drank directly from the bottle.

Already the numbness was spreading through him, his head whirling.

Too soon, the bottle was empty. This, too, he hurled at the stained wall, the sound of the heavy crystal shattering making Bryce laugh outright.

"Well," Diedra cooed, standing in the doorway to his bedroom. "I didn't expect you to be quite so jolly."

Bryce stood for a moment, surprised she would enter his bedroom parlor without being announced. Finally he said, "I didn't expect company. Especially you, dear sister."

Cold, gray eyes darted about the room. Her delicately shaped brow moved up as she took in everything, her actions reminding Bryce of how much she was like him.

"Tell me, dear brother, are you planning a trip?"

Bryce and Diedra simultaneously looked at his matching leather bags neatly stacked by the door.

"Actually, I have planned a trip . . ." Bryce didn't finish, merely shrugging his shoulders indifferently. The indifference was a lie. Inside rage tore at him. Ariel would have been his; tonight would have been their wedding night.

Had Diedra known his thoughts, she might have held her tongue. "Yes, that's what I've been told. Too bad your plans were changed. I know how much you had your heart set on marrying her."

Bryce had no tolerance for her games. "Diedra, do you have a purpose for being here, or did you come just to gloat over my loss?"

Then, even before she replied, he had another thought. "I would think you would be down, darling. After all, you had your heart set on Dylan."

This didn't seem to dim the glow in her eyes, and Bryce became suspicious.

"Yes, I admit I wasn't happy to hear your little love ran to Dylan. And I was even less happy to hear he married the conniving witch."

She paused a moment, running her finger over a porcelain statue, pretending to study it. Bryce was not fooled.

"I intend to kill him. Would that please you?"

This brought Diedra's wandering gaze back to him. "Oh, Bryce." She stomped a pretty foot. "You wouldn't."

"Why not? He deserves to die. Besides, I'd have

thought you would want him to pay."

Diedra seemed to give this some thought, then asked, "And what of Ariel's rejection of you? Is she going to pay, too?"

A cold smile twisted Bryce's features. "Of course." He envisioned the moment she would come back to him.

His sister shivered with apparent delight.

"It is quite a tempting offer, and I'm beginning to see it your way."

"You always were bright, Diedra."

She smiled. "You must always consider your options, Bryce. I like to be flexible. It makes life a bit easier. Dylan was a good choice, but there's got to be easier, less trying opportunities. Don't you think?"

"Yes, I agree." Bryce laughed at her fickleness. "So much for true love."

This brought on Diedra's laughter, its high-pitched notes filling the room. "Love? Really, Bryce, I can think of a lot of feelings we may have, but love isn't among them. Lust, desire, obsession, even hatred, but not love. Surely you don't think you love Ariel?"

His silence gave her the chance to continue, her voice taking on a lecturing tone.

"Well, you thought wrong, dearest brother. You were obsessed, and certainly you desired her. But you definitely didn't love her. Why, you're going to kill her. That's certainly an odd thing to do if you love her."

Bryce scowled. "I didn't say I would kill her. At least not for a while."

"It's good to see your brain isn't totally muddled by that little tramp. Have your fun, then. Well, we're lucky to be rid of them."

An amused eyebrow lifted, relieving Bryce's face of the cloud. "We're not rid of them yet."

"I know, but I have utmost confidence in you, Bryce."

"I'm so pleased," Bryce drawled, thinking he and his sister hadn't exchanged this much conversation in years, if ever.

Diedra reached out and patted him on the shoulder. "Well, I'll leave you to your plotting. All I ask is that you make their deaths fitting. Do you know what I mean?"

"I think I do."

Bryce watched her open the door, then turn back to him.

"Oh, dear, I almost forgot to tell you something."

"What's that?"

"Ariel's gotten passage on a ship bound for India. *The Indian Princess*, I believe. It sails tonight, so you'd best hurry. I've got to go, dear. Let me know how it goes."

In a swish, Diedra was out the door before he even had a chance to digest her latest bit of news. Suddenly her nonchalance at killing someone struck him as funny. She certainly was like him, that was for sure.

When his laughter died, so did his humor. Bryce assessed the new situation with a calm attitude. A flustered hunter never got his prey.

"So," he said smoothly, his delight over this new event lifting his spirits. "My little witch has run

215

away from everyone, including you, Dylan, old
friend."

All the warmth left the shipping office when the
sun went down. The breeze coming off the water
seeped in through the cracks of the walls. Ariel's
teeth chattered, and still she felt hot. Her head
ached so badly she feared she would be sick. A
hand touched her arm.

"Are you all right, lass? You dinna look so well."
The big Scotsman was gentle, his caring look
touching from such a large, burly man. His brogue
was strong yet held a softness in it. Ariel liked this
man called Mr. MacDonald that managed the shipping office.

"I'm fine . . . well, perhaps a bit under the weather, but I'll be all right."

"How 'bout a cup o' hot tea? Will do you good."

"Please don't go to any trouble on my account,
Mr. MacDonald. I'm fine."

A clicking sound came from deep in his throat.
"Now, lassie, ye'd never be no trouble. 'Tis my
pleasure."

It wasn't a moment before she was sipping the
strong tea, its heat seeping through her, relieving
her chills for the moment.

"It won't be long now n' we'll have ye snug on
the ship, lassie."

Ariel smiled in gratitude for his kindness—and
for taking the gold wedding band as payment for
her passage. She hoped it wouldn't be long; she was
so tired. Just keeping her eyes open was exhausting.
Giving in, she closed them, just for a moment.

* * *

Bryce watched Ariel from outside the shipping office, his fury nearly out of control. How he wanted to grab her and . . .

And what?

Carefully, he pulled rampant emotions under control, then examined the question more thoroughly. What did he plan to do with her? In the end, Ariel must die. That was the only thing he was certain of. In the meantime, he wanted many things. He wanted her to pay for what she had done. He wanted her to suffer.

This brought a smile to his lips. Yes, he wanted her to suffer. He had to fight the urge to just barge in and be off with her, but the old fool of a Scot was hovering about like a mother hen. The man hadn't been out of sight for a moment since Bryce arrived.

His patience sorely tried, Bryce paced outside the building, stopping every now and then to glance in the dingy window to see if she was alone.

Bryce's chance never came. Before he could even react, Mr. MacDonald escorted Ariel to *The Indian Princess* and settled her aboard. Bryce walked back to where his driver and carriage waited, frustration pounding with every step.

"Go back and get my baggage. Then return here and see it gets put aboard *The Indian Princess*. And hurry!"

Just remembering that his manservant had packed those bags for his trip with his new wife-to-be only hours before galled him. How on earth had he lost control of everything?

"No matter," he mumbled under his breath as he moved toward the door. "I'll not lose control again." Even if he had to follow her to the ends of the earth.

It didn't take long for Bryce to be settled aboard *The Indian Princess*, his servant thorough as usual. He sat for the longest time just staring at his door, knowing her cabin was just beyond. Unable to stop himself, he went out into the passageway. He walked over and stood in front of Ariel's cabin.

Bryce laid his hand on the smooth wooden door, the feel of it cool against the heat of his palm. The ship swayed beneath his feet, the rocking motion pulling him further from reality. He heard the beat of his heart as it pumped blood through his head, the rush leaving him breathing hard. Sweat popped out on his upper lip as he considered the woman who lay just beyond, probably sleeping.

He closed his eyes, envisioning Ariel's beauty lying before him, her hair spread out in a glorious ring of reddish-brown. His hand slid down the door's surface, his mind imagining the long length of her neck beneath his fingers. He could feel it, so soft and silky, so delicate. So easy to break. His fist clenched, and his nails raked along the wooden surface.

"Can I help you, Lord Harrington?"

Bryce pulled his hand away from the door and turned to the man who had spoken. "I was just about to retire to my cabin."

"I'm afraid you have the wrong door. You're next

door." The doctor pointed to Bryce's door. "It's easy to do, to get the wrong cabin."

"Yes, I suppose it is."

"Good thing I stopped you. Wouldn't want you to disturb Miss Lockwood." He reached out and twisted the doorknob. "She's not feeling very well."

Bryce turned his attention back to the portly man, his interest peaked. "Nothing serious, I hope."

"Probably a touch seasick is all."

The doctor disappeared into Ariel's room. Bryce stood for the longest moment, staring at the closed door and listening to their hushed voices.

Patience. The time would come.

Chapter Nineteen

"Ariel." Dylan eased open the door and stepped into the dark room. Quietly, he moved across to the bed.

"Ariel," he said in a loud whisper, reaching out to shake her awake. Instead of finding Ariel's soft curves, Dylan encountered only pillows and blankets.

A dozen places she could be tumbled through his head as he lit the table lamp. Not one to panic or jump to conclusions, Dylan checked the bath, then returned to check the room again. That was when he discovered her tapestry bag was gone.

Where would she go?

He searched the house, starting with the top floor and looking into each room with care, one by one, floor by floor, until there was no place left to look. Suddenly, hopefully, it occurred to him she must have gone to her aunt and uncle's.

"Of course," he said with a sigh, his heart easing. Dylan ran out to the stable, saddled his horse and mounted. It had started to drizzle, the cloudy day keeping people inside. For that small favor he was thankful.

Dylan urged his stallion into a run, cutting across the park to save time. It wouldn't take long to get to Witherspoon's townhouse, but each second that ticked by was too long for him. Questions pounded his mind.

As he stood in front of the door, Dylan felt a fear he had never experienced before. Carefully he put aside the rush of emotions and banged the door knocker. He waited with as much patience as he could summon for Henry and Margaret to see him.

It was difficult to look calm, but he certainly didn't want to panic them. Yet, as hard as he tried, he could not hold back the question that plagued him.

"Would it be all right if I see Ariel?"

The confusion on Henry's face was his answer, but he waited for confirmation. "Why, she isn't here, Dylan."

The pain returned twofold, and he flopped down into a chair in defeat. "Ariel didn't come here?"

"No," Margaret whispered, her face pinching with worry.

"Are you sure?"

"I left her with you, Dylan, just this morning. I don't understand." Henry looked from Dylan to Margaret, as if uncertain who could settle the matter.

Dylan felt lost himself. His shoulders sagged under the weight of it. "She left."

Margaret got up and crossed to her husband, taking the hand he offered to her. "Ariel left you, without saying anything?"

Running his hand through his hair, Dylan shook his head, the movement showing how he felt. "Not a word."

Silence engulfed them. Finally, Dylan stood. "Where would she go?" And more important, why?

"I don't know. She always stayed so much to herself. I'll go check her room and see if she left a note."

As soon as Margaret was out of hearing, Dylan exploded. "Damn it, Henry, why would she just run off? Have you told me everything about Harrington and his hold on you?"

"You know everything, Dylan."

"Somehow I don't think I know everything," Dylan mumbled, his mind recalling all the strange happenings of late.

Henry's look brought his mind back to the present. "I didn't mean to imply you were keeping anything from me. I think she's in trouble. It's something I think even you don't know about, Henry."

"She's an independent one, that's for sure. Even after her aunt's attempts to transform her. Margaret meant well, but Ariel's . . ." He shrugged, looking for the right word. "Ariel's . . . Ariel. Sometimes I wonder if we should have left her in India, running free in the jungles with that pet of hers."

Dylan might have agreed, but at that moment Margaret returned.

"Margaret." Dylan's voice was soft and gentle. "Did you find anything?" She shook her head no. "Do you have any idea why Ariel would leave?" A tiny note of desperation shook his own words.

Margaret's look was sympathetic. "I'm sure it was not because of you, Dylan."

"Then what?" His voice rose, and it took a great deal of control to bring it back to a calm level. "Then what? I know something dreadful has happened, but she will tell me nothing."

"I wish I could be of more help to you, Dylan."

"Do you have any idea where she might go?"

"I think she would go home," Margaret said tenderly.

Henry shook his head. "But she's not here."

"This isn't home, Henry." Margaret's face was sad, as if Ariel's own misery was mirrored on it. "It never has been. India is where she longs to be."

Dylan was truly surprised. "Why India? She has nothing left there."

"Her memories are there. And perhaps Kala Bagh still waits for her."

Henry somewhat grunted. "I doubt that."

"What do you mean, memories?" Dylan's curiosity was running wild, his mind reacting to every thought.

A single tear slipped from Margaret's eyes. "It nearly destroyed Ariel when she heard of my brother's death. She has nightmares all the time. She doesn't sleep well."

"But why would that make her go home?" Dylan

pursued, Ariel's reasons still unclear to him.

"She's gone home to say goodbye to her father." Now the tears flowed freely. "Ariel never got to say goodbye. It's the only way she can rid her heart of the grief."

All the way to the waterfront the words echoed about in his mind. *Never got to say goodbye.* His heart constricted tighter within his chest each and every time it rattled about.

"Damn," he cursed himself. There was so much he didn't know about her. "Hell, I don't know anything about her really."

Yet she was legally his wife.

His wife. That sentiment now replaced the other in his thoughts. If he got to the ship in time, what would he do? What would he say?

Frustration filled him, eating at his insides like a bad wine. His thoughts stampeded, one into another, drifting incoherently from subject to subject.

Again a surge of anxiety brought him full circle to an old question. What was she involved in? Dylan ran his hands over his face.

Carefully Dylan examined everything since his return to England, backtracking over the last few weeks. It had actually started before with the message from his father, asking him to check into Lockwood's death. Was this somehow connected to Ariel? He had come here to ferret out the truth. His gut instinct told him Harrington was behind the so-called accident. In turn, Harrington was blackmailing Henry to make Ariel marry him. Did he first kill her father to clear his way?

"My God," whispered Dylan as the clouds began to clear. What else was Harrington capable of?

This he didn't know, but he wondered if Ariel did. Dylan also realized his own marriage to Ariel wouldn't stop Bryce. Of that he was certain. He would watch his back, but who would watch over Ariel?

He didn't or couldn't allow himself to delve further into this question.

Finally he reached the docks and his first stop was at the ticket office. Mr. MacDonald was very obliging, giving Dylan the information he needed about the ship Ariel had sailed on and when. Next, he headed for his own ship that was harbored nearby.

Within a few hours of discovering Ariel gone, Dylan strode aboard, yelling orders to his men.

"We kin have her ready t' sail with the tide, Captain."

"That's too late, John. *The Indian Princess* has already sailed with Ariel on it."

"We canna' row her out t' sea. We have t' wait for the tide."

"I know." Dylan's voice lowered its pitch and he felt tired. "I know. Do your best, John."

"We'll catch her, Captain. *The Indian Princess* is a passenger ship. It'll be going ashore for more passengers 'n we kin be in Alexandria afore she is."

"You're right."

"She'll be fine, Captain."

Dylan's thoughts were not so confident. He recalled how feverish she had been. What else could possibly go wrong?

*   *   *

Bryce lay in his bunk, sleep a stranger. The rocking of the ship lulled him, but his eyes wouldn't close. Sweat ran from his forehead into his eyes. He rubbed the sting away.

She *would* be his.

He drew in a ragged breath. His body ached for her.

"Witch," he mumbled hoarsely, his hands clenching into fists. "Witch, I'll have you; then I'll destroy you."

Ariel came awake, the fear that clouded her mind very real. She pushed the covers away and swung her legs over the side of the bunk. Dizziness and pain kept her from standing.

She looked around, but darkness kept her surroundings a mystery. It wasn't until she felt the sway of the ship that she remembered where she was and where she was going. She sighed, but it came out a wheeze and ended in a cough.

Ariel wanted a drink of water, but instead she slumped back into the bunk and pulled the blanket back over her. Warily, she stared into the blackness that engulfed her, wondering what had wakened her. Fear choked her, taking the air from her lungs, the heat from her body.

She sensed danger. She could smell it, she could taste it, she could feel it crawl over her. But she couldn't see it.

Where was it? What was it?

No, she was imagining it. She was sick. It was the fever. Finally, her eyes closed in weariness.

When Ariel opened her eyes again she had no idea if only a few moments had passed or a day or maybe more. It was still dark; that was all she was able to discern.

She was hot. She had kicked the covers off on the floor. Ariel forced herself to sit up. The room was stuffy. It smelled of sickness. She needed fresh air.

Ariel set her fevered mind on standing, ignoring her body's warnings it was not up to it. Her legs were so shaky and weak she immediately sank to her knees. Gritting her teeth, she pulled herself back up.

Fresh, cool air was what Ariel needed. Slowly she inched her way to the door, her eyes adjusting to the pale sliver of light the moon cast through her tiny porthole.

Ariel felt like a child taking its first toddling steps.

The door seemed heavy, but it eased open with persistence. Suddenly the ship rolled over a swell in the water and sent her stumbling to the far wall of the narrow companionway, the door shutting behind her. She clutched at the wall to stay upright, depending on its rigidness when her knees seemed to be failing her.

"Please, God," she whispered, closing her burning eyes for a brief second. "Just a breath of fresh air. That's all I ask."

Ariel could not bear to think of returning to the cramped cabin without some fresh air. She shivered, more from the dread of confinement than the chill sweeping down the long passageway. She smelled the salt of the sea air and felt renewed energy as the breeze cooled her heated face.

It wasn't so far.

Taking a ragged breath, Ariel moved on, slow and unsteady, yet she managed to put the length of hallway behind her.

Looking up the steep flight of stairs, Ariel felt the urge to cry. Tears came to her eyes, but she wiped them away. She had climbed too many trees in the jungle to let this stop her.

Grabbing the rail, Ariel dragged her weak, betraying body up. One, two. She counted each step, feeling victory as she traversed each successfully.

As her head peeked out onto the deck, the sea misted her face, and the cool spray relieved her of the fevered heat that burned her skin. She drew in deep, cleansing breaths of crisp air, dispelling the stench that clung to her. She tasted the salt hanging in the dampness, licking the moisture from her lips.

She moved to the rail, grasping it to stand and cleanse the staleness from her lungs. Clouds played tag with a crescent moon. Memories ran through her mind like the clouds. They came and went in a rush of emotions. Ariel thought of the jungle, the air heavy with dampness from a sudden rain, the thick growth of trees dripping down on her long after the skies cleared.

Her homesick sigh was lost on the wind, but the feeling was not so easy to dispel. Her heart beat faster as she saw in her mind's eye Kala Bagh springing through the trees, coming to her. Soon they would run free again.

"Free."

The sound rushed from her in a whisper of hope. What she would do once in India, she didn't know. It didn't matter. She would be home.

"I'll be home soon, Papa."

"Sooner than you think, my sweet."

The words fell upon her from the sea breeze, chilling the heat that scorched her body. She whirled about to see who had spoken, the quick movement sending her balance askew. Ariel stumbled and fell to her hands and knees. Pain stampeded in her head, making it difficult to stand again.

She heard footsteps moving closer, close enough for her to see. But as she used the last of her strength to raise her head, the black boots disappeared across the wet deck.

"Good God," muttered Dr. Thompson as he ran to help Ariel. "What on earth are you doing out of bed?"

Ariel allowed him to gather her up and carry her back to the cabin. If he expected an answer, she was unable to give one. Her eyes were closed; only the tears on her cheeks revealed she was conscious.

How long he fussed about, she wasn't sure. Time no longer registered. Only her dreams and nightmares held meaning.

"Ariel."

"Papa."

"Help me. I need you."

Ariel lifted her heavy legs, the effort taking all her strength. "I'm coming, Papa. I'm coming."

Each step was agonizing, like a bog sucking her legs into the wet earth, keeping her from him, holding her back.

"I'm coming!"

Yet as hard as she struggled, Ariel made no progress.

"Papa!"

"It's too late, my sweet."

Her father crumpled to the ground. Above him stood Bryce Harrington, a smile on his face. He held a knife, and from its gleaming tip dripped her father's blood. It fell upon her hand, and she wiped it away in horror. But its stain grew, smearing across her palm, then across her face as she covered her eyes against what she saw.

"No!"

Ariel cried out, jerking awake to the horror of remembrance.

"Oh, Papa, why did you send me away?"

"Did you say something, Miss Lockwood?"

Ariel felt herself drifting away again. "I never got to say goodbye."

"There now, dear. You go back to sleep. You need your rest."

He stroked back her damp hair, and she relaxed under his soothing touch. He was kind and good. Abruptly visions of Harrington crowded in, causing her to pull away from the doctor's ministering.

"Papa."

Dr. Thompson tucked the blanket about Ariel. He unhooked the wire pieces from his ears and pulled the glasses off his face. He rubbed his tired eyes, then carefully replaced the glasses. He stared for some time as Ariel slept fitfully, wondering about the young lady in his care. Standing, he walked over to the washbowl, wrung out the cloth once again and returned to his patient. Gently, he wiped at her feverish brow.

"Papa," she mumbled in her half-sleep.

"Ssshhh," he whispered.

"Is that you, Papa?"

Dr. Thompson patted her hand in a comforting manner. "Yes, Miss . . ." He stopped, then corrected himself. "Ariel. It's your father."

A smile touched her lips, and Ariel drifted back to sleep. Dr. Thompson continued to cool her heated skin with the damp cloth. It would be a long trip.

Dylan stood on deck of his ship staring out into the darkness, the sound of the wooden hull slicing through the waves his only comfort at that moment. Sleep was becoming a rare relief.

The breeze ruffled Dylan's hair. He rubbed the stubble on his face. He felt haggard. Dread had lain in the pit of his stomach the entire day, yet he could do nothing. Nothing.

He clutched the railing.

"Damn you, Ariel. Why did you run away? I could help you. What must I do for you to trust me?" Trust. Why would she trust him? They didn't know each other. They were all but strangers.

"I will teach you to trust me, Ariel. I promise."

Chapter Twenty

The dock was busy, near overloaded with peo
ple and cargo. The clamor of many language
was accented by all color and manner of dress
Horses snorted, donkeys brayed, chickens clucke
and geese honked, each adding their distinctiv
sounds and smells, their odors mingling pungen
and sweet. Ships crowded the sea's horizon. Hig
turrets of mosques reached into the city's skyline

Dylan pushed past the surge of people. He ha
lost his patience watching everyone disembar
from *The Indian Princess* and started aboard.

"Excuse me," he mumbled, bumping into on
person then another. It was like swimming up
stream; for each step he took forward, he was force
to take another back. Finally, he stepped onto th
deck. Quickly he scanned the ship and located th
captain as he oversaw the unloading of the cargo

He wasted no time. "Captain."

The man turned his attention to Dylan. "Yes?"

"I'm Dylan Christianson, sir. I've been waiting for my wife, but I don't see her."

The words were calm enough, but the worry he felt came through and the captain caught it. "I don't recall any passenger by that name. We had only one young lady traveling alone. A Miss Lockwood."

Relief swarmed over Dylan, a flush of warmth. "Yes, Miss Lockwood is my wife. We were just married."

"Yes." The captain smiled.

Dylan wasn't certain what his smile meant, but it really didn't matter. Only that Ariel was aboard.

"Miss . . ." The captain corrected himself. "Mrs. Christianson is still in her cabin. The ship's doctor is with her."

Relief was replaced by worry once again. "The doctor?"

"Your wife's been very ill. Dr. Thompson has been with her day and night for the entire trip."

His first instincts were to rush to Ariel to see for himself she was all right, but Dylan refrained. "Could you take me to her, Captain?"

"Certainly."

They walked towards the companionway, and Dylan added, "I appreciate your helping my wife. I would like to pay you for your troubles."

"Dr. Thompson's the one who tended to her. You might talk with him."

They reached a door, and the captain knocked softly.

Dylan shook the captain's hand. "My thanks." Then he stepped into the dim room.

"Ariel."

"She's resting."

Turning to the voice, Dylan allowed his eyes to adjust to the darkness before moving further into the room. "You must be Dr. Thompson."

"Yes, and who are you, sir?"

"I'm Ariel's husband."

"Oh."

It was all he said, but Dylan winced at the judgment in that one word.

"Is she going to be all right?" He dared a look at the small cot, Ariel's form lost in the shadows. His heart skipped a beat then lurched forward. He held his breath, waiting for the doctor's answer.

"I think the worst of it is over. She needs to be taken care of; maybe let another doctor look in on her. I've done all I know how."

Dylan had to swallow, to relieve the dryness of his mouth. "I'm grateful for all you've done."

The older man lifted his hand and swatted the air. "No need. Just promise me you'll take good care of her."

"You have my promise." Dylan stepped to the bed and gathered Ariel into his arms, gently wrapping the blanket about her. "I have a carriage waiting."

"Here." The doctor handed him her tapestry bag. "It's all she had with her."

He took it, then started for the door. He paused, then turned his head to the doctor. "I'm forever grateful."

The man nodded, then went about gathering up his things. Within minutes Dylan was in the carriage, the driver heading to the hotel in Alexandria.

"I'll take care of you, Ariel," Dylan whispered in her ear, kissing the warm blush on her cheek. Brushing the hair from her fevered forehead, he studied her face, her eyes still closed in sleep. Every once in a while she stirred, a soft moan escaping from her chapped lips.

"Why did you run off? Why?"

Bryce stood in the throng of people and watched the carriage roll away. He was not totally amazed that Dylan Christianson had turned up on the docks of Alexandria.

Perhaps this could work to his advantage. Perhaps he could have his revenge on them both. Visions danced through his mind, teasing him with delight to come. The possibilities were endless, and this pleased him further. Christianson's death would be a moment to savor, just as his conquest of Ariel would be.

His mind conjured up dreams of her submission, her shapely body squirming beneath his. Pain and ecstasy were his to give, life and death.

The power of it was exhilarating; his pulse pumped faster, the blood in his veins running strong. Bryce pulled out a white handkerchief and patted at the sweat popping out on his forehead.

Soon, very soon. Anticipation was like a drug, its elixir working on his mind as well as his body.

"I need a woman," he mumbled, then walked away, heading for his carriage. "Maybe two."

* * *

Dylan had to use every bit of self-control to stay put in the chair and wait. It was only a short while, though it seemed like hours, before the door opened and the doctor came out.

This time he allowed himself to stand.

"Your wife will be fine. The fever's broken. She'll start to feel better in a few days, but make her rest. Plenty of rest. That's what she needs."

"I'll take good care of her."

"Good. She may just sleep for a day or two. Don't be too alarmed by it. She's had a rough bout."

"I'll call you if she gets worse again."

"Yes, do that. I'll stop by tomorrow to check on her."

"I'd appreciate that."

As the doctor started out the door, he paused. "I've left a bottle of laudanum. If her sleep becomes fitful, just put a few drops in a glass of water and give it to her. She'll sleep better."

"Thanks. I'll see you tomorrow."

Dylan watched the door close. He brushed his hair back, walked into the bedroom and looked across the room at Ariel, sleeping in the large bed. She cried out softly. He crossed to stand beside her, staring down at her as she slept. Her hair spread out over the white pillow, red highlights sparkling in the light from the lamp on the side table. The delicate lace trimming the bedcover framed her face, and it made him think of how fragile she was.

Another whimper escaped. Dylan sat down on the side of the bed. He stroked her bare arm and whispered, "It's all right now, Ariel."

Ariel stirred, her topaz eyes opening large against the paleness of her face. Tears swam in their depths and slipped from her darkly lashed lower lids.

"Papa?"

Dylan started to reply, to tell her he wasn't her father, but he didn't. The words seemed to stick in his throat; maybe it was the look on her face. Love and sorrow were intermingled in her eyes, breaking his heart.

"Papa," she whispered hoarsely, her voice cracking from dryness. "I've come to say goodbye. We never said goodbye."

"I love you, Ariel." Whether it was his own words or her father's, he didn't know. Either way, it made her smile, and he felt happy.

"I love you too, Papa." Tears rushed down her cheeks. "Why did you send me away? You needed me, and I wasn't there. I wasn't there."

"Oh, Ariel." Dylan pulled her into his arms and rocked her, her sobs tearing at his heart. "It's all right, darling."

Slowly, the sobs subsided, and he gently laid her back down, tucking the covers around her. "Sleep, Ariel. I'm here to take care of you."

A breeze swirled the white sheer panels out from the tall windows, the delicate fabric drifting silently. Palm trees just outside waved their giant fingered leaves, their soft rustle floating on the air. The sun's light bathed the room in a golden spray.

Dylan closed his eyes and allowed tension to drain from him. Two days had passed, and still

Ariel slept. The dreams no longer bothered her rest, her slumber deep and sound. The worry of her illness was relieved, but other thoughts and troubles continued to plague him. He wanted her to sleep, to recover completely, but he wanted her to wake up so they could talk.

"Talk," he mumbled, rubbing his hand over his tired eyes. Would they talk? Would Ariel trust him enough to tell him why she ran away?

He turned away from the window, the beauty of the city a hollow thing. His gaze rested on the canopied bed, Ariel's petite form lost in a mountain of white lace and pale blue satin. His gaze traveled to her face. Dark gold stopped him, the depths clear and alert.

Her lips quivered into a small smile, a flash of happiness sparkling in her eyes. "Dylan?"

Never had he been so delighted at hearing his name, yet he understood the confusion that underlined it. Her gaze moved away from him and looked about the plush room, her distress evidencing more with each passing second.

"Where am I?" She turned back to him, despair in her look. "How did you . . . ?"

Ariel couldn't finish. She turned her face into the pillow. The sobs reached Dylan, nearly defeating all the hope he had mustered in the last few days. He wanted to go to her, but he was afraid.

Fear. It was an unusual feeling, one he had seldom ever experienced. Yet one little sob from this woman, and he turned to jelly.

"Lordy," Dylan sighed. Taking a deep breath, he walked over to her bed. He laid his hand on her head, smoothing the tangles of reddish-brown hair. Her sobbing got worse at his touch.

"Ariel," he whispered in agony, "don't cry."

He couldn't stand to hear her cry, but she didn't stop. Dylan felt awkward, another feeling he rarely had to deal with. Finally he pulled her up into his arms and held her. He wanted to say something. Anything! Instead, he just continued to hold her. All the questions that haunted him were left unasked. He held her close to him.

How much time passed before Ariel stopped crying, Dylan didn't know. Soon her even breathing hypnotized him, and he fell asleep, still holding her tightly in his arms.

Slowly, lazily, Ariel came out of her deep sleep. She heard the steady beat of her heart, loud in her ears. No, not hers, but . . .

She tilted her head up, the warmth of flesh beneath her cheek. With effort, her eyes fluttered open. She saw the tip of a chin, Dylan's chin, the dark markings of his unshaven beard blending into the bronze tan of his face.

This time it was the beat of her own heart sounding inside her head, charging ahead in abandon. His warm breath was like a caress on her face, his nearness bringing a warm flush to her. Many emotions rested uneasily in her mind.

How did he find her?

This question was easily answered. Ariel figured it wouldn't have been so difficult to know she would go to India, to find out what ship she was on. But how she came to be here was unclear.

Ariel vaguely remembered being ill, and that someone, a kindly older man, had cared for her. All else remained a jumble of confusion.

Part of her was overjoyed Dylan was here, and the other wished him gone. Nothing had changed. She was still in trouble.

A tremor of remembrance bolted through her as Bryce's threat drifted to her mind.

Sooner than you think. Sooner than you think.

Ariel's gasp caused Dylan to stir. His hold on her tightened. She knew he was awake even before his eyes opened. Panic seized her. She knew it was impossible for Bryce to have been aboard *The Indian Princess*. Or was it? She couldn't still the gnawing fear.

She tried to pull away, but Dylan wasn't about to let her escape him. What would she say? What could she say?

Tears stung her eyes, yet she blinked them back, determined not to cry again.

Dylan felt Ariel tense. Guilt rushed forward at having kept her from getting up. She had felt so good, her warmth a comfort to him. Unwillingly, he let her go and watched her stand on shaky legs.

He wanted to say something, anything, but no words seemed right. The look on her face was fearful.

"I didn't mean to frighten you," Dylan finally said, reaching out his hand to her. "Please come back."

Ariel did not move. The flush left her face. Her skin paled, alarming Dylan. He saw her trembling and was just in time to keep her from falling to the floor.

"You're weak, Ariel. You must lie back down. It will take some time before you regain your strength."

He lifted her and carried her back to the bed. She did not speak. "I'll have some soup brought up for you. You must be starved."

Like a mother, Dylan tucked and fluffed, making sure Ariel was comfortable. "There." He smiled, patting the pillow one last time. He turned away but paused, his gaze catching hers.

"Ariel, I . . ."

What? What did he want to say? Never had Dylan felt so confused. And to make matters worse, Ariel remained silent.

"I'll be right back with a tray."

It was inadequate, but he didn't want to push her. Ariel would have to tell him in her own time. He would have to show her she could trust him. That no matter what . . .

No matter what. All kinds of horror crossed his mind as he once again could only guess at the cause of the fear in her eyes. It was driving him crazy—not knowing, Ariel not telling.

Dylan closed the door to the bedroom, feeling Ariel was shutting him out in the same manner. He stood for a moment, fighting the urge to go back and demand she explain.

He grasped the doorknob but did not go in. With a sigh, he let it go and walked away.

Ariel stared at the closed door, her heart aching, her heart breaking. She needed to think, but her

241

eyes drooped, her concentration scattered.

Sleep clouded her thoughts, and others moved in to take over. Memories of that night in the park drifted across her mind's eye, the horror of it terrorizing her. She must go home.

Chapter Twenty-One

"Can we go into Alexandria today?"

Dylan looked up from the letter he was writing. "Are you feeling strong enough?"

Ariel moved toward him, each step a graceful statement. She looked better today than she had since her arrival; even the natural blush was back to her cheeks. She wore an attractive green dress, and Dylan couldn't help but notice the gentle curve of her hips, the rise and fall of her breasts just beneath the bit of frill at her neck. She was beautiful, and he was finding it hard to keep away from her bed these past few days.

An almost shy smile curved her full mouth. "I'm strong enough to feel confined by this room. Please, Dylan. I promise that if I get tired, we'll come back."

"Well," he drawled, teasing the tiny smile into

a full one. "I don't know. You look a bit pale to me."

"You mother me too much," she complained good-naturedly.

"Oh, all right. We'll take in the sights, my sweet." Once again he saw the instant uncomfortable look at his endearment. Not once in the last week had he been able to get past a simple intimacy. "You get ready. I'll hire a carriage."

Dylan's disappointment was obvious, and Ariel regretted her uncontrolled reactions. Too many conflicting emotions churned inside her, taking away any pleasure his sweet words might have given. Fear and guilt held her in sober reclusion. All his efforts to comfort her only pushed her further away.

Ariel knew he wanted to ask her why she had run away, but he didn't. She was grateful and didn't offer an explanation. They had yet to discuss returning to England, but she knew it was unavoidable. Ariel's determination to go to India had not diminished, but how she was going to get there was beyond her at that time. She would figure it out. She had to.

Hearing Dylan returning, Ariel quickly gathered up her things and met him at the door. She would face all this later. Today she would see the city with her husband by her side.

"I'm ready."

The twinkle in Dylan's blue eyes told her everything was all right. Ariel slid her gloved hand onto his gray-jacketed arm, the muscle beneath hard. Her illness was all but a memory, her health returning quickly under his tender care, along with the stirrings of desire he so easily ignited.

"Shall we go?" she asked, needing to escape the heat of his gaze.

The day was beautiful, its sultry heat welcome. She had been cooped up for too long. The sky provided a canopy of blue over the city and its buildings of sun-baked bricks with high turrets of all sizes and shapes. Tall stone pillars with ancient writings, elegant mosques with round domes, and spiraling towers spread out before her curious eyes.

They strolled through the many stalls and shops of the busy bazaar, stopping often to examine antiques and wares. Silver and copper objects of every sort were offered, while perfume and spices added their array of scents to the pungent air. Beautiful weavings of silk, wool and linen lined makeshift walls, their rich texture and patterns, florals and landscapes, in vibrant blues, greens and reds attracting their gazes.

Craftsmen called to the throng of people, each trying to draw shoppers to his wares, each with a strategy, a trademark, revealing the man's character. The sounds, the smells, the feel of the open market were tantalizing, and Ariel felt vibrant and alive. She forgot the past weeks, the horror of it all fading in the magic of the old city. For the moment, she was happy.

Ariel touched a small hand-carved bird, admiring the intricate detail achieved by the artist. Dylan came up behind her, the heat of his nearness warming her.

He leaned over and said, "Stay right here, Ariel. I'll be right back."

His breath tickled her ear, but it was the hidden promise in his words that intrigued her. She looked up in time to catch a glint in his eyes. "I'll be right here."

Dylan moved off into the crowd, his height making him easy to follow until he turned and disappeared from sight. Ariel wondered at his mysterious mood, then returned her attention to the carving she held.

It began as an uneasy feeling, crawling up her spine. It came to rest in her mind, pulling her full, undivided attention. Ariel looked about, searching the many strange faces for a reason for her anxiety. Slowly, the feeling intensified, raising the hair on the back of her neck.

She tried to concentrate on the vender jabbering at her, pushing different objects at her to examine, perhaps to buy. The smile she gave the bearded man was forced, but it prompted a wide toothless grin from him.

"She'll take this one."

Ariel's heart nearly crashed from her chest. The blood rushed from her head too fast, and she had to grip the small table to keep from falling.

Casually, Bryce paid for the carving, acting as if nothing was out of the ordinary. He took the fine work of art; then taking her hand, he placed it in her palm, folding her fingers around it.

"A wedding gift," he whispered.

She tried to pull away from him, his touch sending chills through her. She felt ill.

"Oh, dear," he scolded. "You're not going to faint on me, are you?"

Jerking her hand free, Ariel gathered her wits before they scattered completely. "Don't touch me."

"Ariel, my sweet, there's no need to be rude."

Bryce's use of the same endearment Dylan had used earlier distracted Ariel. It made her wonder that one man's words could make her want to melt in his arms, while the other made her feel dirty, made her want to scrub the filth of his words from her. "What do you want from me?"

His chuckle caused the same reaction, making her skin crawl. "What do I want? You ran off and married Dylan. Then you ran off from your husband. Now, why are you doing so much running away, Ariel?"

"Why do you think?" she snapped, fear weaving its way through her mind, tying knots in her runaway thoughts.

"What have you told Dylan?"

"Nothing."

He grabbed her hand again, squeezing it until the object she held bit into her flesh. "I find that hard to believe, my dearest. Especially when I see you two together."

"I told you it would be our secret. You've made more than clear what will happen if I should be so foolish."

Bryce's head shook back and forth in doubt. "I don't know. How can I be certain?"

"You've threatened my family—"

He interrupted her, putting his hand to her lips. "That's not enough."

Ariel swallowed hard, then spit at him, "Then kill me. That would solve your problem, wouldn't it? Do it now. Kill me!"

A strange smile twisted his lips as he considered this. His hand moved to her neck, his fingers running down the long length of it. Her flesh crawled beneath his touch, but she did not move away this time.

"That's such a tempting offer, but that would be too easy."

"No challenge?"

His smile grew. He appreciated her spirit. "No challenge at all." He pulled his hand away. "On the other hand, I think Dylan would be—a challenge, that is."

This came from nowhere, something she had not suspected at all. The meaning of his threat took away her fight.

Bryce pulled her into a stall of rugs, the overcrowded space blocking them from the view of those who passed by. He drew Ariel's face up close to his; the look she saw told her as much as his words.

"He took you away from me. I can't let that go unpunished. I've gone to a lot of trouble to get you, and I'll not stand for his interference."

His words came out in a rush, a glaze settling over his eyes. This frightened her even more. "I had no intention of marrying you, even without Dylan's interference."

"You lie!" Bryce's grip on her tightened.

Ariel's mind was working quickly, trying to find some sort of reasoning Bryce would comprehend.

248

"If you kill him, the police will know it was you. You two fought over me. Everyone knows that."

She could almost see his mind churning, digesting this thought. "You are very bright. That is one of the many reasons I was attracted to you."

Relief came in such a rush, she could not still the look that reflected it. Bryce immediately dispelled any illusions she might have formed in that brief moment.

"Don't be so gullible. There are other ways. Accidents can cover many a motive."

"If you even consider such a thing, I *will* tell what I know."

Bryce's laughter nearly undid the little composure she had left. She wondered if it was all a bizarre dream.

"I'm no fool, Ariel. Nor am I a novice at these things. I do admire your gumption, but an accident is just that, an accident. Purposely prompted or not. I'll be sure of it."

"You can't get away with it," she hissed.

"Of course I can. No one's ever questioned your father's accident. No one will Dylan's."

A sweep of emotion took the stiffness from her legs, but she would not succumb to her weakness. With every bit of any determination she had, Ariel faced him squarely. "What do you know of my father's accident?"

Another smile broke his stony features, but it did not influence the steely look remaining in his eyes. "Only that it was not an accident. Well, not totally."

Ariel found it difficult not to claw his face as anger swept through her. "You shot my father?"

"It was an accident, the first time. We were in the middle of a hunt, and the fool came out of nowhere. But as he was lying there, I thought of how he had said I wasn't good enough for you."

Ariel opened her mouth to speak, but shock kept the words frozen in her throat. She forced them out, the sound of them cold in comparison to the heat that scorched her. "What are you saying?"

"You didn't know I had gone to your father and asked for your hand in marriage, did you?" His hand shot up to touch her cheek; then he grabbed her face, hurting her. "So I shot him again. I shot him *dead*."

He'd killed her father. The vision of this horror loomed in her mind. His confession was so blunt, so clear, the impact of his statement numbed her body. Even the fire of anger was doused beneath the coldness of his words. He was worse than an animal. He killed for pleasure. Ariel felt sick.

Bryce shook her. "Don't you pass out on me yet!"

He was almost yelling, his eyes taking on a distant look. "I've done it all to have you. I'll stop at nothing. Then, and only then, will I kill you."

"No," Ariel mumbled, trying to deny it all. Yet she knew it was true. He meant to kill her and Dylan, too. She was beyond fear.

"This is yours, Ariel."

He dangled her necklace in front of her. Slowly, she reached out and took it.

"I don't need it any longer." Bryce smiled, but only one side of his mouth lifted. "I'd rather kill you myself. It will give me such pleasure."

"Ariel."

She heard Dylan call for her and turned to find him. When she turned back, Bryce was gone. Were it not for the carved figure she still clutched, she would have thought his visit a bad dream.

"Ariel." Dylan appeared right before her. "You promised to stay put. You gave me a scare."

She gave him a scare. This thought struck her as funny, and she laughed.

Dylan smiled, but it was an unsure smile and disappeared as her laughter grew odd, almost hysterical. "Are you feeling ill again?"

Finally Ariel sobered and answered him. "Can we go home?"

"Certainly."

As their carriage headed for the hotel, Ariel wanted to cry but couldn't. She wanted to find she had been asleep and this was all a terrible nightmare, but she knew she wouldn't. Instead she sat quiet and withdrawn, saying nothing, doing nothing.

"You look pale," Dylan commented.

The look on his face prompted Ariel to comfort him, to ease the worry. "I just overdid it a bit, that's all." She forced the words out.

She had the urge to fall into the protection of his arms and never leave them. That, too, she did not do. When the numbness began to wear off, the barrage of questions came.

She knew she should warn Dylan; still, no words came out. She was afraid. Her own life seemed of little consequence, but she feared for Henry and

251

Margaret. If she told Dylan, then what? Bryce was out there watching, waiting.

Bryce was mad. She had been a fool to think she could run from him. Now, because of her, they all were in danger. She shivered as she unwillingly remembered the asylum. She felt caged now, with nowhere to run, no one she could turn to. She was alone.

They arrived at the hotel, and Dylan helped Ariel down and hurried her inside. She watched him as he bustled about, his tender care touching her. Looking at Dylan she saw a virile man, his strength and power undeniable. He was much like an animal. His vitality was pure, raw. But the last week had shown her the most gentle of men; his mothering and devotion amazed her.

"I'll have the maid draw you a bath. You'll feel better in no time."

A sad smile moved her mouth but faded just as fast. Dylan's expression changed as he watched her, and she knew the question was coming before even he did.

"What happened at the bazaar?"

She just watched him, his feelings so clear on his face. "Nothing happened, Dylan. I just wasn't ready for such a long day." Ariel hated lying; still, she found herself doing it with ease. She didn't know how to tell him. Bryce's threats clung to her, giving her no respite. Her hand tightened over the carving, the sharp edges digging into her flesh. This pain was better than the hurt she caused herself by her silence.

Dylan just stood there, looking disappointed. He turned and left the room without saying what he had obviously wanted to.

Ariel opened her hand and saw blood in her palm. Tears dropped into the dark red, mixing together, like the emotions within her.

She was lying to him. Dylan jerked his jacket off and flung it across the room. Didn't she know she could trust him? What had brought her to this point? Pain kicked him in the gut. Unable to breathe well, he loosened his collar.

"Damn," he swore, then turned and stomped back out of the room.

Ariel heard the door slam and knew he was gone. She sat for the longest time staring at the door. The room grew dark, yet she didn't move. Her tears had dried; there were no more. Her heart felt emptied of all feeling, her mind void of any thought.

She stood and crossed to the dressing table, then sat. The moon's glow gave enough light for her to see her reflection in the large ornate mirror. The woman who stared back was a stranger, someone she did not know, someone who lied.

Perhaps Bryce would not take his revenge on Dylan if she went to him now. Once the thought had formed in her mind, she knew the absurdity of it. Ariel sighed and threw the carving across the room. She had no heart for any more lies.

Dylan's kiss was magic. The heat of his lips warm against her flesh. She longed for his tender touch, to feel the long, muscled length of him hard against her softness. She opened her arms to him, inviting him to her.

He came closer, his breath warm against her face. His laugh tickled her ear, but then it turned into an evil sound, wicked and cruel. Ariel pulled away and found Bryce's face before her, not Dylan's. She screamed and tried to crawl away, but he grabbed at her, his face distorting into a large, gaping mouth. As if she were nothing but a rag doll, he drew her back to him. He opened wider.

"No," *she screamed again.*

He only laughed louder.

"No!"

Ariel struck out in hate and fear, fighting the man who had made her life a living horror.

"Ariel, stop."

She fought harder.

Hands forced her fists down to her side. "Ariel. Please. It's Dylan."

She opened her eyes fearfully and found Dylan's face.

"It's all right." Gently, he pushed her hair back from her face. "It was just a dream."

"No," she mumbled. "It's not just a dream."

Dylan pulled her chin up, to look straight in her eyes. "Don't you know you can trust me? That you don't have to face this alone?"

"No, I don't."

It was an honest answer, one he had expected. "What must I do to prove it?"

Ariel bit her lower lip and considered this seriously. "Take me home, Dylan."

"We can take the next ship to England. I promise."

"No, England's not home. I want to go home to India."

"But you have no home in India, not yet anyway. I've got my solicitor working on getting your estate back. I wanted to surprise you . . ."

She interrupted him by placing a finger on his lips. "The jungle is my home. I want to be there. I need to be there."

"We must go back to England."

"I can't." Ariel felt near tears. "Don't you understand? England smothers me."

Somehow, he did understand. "If I take you home, will you be able to trust me, to tell me what's causing the fear I see in your eyes?"

She hesitated, then nodded in agreement. "Yes. Just take me home, Dylan."

Dylan looked at her, the longing so clear on his face. She could feel the heat of his body as he sat on the bed beside her. Ariel couldn't resist the urge to touch his square jaw.

Dylan's eyes closed as her touch moved over his stubbled flesh. Ariel leaned forward and whispered, "You feel so good, Dylan."

Dylan wrapped his arms around Ariel, and he drew her close, his lips taking hers. His tongue traced the line of her full lower lip just before he took it into his mouth, the taste of it sweet.

"How I have missed holding you at night. I beg you not to let me suffer so again."

She smiled shyly. "I shall try not to let you suffer again." Her fingers walked through the mat of hair on his chest, her look taking on a teasing quality. Brazenly, she hooked her hand behind his neck and pulled him down to her. "Never again."

She felt Dylan's smile beneath her lips. Playfully she bit his lip, then pulled away.

"You've nowhere to run," he threatened sweetly.

"I have no intention of running, ever again."

Dylan understood. They had just taken a giant step forward. He reached out and pulled at the satin ribbon of her gown, one persistent tug parting the filmy material to expose the fullness of her breasts to his gaze.

A tremor of passion shook him, but he knew his feelings went much deeper. His heart ached from the power she held over him. Not a painful ache, but a warm and wonderful one.

He bent down and kissed the smooth curve of her shoulder, the long length of her neck. He smelled the scent of jasmine that lingered on her skin, the same sweetness in the mass of tangled curls cascading about her shoulders in disarray. He caught a single strand of hair between his fingers, twisting the end around the tip of his finger.

He looked into the darkened gold of her eyes, her sultry mood reflected on her face. Lush full lips were parted slightly, the tiniest flash of white in between. Dylan outlined their shape with his finger but paused in his drawing when the tip of her tongue touched him, her mouth sucking his finger into the warm wetness of her mouth.

Patiently, he waited as she nibbled her way over his hand and up his arm; every inch was covered by the heat of her kisses. Dylan pulled her to him, taking her lips with his own. The warmth within him fired, consuming him with its fierceness. His kiss deepened, and in response, so did hers.

Ariel lay quietly in Dylan's arms, her head cradled on his chest. The beat of his heart was strong in her ear, the sound a great comfort to her. The security he provided kept the warmth of their lovemaking alive inside her. She refused to think of tomorrow, what it might bring. Only this moment and the tender feelings of love she was experiencing were important. Even the horror of Bryce's sudden appearance did not dampen her mood. For the moment, all was perfect.

Dylan waited for Ariel's breathing to settle into sleep's even rhythm, but it didn't come.

Still, he said nothing. It was good to lie with her in his arms. He didn't want to disturb the easy feeling between them. It provided something he needed.

Ariel's lovemaking was always free and abandoned, natural, uninhibited, without artifice or pretense. He was beginning to understand this was Ariel, the Ariel he had felt the first time he had seen her coming from the jungle in the rain.

England smothers me.

Her words echoed in his thoughts, and he understood for the first time what she truly meant. England had nearly put out the fire inside her, destroying the quality that made her the woman she was.

His arms tightened about her as he considered what he had nearly lost. Tomorrow he would make travel arrangements to go to Cairo. He would need to send a letter to Henry and Margaret.

But that was tomorrow. Tonight he wanted to hold Ariel.

Chapter Twenty-Two

Leaving Alexandria they quickly moved from the lush, fertile green of the city to arid desert. The sun was high, reflecting off the vast expanses of sand that stretched out before them. Their small caravan barely dotted the landscape as they moved toward Cairo.

The trip was an exciting excursion, the thrill of traveling across the desert by camel a rare one. Even Ariel found her spirits lifting as the day wore on; the further away from Alexandria and Bryce she got, the more at ease she felt.

The desert was the opposite of the jungles Ariel loved, yet it held an appeal all its own. The dry heat and barren landscape stretched out before her giving no hope of relief, the challenge of it bringing forth the inner part of her that had lain dormant for so long. Slowly, it awakened, unfolding like the bud of a flower.

Light chatter drifted to her ears, the steady plodding of the camels' feet, scored by their occasional bawls. The warmth and steady rocking of the saddle eased her into a relaxed, sleepy mood.

At first, the specks on the horizon caused no alarm, but as they became black-clad figures on horseback, the travelers around her became cautious. The members of the caravan were assured by their guides that attacks were no longer a great concern; even the fierce Bedouin would not dare such a thing. Ariel knew differently, her instincts giving her warning.

As the nomads rode nearer, their greater number increased her anxiety. The guides continued to assure them there was no danger. Ariel could see Dylan tense, his eyes taking on a dangerous look. The dark-faced, dark-eyed Arabians drew in about them, and Ariel felt the persistent nagging of fear increase.

Dylan edged his camel closer to Ariel. He held up his hand to the man just ahead of them and said, "Don't be a fool."

This stopped the younger man from pulling his pistol from its hidden place in his jacket.

"They outnumber us four to one. We've got to think of the women and children. Don't provoke them."

Ariel looked about her, finding Dylan was right. The guides were trying to talk to them, but they were bluntly ignored. At first, the newcomers showed no signs of violence but merely rode alongside them. Ariel did not like the way they slowly spread out until the caravan was completely surrounded. Finally, they brought everyone to an abrupt halt. Slowly, a single man rode among them, as if searching for something or someone. The caravan leader made every attempt to speak with them, but he was pushed aside, ignored like a pesky insect. Ariel could see the muscle in Dylan's jaw move as he ground his teeth in frustration. The look on his face was dark and menacing, but he said nothing.

As the Arab neared her, Ariel felt a prickling on the back of her neck. She did not move, even when he stopped. Black eyes searched hers, the look she saw within their depths a familiar one. He kicked his mount forward, drawing alongside her camel. The man reached out to her. Ariel heard Dylan's growl as he moved to protect her. Every Bedouin pulled his weapon. Guns and swords were drawn.

Ariel glanced back to see the men surrounding Dylan, their weapons keeping him in place. Only his eyes and the twitch in the muscle of his jaw revealed his immense anger. Her attention was drawn back to the man beside her as he pulled at the hat she wore. Irritated, he finally jerked it off, the pins holding her hair up going with it.

Her hair fell about her shoulders and down her back, its dark reddish-brown color reflecting the sun's light, fire in its length. The Bedouin leaned closer and took a handful of the silky hair. Dylan lurched toward them. Before he reached them, he was taken down by four men.

Ariel tried to jump down, but the hand in her

hair tightened, keeping her in place. When she saw the rifle lift and descend on Dylan's head, she nearly tore the hair from her head as she leaped toward him. Strong arms grabbed her about the waist and pulled her from her camel onto his horse, the grip nearly keeping any air from reaching her lungs.

"Let me go," she screamed, kicking and flailing at her captor.

He jerked her head up cruelly so his hard look bore into her mind. "Be still, or he will die."

She stilled, fearing even to breathe. Dylan was thrown across a horse, and before she was even clear on what was happening, they rode off. Ariel twisted around to see the people they were traveling with grow smaller and smaller until they disappeared altogether.

Turning back around, she yelled, "Where are you taking us? And why?"

The dark eyes looked down, and she knew he smiled by the crinkles that appeared around his eyes. He said nothing but urged his horse into an even faster run.

It was well past dark before they stopped, riding into a camp in an oasis. Ariel's captor lowered her down, but she no longer had feeling in her legs and she crumpled to the ground exhausted. The Bedouin dropped beside her and stood looking down at her. His robes flowed out in the breeze, giving him an ominous look. She wanted to crawl away but couldn't. Then he swept her up into his arms and carried her into a tent, where he carelessly dumped her onto a pile of cushions.

Ariel remained still, taking the opportunity to

recuperate from the long ride and to study the man who loomed above her. She had been unable to see where Dylan was taken or even if he was all right. Her mind would not allow her to consider he wasn't.

The Bedouin didn't say a word, but within minutes of their arrival four women hurried into the room. He spoke to one of the four, and she left him to tend Ariel. Quite gently, she urged Ariel up, then led her to the back of the tent. She pulled a curtain aside and motioned for her to enter.

Ariel was uncertain whether to comply and glanced back at her captor. Two of the women were removing his dusty robes. Ariel quickly made up her mind and sought refuge behind the curtain. Another woman joined them, and they immediately began to take her own clothing off.

Resisting, Ariel pushed the hands away, shaking her head no to show her objections. They merely smiled and persisted. Their four hands were quicker than her own, and Ariel found the layers of her riding habit disappearing. Their smiles turned to giggles as she did her best to fend them off.

Large jugs of water were brought in, and, much to Ariel's dismay, she was scrubbed from head to toe, like a child by a mother. Standing in a large copper pan, Ariel sputtered and coughed in embarrassment as they poured the final rinse water over her, her hair falling in her face, totally blinding her. Puppetlike, she was moved about as they needed, her arms raised, then lowered, the humiliation complete when they buffed her dry.

Freeing her hands, Ariel pushed the heavy

strands of wet hair from her eyes, then wished
she had remained ignorantly blind. Her gaze met
the Bedouin's, his eyes reflecting his pleasure as
hers, she knew, mirrored her alarm.

Jerking free of the women's hold, Ariel reached
for the first thing she could find, an empty jug.
With a scream of anger, she hurled the large object
at him, but he was quick and easily dodged its bulk.
As the crash sounded, he smiled, the appreciation
on his face apparent. This only made her angrier.

Mortified, Ariel turned her back to him, as much
to hide her tears of shame as her nudity. She did
not want to give him the satisfaction of seeing her
cry. Searching the room for something to cover
herself, Ariel was unaware he had moved closer.

She felt silky fabric brush her arm and turned
her head to look, thinking one of the women was
offering it. Instead, it was the tall Arabian. He
loomed above her. Ariel snatched the robe and
stepped away to slip it on.

"You are most beautiful."

"*You* are most annoying." She was surprised he
spoke English, but her anger overruled her curiosity.

His laughter made her flinch, its deep warmth
lost beneath her fear of the man.

"Annoying," he repeated, still chuckling. "No one
has ever called me annoying."

"Well, you are." Ariel turned to a question that
had nagged her since their capture. "Is my husband all right?"

"Your husband?"

"Yes, the man you struck on the head."

"Yes, he was quite protective of you. He had to be stilled."

Ariel bit her lip, trying to be patient. "Please . . . he did not look well."

The man seemed to consider her request for information with no hesitation. "You love this man?"

It was not what she expected, but she answered without hesitation. "Yes, very much."

"And if he does not live?"

"I . . ." Ariel had to swallow, relieving the dryness that choked her. Her heart was racing hard and fast within her chest. "I don't know. He is my life."

This did not please him. He frowned gruesomely. "He lives, for how long I cannot say."

"I must go to him," Ariel said quite plainly, yet she held her breath in fear of what he might say, or worse, what he might do.

"He does not need you."

"But you said he might not live." Ariel was too near tears this time, her face revealing all her feelings to him.

"No, I only ask *what if* he does not live. The bump on his head makes it ache, nothing more."

Ariel was confused. "What do you mean? Explain yourself."

She had taken on a tone that held a note of impatience mixed with anger. This brought his eyebrow up as he studied her closely.

"I explain myself to no one. Especially a woman."

"You insufferable bore. Let me explain something to you. I have no intention of staying here, and I have no intention of letting you get away with this." Ariel paused in her lecture, then added "Whatever it is you are doing."

His amused look returned. "You are free to go whenever you wish, little one. I doubt you would last two days in the desert. You would wilt like a flower in the heat."

"Dylan and I will manage just fine," she boasted, but she knew he was accurate enough in his assumptions.

Lifting a finger he wagged it at her. "No, no. I did not say he was free to go."

It was not what she wanted to hear. "And why not? Are you planning to ransom him? Is that why you kidnapped us?"

"Of course not," he objected, looking offended at such a suggestion. "I plan to kill him."

Ariel was horrified. He looked almost proud that his intentions were above kidnapping, killing clearly a more prideful act. Confusion struck head-on with her fear, creating a bizarre feeling. She felt like laughing.

"And what do you intend to do with me?" she asked almost casually.

The big man considered this, all the while his dark eyes watching her closely.

"My plans were to sell you. There is a man who would pay any price to have you."

This did not surprise Ariel as she assumed this whole thing was Bryce's doing.

"But I like you. You have a fiery spirit. I think I will keep you."

"Keep me?" she echoed, finding the entire situation and what he was saying unbelievable. It was like another person was walking and talking, acting out this farce while she looked on.

"Yes," he repeated quite matter-of-factly. "I will make you my wife."

This time Ariel did laugh. It had to be a joke, a bad joke of some kind.

"Your wife!" She seemed unable to say anything except to parrot his ludicrous words.

His head nodded in agreement, his smile widening with that odd pride of his. "My fourth."

Her laughter turned into a howl, and she nearly stumbled to the floor over large pillows scattered about. His look faded under her uproar.

"I see nothing to laugh about."

Tears rolling down her cheeks, Ariel tried to sober up. "You are joking, aren't you?"

The seriousness on his face told her he wasn't. She swallowed back ill feelings and tried to think. "I cannot marry you . . ." Ariel paused, not knowing his name. "Sheik." She put up her hands in emphasis. "Though I am flattered you would consider it."

She decided it best not to offend him further, if it was at all possible. "But I'm already married. I can't possibly accept your generous offer."

"But I plan to kill your husband. You will not be married long."

For a moment she did nothing but stare, her mind clamoring for a logical thought. "Then I shall stick a knife into your cold, unfeeling heart the first chance I get."

Never had she said anything so calmly, and never had she meant anything more.

"You would soon forget him," he said, a certain arrogance twinkling in his eyes.

"Never," Ariel whispered, the soft word so strong in meaning his look changed. "I promise you, I would never forget that you cold-bloodedly murdered the man I love with all my heart and soul."

"You do not mean what you say."

She bravely walked up to him, ignoring his imposing height and physical strength. "Are you willing to take that chance, Sheik?"

"It is a tempting thought to die for such a delectable morsel." His hand brushed her cheek. "But I am a patient man. We shall wait and see."

Wait and see. Ariel wasn't certain what it meant, only that it sounded better than his previous plan. Still, a nagging fear made her ask, "And my husband?"

Dark eyes watched her closely, perhaps waiting for her to turn away from his close scrutiny. She did not. "He shall be well taken care of. You shall remain here, as my guest."

"I would prefer—"

His hand shot up and stopped her short, his look turning quite hard. "You will stay here as my guest. Should you consider otherwise, it would not go well with your husband."

This was quite clear. Ariel said no more. He seemed pleased.

"You are a very wise woman," he said. Then he turned and left the tent, leaving her to stand alone in her strange, lush surroundings.

Suddenly, Ariel was exhausted. For the moment

she knew of nothing better to do than rest. Just a little rest would help her think clearly. Seeking out a pile of plump pillows, she curled up on them and in minutes was fast asleep.

When Ariel woke it was daylight. It took a few moments for her to shake off the sleep and realize where she was. A moan of despair shook her. She buried her face into the velvet pillow.

Someone tugged at her hair, and Ariel whirled around, startled, batting at the hands disturbing her. Two women stood looking down at her; another stood behind them.

They giggled and glanced at one another as one braved another tug at her hair. Only their eyes showed above their veils, but Ariel saw they were smiling.

One spoke to the woman behind them, and she nodded.

"They are fascinated by the color of your hair. And that you have no veil over your face."

Ariel stood and tried to collect herself. "You speak English, too. I'm surprised."

The oldest of the three women motioned for the other two to move aside, and she stepped forward, her eyes summing up Ariel quite effectively. "My husband attended one of your English universities, and he taught me."

"The sheik is your husband?"

"Of course," she answered, the same superior air about her as the sheik had. "I am Saree, first wife of Abdul Hakeem. This is Leila, second wife, and Tabina, Abdul's third."

"I am Ariel Lock—" Ariel corrected herself. "Christianson."

Saree seemed to observe this. "You are wife to the man my husband brought back last night?"

"Yes." Ariel nodded, then asked, "Is he . . . ?" Fear kept her from finishing.

"He is well," Saree said, relieving the worry she read so clearly on her face.

"Would you take me to him?" Ariel knew she risked much by asking but could not keep from it.

Dark eyes gazed into her own, and Ariel saw the dislike in them. Disappointment flooded over her even before the Bedouin woman answered.

"I will take you to him."

She could not keep her surprise from showing. "Thank you, Saree."

A cold gaze chilled Ariel. "There is no need to thank me. I have my own reasons for helping you."

"Fair enough," Ariel said, already excited by the thought of seeing Dylan. Without any further conversation, Ariel followed Saree into another section of the large tent.

She picked up a hooded robe and handed it to Ariel. "Put this on and cover your hair and face well."

Ariel did as she was told, making certain all her hair was tucked beneath the hood and the veil covered her face. Saree left the tent. Ariel followed right behind. They moved through the compound quickly, avoiding as many people as possible. Saree stopped behind a tent, carefully looking about before pulling the flap aside for Ariel. Ariel slipped through.

It was dark, no light penetrating inside. It took a long moment before her eyes adjusted. Ariel looked about but didn't see Dylan.

"Dylan," she called out in a loud whisper.

"Ariel."

Her heart lurched ahead of its normal pace. She turned to follow his voice. "Where are you?" She still did not see him.

"Here."

She moved farther into the tent and finally saw him, his hands and feet bound to a tether about his neck. The sight took her by surprise, stopping her.

"Are you all right, Ariel?"

She heard the tortured tone and understood the underlying question. "I've not been harmed, Dylan. Are you all right? They struck you so hard. It frightened me terribly."

"I've a bit of a headache, but I'm fine."

Tears stung her eyes as she looked at her husband, tied like an animal. She found herself unable to step closer, her own fears crowding in upon her, keeping her still. Flashes of the asylum and of the tiger at the zoo confused her.

"Ariel."

Dylan's voice broke through her barrier of fear, his need making her move to him. She reached out and placed her hand on his, wrapping her fingers about his larger ones.

"What are we going to do?"

His voice was calm and soothing. "We are going to get out of here, I promise."

His words struck chords of fear in her mind.

"Don't do anything foolish, Dylan. Abdul Hakeem will kill you."

A strange look came over his face. "Abdul Hakeem?"

"Yes, the sheik."

"The sheik?"

Ariel felt his touch tense and went on. "Saree, his first wife, brought me to you, Dylan. Please, do not act in haste."

"What's wrong, Ariel? You're not telling me everything."

"We must go."

Ariel turned to see Saree just inside the tent, her silhouette dim in the shadows. Ariel turned back to Dylan. "I will come back as soon as I can."

"Will you be all right?"

Once again, she understood the hidden meaning. "Don't worry over me. Take care of yourself." She stood on her tiptoes and brushed her lips against his. "Promise me you'll be good."

"I'll promise no such thing, Ariel."

"Then I'll not go," Ariel objected.

"You will go." His voice turned steely, and he pulled away from her. "Go."

Saree pulled on her arm, and Dylan turned away.

"We must go," Saree repeated, her grip unbreakable as she nearly dragged Ariel from the tent.

"Please," Ariel pleaded with Saree, clawing at her hand on her arm. "I must go to him."

Saree stopped dead in her step and turned to Ariel. "You must leave him alone. A woman must not interfere."

Anger chased Ariel's fear away. "And if I do not

interfere, Dylan will try and escape. Then your husband will have a reason to kill my husband. Then he will make me his fourth wife, and I'm not particularly thrilled by the idea."

The look in Saree's eyes told Ariel she had not known her husband's plans. "Abdul has said this?"

"Yes."

She still looked doubtful. "Abdul would not take you for his wife." Saree stomped away. "He can have you without taking you as wife."

Ariel reached out and stopped her, whirling her about. "Over his dead body!"

Slowly, Saree understood Ariel's meaning. "You would harm Abdul?"

"I certainly have no intention of letting him take me or marry me."

"What will you do?"

Saree's question deflated all of Ariel's anger, leaving her feeling helpless and confused.

"I don't know," Ariel confessed softly.

Taking her hand, Saree led her back to the other tent. Ariel couldn't determine the look that now lit her eyes, but she shook the thought off as quickly as it came. Other matters dominated her mind.

"You must eat," Saree commanded, handing Ariel a morsel of food, holding it to her lips to tempt her.

Ariel shook her head, food she had eaten merely sitting like rocks on her stomach. She turned away from Saree's attempts.

"Saree, my wife, our guest does not look happy."

Saree turned to her husband, who now stood

before them, her eyes lowered in obedience. "She worries much over her husband."

"I do not want her growing thin," he mused, his gaze openly admiring. "You must do better, Saree."

Her eyes remained focused on the floor, but Ariel saw her hands twisting in her lap. A flash of heat caused Ariel to shout, "I can take care of myself. You needn't bother over me."

Saree's wide, dark eyes looked up, horrified Ariel would speak in such a way to Abdul Hakeem, but Saree's horror ended quickly when her husband merely laughed. Ariel saw anger take its place.

"You are not like other English women." His smile widened. "You have a sharper tongue than most. And more fire in your eyes."

Ariel turned away to ignore him.

Abdul Hakeem's laughter filled the tent once again. All those who watched finally joined in, but Ariel's audacity clouded the air with tension. The sheik returned to his seat among the men, his jokes lost on Ariel as he began speaking in Arabic. After everyone tired of the food, more drink was brought in, and dancing girls followed.

Unable to resist, Ariel turned her attention to the dancers, their colorful dress catching her eye. Everything was intoxicating, the colors swirling, the strange music blaring, the food, the drink. Even the sheik had a certain charm.

Ariel turned her gaze to Saree and wondered what she would look like without the veil. From the look of her eyes, she was very beautiful, as were Leila and Tabina. It was obvious Saree's position as first wife gave her a higher position in the household, one she enjoyed.

Ariel couldn't help but envision herself, veiled and subservient, standing in the background as number four.

Not in this lifetime.

When the dancing girls left, Abdul clapped his hands to silence the crowd and called out for Jena. Immediately the room hushed. Everyone seemed to be waiting.

The tent flaps were pulled aside, and an old woman shuffled in, her long hair white as snow, her flesh wrinkled with age. She leaned upon a cane for support, the many chains of jewelry seeming to bend her back with its weight. The jingle of silver, gold and brass filled the room.

Abdul gazed at her reverently, patient with her slow pace. Ariel's curiosity got the best of her, and she whispered to Saree, "Who is she?"

"She is our seer."

"A seer?"

Saree turned to look at Ariel. "She sees the future."

A tingle ran up Ariel's spine. At that very moment, the ancient Bedouin woman stopped and turned toward her. She said something, and Saree touched Ariel's arm.

"She asks you come forward. She cannot see you in the shadows."

Ariel would have preferred to remain hidden among the other women, but she did as she was asked. All were aware of her presence at dinner, yet this was the first time she had been near the fire's light. Had she known what a picture she presented, she would have remained in the dark.

Everyone watched her closely, but it was Abdul who was especially attentive. The flames from the pit danced against the red strands of her hair, as its length swished softly down her back. The fire's warmth painted a blush on her cheeks. The satin robe clung around her hips, bringing him definite heat.

The old woman studied Ariel intently. Gnarled and knotted hands reached out and touched her cheek, then picked up a wild curl. Then she turned away and moved toward Abdul. She waved for Ariel to follow.

It took a moment for Jena to settle down, her old bones moving slowly. She patted the plump pillow next to her, and Ariel sat beside her. Without drawing attention, Saree moved to sit beside her. Ariel couldn't understand her gibberish, but the meaning of what she was doing seemed clear.

Dark eyes watched her. She felt uncomfortable under Abdul's stare. Finally, when the seer's words reached a fevered pitch, he turned away.

She tossed ancient stones upon the floor, their wisdom falling into place as the future was revealed to her eyes.

"What do the stones tell you tonight?"

Quietly, Saree interpreted.

"The stones are wise," Jena said, looking up at Abdul.

Abdul nodded. Everyone agreed.

"Tonight they tell me much." She turned

watered-down brown eyes to Ariel. "They reveal much of this beauty you have taken."

"And what do the stones reveal?" Abdul's interest showed as he leaned forward to better hear her words.

Jena turned back to her stones. "Her soul belongs to another."

A scowl touched Abdul's face. "Her husband?"

The silver head shook in answer. "No, Abdul Hakeem. Her heart belongs to the man you hold captive. Her soul belongs to a beast."

Abdul snorted in disbelief, then said as much. "Old woman, I think age has addled your mind."

"Pahh," Jena screeched, insulted. "I see what I see. You run to me for my wisdom, yet when you do not understand you claim me too old."

"What else do you see?" Abdul's jaw was clenched in aggravation. His patience was at the end.

Jena pursed her lips, the absence of teeth making them wrinkle like dried fruit. Her eyes narrowed, and she studied Abdul a long time before finally speaking.

"The white horse will run in the race. The race will be his."

This brightened Abdul's look, his anger lost in his excitement. "Are you sure?"

The pursed lips were set and determined. "I see what I see."

Chapter Twenty-Three

"You do not like my home?"

Abdul's question brought her gaze up to his, the smoky-gold color of her eyes sending a rush of emotion through him.

"It is very beautiful."

"Tell me, Ariel, what would bring a smile to your lips?"

"You know the answer to that, Sheik."

"Yes, I do, but it is not something I can do."

The eyes he loved to watch turned away, and he felt the disappointment immediately. They continued to walk, neither saying anything.

A cat's cry reached them, the sound carrying on the soft breeze that stirred the giant palms. Ariel stopped and listened, another cry piercing her soul.

Without asking Abdul, she started toward the

part of the camp the sound had come from. Her walk picked up until it turned into a full run.

At the edge of the village she found the frightened animals, two leopards pacing back and forth in the tiny confines of a cage. A black-clad Bedouin was poking a large pole in between the bars, striking the leopards viciously.

One screamed, and the other growled in anger.

"No," Ariel yelled, drawing the large man's eyes toward her for only a second. Then he turned back to the animals, beating the cat that was growling.

Before she gave it a thought, and before the sheik could stop her, Ariel ran and picked up a pole like the one the Bedouin held. She struck out, slamming the wooden instrument into his back. This brought his full attention to her.

"You sorry excuse for a man. Leave them alone!" Ariel was beyond thinking, beyond control.

She hit him again, driving the end of the pole into his shoulder. "How does that feel?" With the quickness of a snake, she struck again, then again.

At first the man had been surprised, but now he was furious. He yelled something at her, trying to catch the pole as she struck him.

"Ariel."

Abdul walked up to her, his voice breaking her anger. "Ariel, put it down."

She drew back, but not in defeat. "What is he doing?"

"He takes care of my cats. You have no right to interfere."

His words were hard, the warning they held clear.

Ariel chose to ignore him. Even as others gathered around, she stood her ground.

"He has no right to treat them in such a way." Her makeshift weapon struck again, slapping him directly on the side of the head.

"Ask him if he likes that? I can assure you the cats do not." For one second she looked away, and the Bedouin grabbed the stick, jerking it from her hands. In two steps he had her by the hair, twisting its length about his hand.

Ariel reacted just as harshly, bringing her knee up into his groin. The man let out a strangled cry, then sank slowly to his knees. Disgusted, she took her foot and shoved him into the dirt.

She turned to the sheik, her fury complete. "Why do you have them?" Suddenly the anger fled, leaving only her pain. "They are meant to be free."

Ariel stared at him, disappointment clear on her face.

"They were a gift."

"Then you should treat them as such. Exactly what does he think he is doing?"

Abdul asked the Bedouin and then answered Ariel. "He takes care of them." He pointed to the man's cheek. "They clawed him, and he was calming them down."

This only brought the anger back. "The man must be daft if he thinks that beating them will calm them down." Abdul's eyebrow rose, and Ariel knew she was only amusing him again.

"And what is the right way, little one?"

His attitude irritated her further. "A little love goes a lot further than a lot of hate."

"Why don't you show us what you mean?"

The challenge was in his eyes as well as his words. Ariel couldn't resist. She looked at the leopards, their agitation still high. Without fear, she moved to the cage.

Her voice was soft and soothing, none of the anger she felt evident in the tone. Slowly, she moved to the door, then removed the bar holding it closed. Abdul stepped forward. "Do not interfere, Sheik. It will only frighten them more."

"I did not mean for you to do such a fool thing. I was only making a joke."

"Your jokes are not funny." Ariel stepped up into the cage; the cats moved back hissing.

"Ariel, I am sorry."

Ariel turned a surprised look to him, knowing he was not a man to apologize, even when wrong. A small surge of victory rose, then disappeared. She pulled the door shut behind her as she sat on the floor of the cage.

"You are crazy," Abdul whispered.

Offering her hand, Ariel reached out to the cats, her voice holding their attention. Their hissing stopped. One curiously sniffed her outstretched hand. Soon, she was petting them both, their growls and hisses replaced by rumbling purrs.

"Her soul belongs to a beast. A great cat."

Abdul looked down at the seer, her bent form appearing from out of nowhere. "A cat?"

"Yes. But one with stripes, not spots."

His gaze returned to Ariel, who sat casually with the wild animals—and he believed. When he looked back down, Jena was gone.

*   *   *

"Ariel."

Ariel turned away from the disturbance; she wasn't ready to awaken from the dream, a dream with Kala Bagh.

Saree was more insistent this time, and Ariel awakened. "What is it, Saree? Is Dylan all right?"

"He is fine. Jena wishes to see you."

"Jena?" Ariel was confused, sleep still fogging her mind. "I'll see her tomorrow."

Pulling her back around, Saree was insistent. "Not tomorrow. Tonight."

"All right," Ariel agreed, pulling on her robe.

The night's darkness covered their way, the moon absent from the sky, leaving only an occasional blinking star to mar the inky blackness.

Saree paused by a tent and ducked inside, Ariel following right behind. The interior was dark with only a fire in the center giving any light. The old seer sat by it, staring into the flames. Saree motioned for Ariel to sit across from her; then she too sat down.

They sat for the longest time with no one speaking. Finally Ariel broke the silence. "What is this all about?"

"I do not know," Saree replied softly.

"Then ask her, please."

Saree did so. The old woman turned her gaze to Ariel, then smiled. The snaggle-toothed grin wasn't a pleasant sight, but its meaning made Ariel smile, too. "What does she want?"

Jena started rattling off, her hands as active as her voice.

"She says she saw more in the stones, much more."

Saree translated as the seer elaborated. "The Great White will win the race, but Abdul Hakeem will not be riding him."

This caused Saree to ask a question on her own. "If not Abdul, who?"

Jena replied, but Saree hesitated to tell Ariel.

"What did she say?"

"She said . . ." Saree started then stopped and questioned Jena again.

Ariel pulled her back to her. "Saree!" Her tone was insistent.

"She said you will ride the horse to victory."

"That's crazy!"

"It is what she sees."

"Okay." Ariel didn't wish to insult the old woman. "What about this horse? Where is it?"

"It is a wild horse, a beautiful white one. My husband has been trying to capture him for many years, but the animal is cunning and avoids all traps."

"Then what makes Jena think I will ride him?"

Saree posed the question to Jena and she explained, her speech punctuated as her hands waved about.

Saree nodded, then explained. "This race is held every two years. It is of great importance to my people. The man who wins achieves tremendous wealth as he wins all the riders' horses. With such wealth his power is great."

Ariel was still confused. "Let's assume it's even possible for me to find this horse, maybe even ride him. And if all went well and I won, then what?"

"You would have much to bargain with."

Saree's simplistic statement struck a chord. "Your husband would trade our lives for horses?"

She nodded. "He has a great passion for horses. Perhaps even greater than his passion for you."

Many things were becoming clear. "You love him very much, don't you?"

Again Saree nodded. "Just as you love your husband."

Still, one thing evaded Ariel. "Why are you helping me? You are risking much."

"I do not want Abdul to take you as wife."

Somehow it still didn't make things clear. "But Abdul has three wives. You don't seem to mind Leila and Tabina. So why would it matter so much to share Abdul with a fourth?"

A soft sigh reached Ariel's ears. "It is not that I cannot accept Abdul taking another wife; it is our custom. It is you who would not accept three others, and I fear his infatuation would keep him from my bed and leave me without children."

For being so quiet and unassuming, Saree was quite wise.

"So I must do what I can to make sure it does not happen."

The leather strap tied around Dylan's wrist snapped, his persistence and patience rewarded as he freed his hands. Carefully he removed the tether about his neck, throwing it away from him in anger.

The tent the Bedouin held him in was dark,

remaining so in the daytime as well. He had been able to distinguish the passing of time only by the noises he heard. In the evening the camp would become jubilant as they enjoyed their meal—eating, drinking and dancing. Then all would become quiet as they slept. It was then he would work on the leather, slowly rubbing it against the wooden pole, wearing it away.

Victory surged through Dylan when he was able to stand and walk to the flap in the tent. His legs were cramped and his head still hurt, but he ignored the pain. Anger gave him motivation and strength.

He pulled the flap back and studied the camp. His one guard sat nearby, relaxed and seemingly unconcerned with him. Dylan inched out, making no noise. Slowly, he made his way toward the Bedouin. Just as the guard looked up, Dylan knocked him unconscious with a single, well-placed punch. He moved on.

He must find Ariel.

The fire held Ariel's attention, but she was distracted by Abdul's agitated pacing. She felt the same impatience, yet she willed it to remain hidden.

"The old woman is too old. Her mind grows addled. The race is in three days. If I were to capture him now, he could not be broken in time."

It had become a nightly occurrence, Abdul visiting with Ariel and his wives, though all the conversation was between the sheik and Ariel. Perhaps her English education prompted him to share with her and not his Bedouin wives. At these times, Ariel felt Saree's pain.

"Why is this horse so important? You have many fast Arabians. You can win without this Great White."

Abdul flung his hands up in the air. "Baghhh. You are a woman, so how can you understand this?"

A flush warmed her face, but Ariel kept calm. "I am a woman who understands much. Perhaps what I see and what I understand I do not find attractive."

Black eyes studied her. Then he asked, "What is it you see? What is it you understand?"

"You, as most men, wish to have what you cannot. The horse is wild and free, so you want to tame and cage him."

"And you don't like this?"

"No."

Abdul's look did not change, an intensity sizzling in the dark depths of his eyes. "And you, Ariel, are you wild and free? Is that why you fight me?"

The warmth within her deepened. "I have a husband. I don't need another."

"Are you a wildcat when you are in his arms?"

"That is none of your business."

Abdul turned to Saree. "Is it not time for you to retire?"

Without argument or hesitation, Saree stood and motioned for the others to follow. She was unable to meet Ariel's eyes, shame keeping them cast down.

Ariel tried to leave with them, but Abdul stopped

her, his arm blocking the way. Fear stirred inside her, but she buried it beneath a hard reserve.

When the last of his wives had disappeared, Abdul pulled her chin up so he could see her eyes. "You are so very beautiful. I am hard pressed to keep my distance."

"And why have you been such a gentleman? It does not seem to suit your personality." Briefly, Ariel wondered if she were daft, asking such a thing, but she did not attempt to take it back.

Abdul was surprised by her straightforwardness. "I'm not sure. You speak the truth. If you were any other woman, I would have had my way with you, willing or not."

"Then why?"

"You promised to stick a knife into my cold-blooded heart, remember?"

"And no one else has ever threatened to do the same?" The question was posed in a tone telling Abdul she would not believe him if he said no.

"Many have said as much," he confessed honestly.

Confusion still remained, and Ariel pursued the subject further. "Why would my threat matter?"

He stepped away, looking uncomfortable at her curiosity. "For some reason, I believed you. I believed if I were to kill your husband and take you as mine, you would not forget. I believed you would kill me for my treachery to your heart." Dark eyes looked back at her. "And now that I know you even better, I believe you even more."

"Then why are we here? Why haven't you let us go?"

A sadness touched his face, his eyes turning soulful. "I cannot bring myself to let you go. Besides, I cannot allow such a thing to come to pass. It would dishonor my house to be so weak."

Just as Ariel was about to speak, one of Abdul's men rushed in, his head and body bowed in reverence. He waited for the sheik's approval to speak. His words meant nothing to Ariel, but his urgency did. Then she became aware of noises in the compound, men yelling and running about. Abdul's look darkened, and he turned to Ariel to speak.

"Something must take me away from your charming company. I shall return promptly."

He bowed, then left.

An uneasy feeling crawled into her mind, and she followed Abdul outside. A shout sounded, and men ran to the center of the commotion. The crowd moved toward Abdul, the cries of the men hostile and ugly. The uneasy feeling grew into a full-blown fear.

Ariel stepped forward but froze when Dylan was dragged up and thrown at Abdul's feet. His eye was swelling shut, and his nose and lip were bleeding. A man kicked Dylan in the ribs, and he moaned. Ariel ran forward, but Abdul caught her, actually lifting her from the ground.

"Let me go," she screamed, fighting his strong grip. "Let me go!"

Abdul yelled to his men and stopped their vicious actions. They picked Dylan up and carried him away.

"Dylan!" Ariel called to him. She saw him crane his neck around to see her.

Tears blinded her now. She could no longer see him. "Dylan."

Her whimper turned into a sob, until one sob followed another. Abdul lifted Ariel into his arms and carried her back inside. She no longer cared if Abdul saw her cry; the pain was more than she could bear.

Then a flash of anger shook her, and she struck out at the cause of it. "I hate you," she hissed, knowing she really did not.

Again and again she hit him, her fists pummeling his face and chest. He merely held her closer. He walked to his bed and sat down, his hold tightening as she struggled against him.

"I hate you," she moaned one last time, her energy spent, leaving only a bitter sadness inside her. Soon the tears stopped. Ariel tried to pull away, embarrassed, but Abdul's hold did not lessen. He held her fast.

She looked up to ask him to let her go, but the words never got past her brain. His own pain was so clear on his face it took Ariel's breath away. Ashamed to be the cause of it, she turned away, regretting having seen it at all.

Abdul let her go and stood. "Sleep well, Ariel."

"I did not know if you would be able to come."

Ariel took the reins Saree offered her and smiled, trying to get over the awkward situation. "Even your husband's sudden desire for my company could not keep me away. We must find the Great White. Next time he may not be so patient." In a roundabout way Ariel was trying to tell Saree that nothing had happened. By the smile Saree returned, Ariel knew she'd been successful.

"We have some distance to travel. We must go."

The two women rode in silence, each allowing the other her private thoughts. Ariel's were haunted by the vision of Dylan, his face bloody and swollen. As much as she had wanted to go to him, she knew it was impossible. His guards would be very alert since his attempt to escape. She prayed he would be patient and allow her the time she needed to achieve their freedom.

This led her to analyzing their flight in the night. Ariel couldn't say she had ever disbelieved or believed in fortune-tellers, but somehow she was allowing Jena's predictions to guide her. Perhaps it was desperation making her grasp at any and all possibilities, even a seer's prophecies. Yet some deep-seated instinct told her to trust the old woman.

Thus she and Saree were riding to a place Jena saw in the ancient stones, a place where they would find the Great White.

Pulling her horse to a stop, Saree turned to Ariel. "This is the place."

The two women dismounted and tethered their horses where they could graze. The moon was full, lighting the oasis as they walked further into the tall grove of palms, which stood above them like giant umbrellas.

It was a beautiful night, and Ariel felt a stirring deep inside her. She drew a deep breath of the sweet, night air, a feeling of wildness surging forth. Like a smooth wine, it warmed her, reviving the spirit within her that had lain dormant for so long.

Ariel turned to Saree. "Perhaps you should stay with the horses."

"I do not think—"

"Please, Saree. I'll be fine."

A look akin to relief flooded Saree's dark eyes, and she nodded. "We must return before dawn."

"I promise to be back in time." As Ariel watched Saree leave, she asked one more thing before she disappeared altogether. "Do you really believe the seer?"

Saree did not look back but stopped. "Yes," was all she said, then walked on.

"I hope you are right," Ariel muttered, moving deeper into the trees. She didn't know where she was going. She followed her instincts, stopping only when a small pond blocked her way.

Thoughts no longer interfered with Ariel's mind; it belonged to the wildness inside her. The tiger was awake in her freedom, her aloneness, the night. Slowly she shed the robes she wore, much like the inhibitions that had claimed her only moments before.

The water glistened in the moonlight, the invitation clear. She walked into the crystal pond, its chill inching up her until the wetness touched her lips. Sinking down she rinsed the dust and sweat of the ride from her, leaving only her natural scent upon her.

Ariel swam the breadth of the lake, emerging on the far side. The white sandy beach beckoned to her. She listened. She dug her bare toes deeper into the softness, a smile of contentment on her face.

She wandered over to stand beneath a palm as it gently swayed in the breeze, its music pleasing to her ears. Sitting beneath it, she leaned her back against the wide trunk. Her eyes closed as she listened to the sounds of the darkness. Its quiet wonder soothed the excitement that still lingered from the long ride, and slowly Ariel fell into a restful sleep.

A soft grunt brought her awake, but she didn't move. She remained still, allowing the animal to take its time approaching her. The horse was a magnificent white Arabian, his size imposing, especially from her view from the ground. Still, there was no fear in her, only admiration.

The Great White snorted again and pawed the earth. Any other person would have scrambled away, but Ariel remained. As if this confused him, he rose upon his back legs and screamed his threat. Still she remained.

"The seer was right," Ariel whispered softly to the animal.

The beast jumped away, skittish at the sound of her voice. But slowly he moved back. Ariel put her hand out, and the Great White smelled it, his soft velvety muzzle touching her fingers. She stroked him, and in turn he nibbled at her own flesh, tasting of it, exploring it. Strong teeth nipped at her, but she only laughed, ignoring the discomfort.

"I'll not hurt you, but you can help me." Her hand moved to caress his jaw, his eyes watching her closely. "I am in need of your great speed."

The Great White backed up, as if understanding

her words. Ariel stood, then walked back to the water's edge. Looking back, she paused, then dove into the dark water. Once she was on the other side, she dressed.

The horse's cry reached her across the water, and Ariel looked up to see the stallion still watching her. He took a few steps forward, splashing into the still water, then turned and ran back from the water's edge. He whirled back around to stare at her, stamping his hooves impatiently. Then, unexpectedly, he rushed forward and splashed into the pond.

Ariel watched him swim across the short distance to her. His great strength now stood before her, glistening in the moon's light, water dripping from his sparkling white coat. He waited, offering himself.

Tears choked her, blinding her of the precious vision before her. A soft nose nuzzled her, and she whispered in his ear, "Thank you, my friend."

Chapter Twenty-Four

"This is the most important race of the Bedouin
Men travel great distances to ride, bringing their
very best horses."

Abdul paced back and forth in front of Ariel, his
tenseness over the upcoming race obvious. She
didn't say much, but he didn't seem to care if she
did or not.

"I shall be a richer man after today. All the finest
horses will be mine."

Unable to keep quiet, Ariel asked, "What if you
lose?"

The look he gave her told Ariel she had gone too
far to consider this at all. "Abdul Hakeem does not
lose."

This caused Ariel to experience doubt. If she won
the race, would Abdul be shamed? Would he kill
them rather than free them?

"Then I wish you luck." It was all Ariel could think of to say.

A hopeful look crossed his face, and he sat down beside her. "Then perhaps you would grant me a kiss for good luck."

Ariel was unable to deny him. It was a sweet kiss, yet it did not stir the heat within her Dylan so easily aroused.

"I shall win for you, Ariel."

For a long time after he left, Ariel just sat thinking, wondering if she was doing the right thing and afraid of doing the wrong thing.

"Ariel."

She turned to Saree but said nothing.

"We must go."

Ariel knew they barely had enough time to get the Great White and return before the start of the race. She still couldn't move.

"You are very courageous."

Saree's generous words touched Ariel, and she stood. "You are kind. To tell the truth, I'm afraid."

"The Great White will run to victory."

"I know. I think . . ." Ariel paused, analyzing what she did think. "That's what I'm afraid of."

A confused look entered Saree's eyes. "Why does this frighten you?"

"What will Abdul do?"

"I do not know."

"What—" Ariel stopped herself. It did no good to borrow trouble. "We'd better go."

The stallion was impatient. He pranced beneath Ariel's slight weight. She held him back, waiting for the race to start. Ariel tucked the kubiyah around her face, leaving only her eyes to show, the long white robe she wore completely disguising who she was.

The noise of the men drifted to her from across the compound as they gathered for the race, their clamor mixing with the cries of the horses and the barking of dogs. A crowd had gathered, families and friends ready to root on their favorite rider. Children played among the adults, their laughter and youthful shrieks marking their movements.

Ariel searched the many faces for Saree. She had promised to free Dylan for the race. Saree had assured her that everyone would be watching the race, leaving him bound but unguarded. She would disguise Dylan as a Bedouin so no one would discover him missing. Still, Ariel could not find them, and she realized how important it was to see him. Just one glance was all she needed.

She couldn't see him though, and disappointment gathered within her. It mixed with her excitement and fear, creating a turbulence of emotion. Ariel struggled to keep it all in check. She leaned down and buried her face in the long, white mane of the horse. His scent was like an elixir, easing the tension from Ariel, taking her mind from her self-inflicted torture. Her heart pounded fiercely in her chest as all thought melted away, allowing primal instinct to guide her once again.

As if the White sensed the changes taking place inside her, he stirred beneath her, his excitement entwining with her own, his great speed and strength becoming hers. She was ready.

The noise of the crowd heightened, the yells of

the men echoing above the din. The excitement struck like lightning in the sky, touching her across the compound. In a tremendous rush of men and horses the race began.

Without encouragement, the White lurched forward, taking with him his small passenger. Ariel couldn't see much; the dust kicked up by the other horses blinded her. So she let the animal have his head, trusting him to take her to the front of the pack.

Ariel knew when they had moved in among the other horses, the grunting from the animals matching their heavy strides, the thunder of hooves a din about her. She could smell the sweat of the horses and the men, churning together with the musk of the earth. Its cloud choked her, and its darkness took away all sight. The dank taste made her thirsty. Beneath her, Ariel felt the sinewy muscles of the White moving, straining from exertion; his power surged through her, her blood pumping with its strength.

"Come on, White," she urged, whispering in his ear.

The animal ran even faster, feeling her words more than hearing them. The group of riders moved from the oasis into the rocky hills, and they slowed their pace, adjusting to the terrain. The pack spread out, picking their way more carefully. Ariel allowed the White to find his own way through.

The dust cleared as they rode onto hard rock, riders now in full sight of each other. As she passed many Bedouins, they became aware of the new rider and the White. One man struck out at her with his leather strap, striking her repeatedly across the back. Ariel hunkered down, trying to get away from the painful blows he inflicted on her. Suddenly, another rider appeared, and she was sandwiched in between the two of them.

They moved in, locking her legs between the horses. While one continued to flail her, the other kicked at her. His foot landed in her side, nearly unseating her. She clung to the White's mane but slipped when the one horse moved away, leaving her to hang precariously off the side of her own mount. Slashing hooves loomed up in front of her eyes. Pieces of rock and shale cut her face.

The White slowed his breakneck pace, falling behind the two attackers, leaving them to fight between themselves. Ariel pulled herself back onto his back then urged him on again.

In a flash, they moved in and out of the rocks, reaching the other side and moving into a grove of palms. The subtle quietness of the oasis was shattered by the swarm of riders and their mounts. They descended into the greenness of the trees, devouring the earth beneath their thundering hooves.

Ariel approached a rider from behind but was not prepared for his arm which shot out and swept her completely off the White. She hit the ground, rolled down an embankment and into a pond of water. She came up sputtering.

Her headpiece had come off, leaving her hair to drip down her back. She struggled up the grassy bank, her wet robes twisting around her legs as she slipped and slid and finally reached the crest. As she raised up over the knoll, she saw his dusty boots, then the dirty hem of his robes. Ariel looked up to find Abdul Hakeem watching her, his eyes a kaleidoscope of emotion.

He offered his hand to help her up. Ariel couldn't figure out what to say, so she didn't say anything. The White called to her from nearby, pawing the earth insistently.

"Why are you doing this?"

Ariel sighed and pushed the wet strand of hair from her face. "You have brought me and my husband here against our will. You have threatened to kill him and force me to marry you. That would kill me, Abdul. So I beg of you, do it now. Take your knife and end my suffering."

The sheik stood there in all his arrogance and pride. Yet as hard as he tried, the hurt he was experiencing showed. He didn't understand, or maybe he did. Ariel wasn't sure.

"You are the most unusual woman I have ever known."

Abdul took her arm and led her to the stallion, then offered her a hand up. Lifting her he whispered, "You must win on your own. I will not stop you, nor will I help you."

He turned and found his own horse and mounted. "You must earn your freedom, Ariel. Show me your worthiness of my generosity."

The sheik didn't wait for an answer but whirled his horse around and rode away. Ariel wasted no more time, prompting the White into a run, the other riders far ahead now.

By the time she left the oasis, she saw a few of the stragglers. Ariel recalled Saree's careful explanation of the course they would cover and knew the last major leg of the race was coming up. As she approached the hill, she heard Saree's warning. *All riders will take the path around the rise, the descent on the other side too dangerous. Other riders have died for their foolishness.*

Ariel pulled the White to a stop, the last rider disappearing from sight down the trail. She turned and looked up the slope, then back the other way. She could not catch up if she remained on the trail. She would lose.

Her decision made, Ariel yelled, "Let's show these men what a horse and a woman can do, White." Together they tackled the hillside, the White's strength carrying them step by step. She felt him strain beneath her, his hooves slipping on the steep terrain. His grunts mixed with her own heavy breathing as Ariel struggled just to remain on his back. When they crested the hill, she slowed to spot the other riders, taking mental note of their position. She could not waste a second more. With only one look at the danger descending below, she plunged on, like diving into a pit of darkness and not knowing if there was ever to be light again.

The White bounded down. His speed combined with momentum as if he had taken wings. Ariel lay back as far as she could to keep from tumbling over his head. Another small rise appeared before them, and Ariel took a deep breath as the stallion lifted from the ground and jumped it. The ground all but disappeared beneath them. The steepness of the hill behind them seemed like a pleasant ride in the park compared to what she now saw before her.

It seemed like the White drifted in the air forever before he finally hit solid ground. The jolt ripped the reins from her hands, so Ariel held on to his mane. God seemed to be guiding the White, so Ariel let him choose his own way. Everything whizzed past in such a blur that she had no idea how far they had come, how much further they had to go.

Abdul had never seen such a sight in all his days.

The White plummeting over the edge with nothing below him, and Ariel clinging to his back, her hair trailing like fire behind her. Another first struck him as fear took him in its steely grip, paralyzing him. His breath stilled and did not start again until the horse came to earth. Still the fear remained; her flight was not done.

Riders came to a halt around him and watched her descent in awe. Like a descending angel, the White carried Ariel down the hill. When the stallion had delivered his rider to the bottom safely, Abdul closed his eyes in relief. When he opened them again, Ariel whirled about, her mount rising up onto his back legs, pawing the air. Never had there been a more magnificent horse, nor a greater rider.

Her snapping golden eyes caught his gaze, the challenge lighting them clear.

"I thought you weren't going to help me, Sheik."

Ariel struggled to keep the White back, then finally let him go. She heard Abdul's warm laughter and knew without looking he had let his mount run as well. The high-pitched warble of the Bedouin chased her as they pounded for the finish. Out

301

of the corner of her eye she saw Abdul, his own stallion pushed to the limit. But the White was not about to be outdone, his body stretched full-length.

All noise seemed to fade away as Ariel leaned low over the White's neck. Only the pounding of each hoof as it struck the ground echoed in her mind, each long-legged stride bringing them closer to the end.

Gradually the monotonous scenery of sand was replaced by a blur of color as she moved into the camp. The roar of the crowd took her mind and led her to the finish line.

Dylan couldn't see what was causing the great excitement, but he assumed it was because the riders had entered the compound. He looked down to see Saree straining to see. The old woman, Jena, seemed content with her own visions.

A cry went up in the crowd, and Saree turned tearful eyes to him.

"Ariel is winning."

The shock that went through Dylan was nothing compared to the aftermath of his confusion. He pulled Saree back around to him. "Ariel is riding in the race?"

She nodded. "She is riding, and she is winning."

It was still confusing, but Dylan put it aside, distracted by the crowd's excitement. He moved forward to see better; then he saw her, riding a huge white stallion. Initially, fear struck him, then admiration.

Ariel rode neck and neck with another rider. Dylan leaned down to Saree and asked, "Who is that?"

"My husband, the sheik, Abdul Hakeem."

Dylan's gaze returned to Ariel. She was beautiful—beyond words, beyond description.

Ariel smiled and yelled to the White. "Let's go, boy."

The animal drove forward, his full speed unleashed. She was aware of the end just ahead, of the crowd's frenzy, of the animal moving beneath her. Ariel's heart was pounding in her ears, and as they neared the finish she felt his own great heart working hard, matching hers beat for beat.

Where the exact end was, she didn't know. Only when the crowd burst its invisible seams and swarmed out around her was she sure the race was won. The White came to a halt, but the mass of people frightened him, making him rear and slash the air with his forelegs. Ariel spoke to him gently, calming him, but his body still shook from fear. She slid from his back, her legs nearly buckling from weakness, her own body shaking. She leaned against the stallion, letting him support her.

The White's head twisted about, and he nuzzled her. She kissed his head and whispered to him, "Thanks, my friend."

Out of respect for his size and strength, the crowd had remained distant, yet a tight circle had formed about them. All fell silent. A path parted to allow Abdul Hakeem to the center.

"You have won the hearts of my people."

"I am honored," Ariel replied truthfully. "But have I proved my worthiness?"

Abdul stepped forward and placed his hand upon her cheek, the tears she wept streaking smudges of dirt. "Never has one deserved my generosity more. You have earned your freedom."

Fearfully, Ariel asked, "And my husband?"

At that moment Dylan broke through the wall of people. Saree and Jena followed close behind. Abdul turned to him. Their gazes locked, stilling everyone. Abdul's gaze moved back to Ariel's frightened one.

"He holds your heart. How can I keep you apart?"

Ariel let her breath out with a little cry and ran to Dylan's open arms. He caught her as she all but flew to him, swinging her into the air, his deep laughter mixing with hers.

A cheer went up. Abdul approached them, his happiness dampened by his private pain. Dylan set Ariel down, waiting for him to speak. The other men who rode in the race gathered behind the Bedouin leader.

"As is tradition, you have won all the horses in the race."

One of the men spoke to Abdul, and he translated. "They say their loss today carries no dishonor. To have run against the Great White and his lady is an honor they will tell their children and their children's children."

"I'm flattered." Ariel blushed under such praise. "Perhaps I had a more desperate motivation and more to lose."

"Do not underestimate your victory. I have never witnessed such horsemanship, Ariel."

Ariel's cheeks heated. "I wish to give you all the horses, Abdul."

This seemed to take him by surprise, but he countered appropriately. "I thank you." He turned to look at the White. "And the stallion? Is he a gift?"

Ariel shook her head. "No. The White is not mine to give."

"But you have tamed him," Abdul argued.

"I have ridden him, but I have not tamed him. He is as wild today as he was yesterday. I haven't the right to take his spirit away."

"What are you going to do with him?"

Instead of answering, Ariel walked back to where the White stood, skittishly waiting for her. She stroked his head and said softly, "I will never forget you, my White."

She untied the rope she had used as a makeshift halter. "Run free, my friend."

Ariel watched him run back into the hills and his freedom. Dylan came up behind her and put his arms about her.

Abdul called out to his people. "Now we shall celebrate. Today all riders will keep their horses. I will win them in the next race."

A cheer went up in the crowd.

That night Dylan and Ariel were honored guests of the sheik. The camp was alive with noise as the men and women celebrated, excitement felt by all, even the animals. Dogs barked, horses whinnied, goats bleated, camels brayed—all combining into a weird song of sorts. Meats roasted over every open fire, the smell drifting on the wind. The women dressed in their best finery, the traditional colors distinctive, as were the decorated or embroidered veils of the married women. The oldest wore black, the stark background accenting the colors even more. Even Ariel dressed in the Bedouin way. Saree had taken great care with Ariel so she would look perfect for this night with her husband.

Dylan looked upon his wife with appreciation. Saree was showing her the steps to their dance. He could not help but notice the sway of Ariel's hips as she moved to the beat. Her hair was loose, the fires bringing it to life in their playful light. The bright colors she wore made her skin look even more pale, creamy and soft. The dark kohl lining her eyes made them larger, the gold-tinted topaz dark and haunting.

"Your wife is very beautiful."

Dylan turned away from studying Ariel and gave his attention to Abdul Hakeem. "Yes," he drawled, almost lazily, the wine having taken away any tenseness that had remained between them. "Ariel has an unusual beauty. It's almost more something from within her that radiates. Something as much felt as seen."

Abdul seemed to understand and nodded his head. "How is it that you have Ariel's devotion? She is not easily won."

Dylan knew he was referring to his own failure to do so, obviously his defeat still not resting easy upon his mind. "I can't really say, Abdul. Perhaps it is because I don't threaten her freedom."

This only confused Abdul. "She is a woman and your wife. What freedom does she need?"

Dylan laughed, thinking to himself that Abdul's attitude was his own undoing. "The very first time I saw Ariel she was walking from the jungle, unmindful of the rain that drenched her. And walking by her side was a Bengal tiger, one of the largest I've ever seen. I saw them together and saw, as well as felt, a specialness between them."

"This tiger was her pet?" Abdul asked, amazement reflected on his face.

"He was more than a pet. He was . . ." Dylan wasn't really sure what the right word would be to describe their relationship. "He was her spirit."

Dylan caught Ariel's gaze, and he witnessed what he was saying in the depth of her startling eyes. The intensity he saw stilled the breath he was about to take.

Abdul watched the changes on Dylan's face, then followed his gaze to where Ariel stood. She had stopped dancing, but the air came alive with the emotion between them. At first, Abdul felt a stab of envy, even jealousy; then it disappeared. He began to understand what Dylan had just told him. Then, quite out of nowhere, he felt shamed, an emotion he was not familiar with. He had tried to take her spirit away, to tame the wildness that was Ariel.

He looked back to Dylan and realized why Ariel had given her heart to him. This man allowed her to run free. There was no longer any regret. These two belonged together.

Abdul leaned closer and suggested to Dylan, "Perhaps it is time for you to take your wife and retire. Saree has prepared a tent for you."

"Yes," Dylan agreed, never taking his eyes from Ariel. "It's been a long day."

Ariel's pulse quickened; the warmth that moved within her flashed into a fire, heat spreading and consuming her. She watched Dylan stand, then move toward her, slow and easy, teasing her senses with anticipation. He reached out to her, his tall body near but too far away for her satisfaction.

She admired the broadness of his chest, the muscles that lay innocently beneath the fabric of his open shirt tempting her. She brushed her fingertips over the ridge of his collarbone, the dark tan of his skin stark against the crisp whiteness of his shirt. She tilted her head up so she could read what lay in the blue depths of his eyes. She smiled when they told her what she wanted to know.

Her hand moved around to the back of his neck, her fingers playing with the soft strands of hair falling over his collar. Standing on her tiptoes, Ariel moved her face to his.

She stopped only a sweet breath away, her laughter as seductive as her boldness. "You are incorrigible," Dylan whispered, the movement of his lips brushing their softness to hers.

"Yes, I am."

Dylan looked around. "People are watching us, Ariel."

Ariel felt a lightness in her head. She wasn't sure if it was the wine or Dylan's closeness. "Yes," she purred, "I know." She didn't care who was watching.

"Completely incorrigible," he repeated, his own lips pulling into a smile.

Unable to keep from his lips any longer, Ariel kissed him. Dylan lifted her into his arms and carried her from the tent, cries of encouragement following them into the night.

Chapter Twenty-Five

Ariel opened the tall doors to the balcony and stepped outside. The city of Cairo lay before her like a quilt of intricate detail and color. Earthy sandstone was balanced by vibrant reds and splashes of green foliage. Bright ornate brass and earthy carved wood adorned the city's buildings. It was beautiful.

"You must take time to see what pleasures Cairo offers."

Ariel turned to Abdul and smiled. "We may have some time before we catch our ship to Bombay. It would be wonderful. Can you be our guide, Abdul?"

She was certain a sadness came to his eyes, an almost apologetic look in them. "No, unfortunately I have urgent business I must see to."

"We appreciate you bringing us to Cairo."

"It was the least I could do. Now I must go."

Abdul walked back inside the room, and Ariel followed. "Will we see you again?"

Dylan looked up from the letter he was writing, then stood and crossed the room to them.

"I am afraid we must say our goodbyes," Abdul said, the regret he felt clear in his softened tone.

"Oh." Ariel's dismay colored her response. She had grown fond of the sheik, as she had of Saree and Jena. Her farewell to them had been difficult, and now it must be followed with another.

"Sweet Ariel, do not look so sad. Remember I took you by force. You should be angry with me."

Ariel forced the smile back onto her face. "You are a rogue, without hope of redemption. But a truly honorable one. I shall miss you."

"We both shall miss the company of the Bedouin," Dylan added, begrudgingly admitting he too had grown to like and respect Abdul.

"You have given me a memory I shall treasure in my heart and find a pleasure in my mind forever."

Abdul took Ariel's hand and kissed it, caressing her silken skin with his lips. With regret, he gave it up, just as he had his quest for Ariel.

"Goodbye, Abdul." Ariel's voice was strained, and tears came to her eyes. Unable to stop herself she flung her arms about him and hugged him fiercely. "Take care of Saree."

Abdul only nodded. Ariel knew he was unable to speak, the glistening in his dark eyes telling her of his own emotion. Ariel and Dylan stood hand in hand and watched him leave. Dylan gave her a

311

reassuring squeeze, bringing her tear stained face up to look into his.

"How odd it is to have gained a friend in such a strange way," Dylan mused.

"That makes it all the more precious."

Dylan pulled Ariel to him, holding her close to his heart. As he had sat helpless in the sheik's camp, he'd prayed for a chance to get away. He'd begun to lose all hope after his one opportunity had ended so futilely, leaving Ariel's cries to haunt him. He doubted he would ever quite understand what had happened. He wasn't sure he wanted to know what had passed between Ariel and Abdul. His bliss now was enough. He decided to let it be.

"What do you mean, you haven't got Ariel?" Bryce rose from the chair he sat in, the relaxed air he'd projected slipping from him. He placed his drink on the table and faced Abdul Hakeem. "That is what I paid for. They never reached Cairo."

Abdul didn't blink an eye. "I believe I was very clear in my meaning. I do not have them any longer."

"Any longer?" The blood gathered in Bryce's head, turning his face a brilliant shade of red, his dark eyes almost bulging from their sockets.

"I let them go," Abdul answered casually.

Exerting what little control he could muster, Bryce tried to find out the whole story behind the sheik's strange confession. "You were hired to kidnap Ariel and kill Dylan. Why hasn't that been done?"

"My decision," Abdul said, "is my own. I am returning your gold."

"Just like that?" Bryce yelled, grabbing the bag from the man who accompanied Abdul. It irritated him further when Abdul merely crossed his arms, unaffected by Bryce's anger. "Get out of here! I'll find another to handle your failure."

"There will be no one in Cairo who will do your dirty work."

Abdul's audacity shocked Bryce, and he stood for a moment just staring. Then he sneered, "Cairo is swarming with thieves and cutthroats. It will be easy to find such a man."

"None will dare." Abdul turned and left Bryce's suite, his man following close behind.

"Son-of-a-bitch," Bryce screamed, throwing the pouch of gold he held at the closed door. "Son-of-a-bitch!"

Bryce whirled, his eyes squinting in anger. "What does he mean, none will dare?"

He directed his words to the Arab standing across the room, Bryce's translator while in Cairo. The man fidgeted under his glare, his shifty eyes showing his great discomfort.

"The sheik has placed these two people under his protection. Any man who dares to harm them, or even attempts to harm them, will face his wrath."

"Oh." Bryce's face lightened. "Then there is no problem. Enough gold will convince some men to kill their own mothers."

The Arab did not look so confident. "There are worse things than death, Mr. Harrington."

"Find me a man to do the job, one who will finish this time. Fail me, and I'll show you just what's worse than death."

"Yes, Mr. Harrington." The Arab swallowed hard, then left.

"Bloody Arabs," Bryce cursed, pouring himself a drink.

The fury returned tenfold. "That son-of-a-bitch." What had happened, he would never know. He only knew he would make her pay.

"I swear I *will* make you pay," he vowed. "You will pay!"

Soft murmurs of conversation drifted about Ariel, the café filled with customers of all nations. The variety of languages and dress varied, creating an exotic atmosphere only Cairo offered. Quite unexpectedly, it all faded in the wake of a stronger feeling swarming over her.

"Is something wrong, Ariel?"

Ariel looked up at Dylan, his question making her realize she had raised her arm halfway to take a drink, then stopped. A dreadful feeling had come upon her quite unexpectedly, chilling her to the bone. She was trembling, sloshing the tea over the side. She put the cup back down.

"I'm fine," she said as calmly as possible.

"Good." Dylan smiled, though his blue eyes didn't seem to believe her. "Shall we go?"

"Yes." Ariel picked up her gloves and allowed Dylan to pull her chair out. "It's a lovely day."

They left the café and walked on in silence, a comfortable companionship between them. Ariel's arm rested on Dylan's, the fine material unable to disguise the hard muscle beneath it. Yet with all his strength and power, he was so gentle. A flush warmed her earlier chill totally, leaving her with a loving, safe feeling.

"You look better, sweetness. The color's back in your face."

Ariel looked up and smiled, the heat in his eyes matching her own. "You always warm me up," she whispered, her voice holding an open invitation.

Dylan stopped, his gaze catching hers. "How did I ever find you?"

Her breath stilled, and her pulse quickened. "We found each other."

An outburst of laughter interrupted them, breaking the hold they had on each other. A crowd had gathered a short distance away, and curiosity prompted them to walk over to investigate.

Two wagons were pulled together, and a small sideshow act was pleasing the audience with its antics. Clowns, acrobats, jugglers and dancing women charmed those who watched.

The laughter was infectious. Ariel and Dylan weren't immune, their own gaiety mingling with the sense of festivity. The clowns with their painted faces jumped down into the crowd, their hats out for appreciative donations. One grabbed Ariel and twirled her about, his oversized shoes making the dance comical. When he let her go, she whirled away.

Ariel felt someone stop her reckless flight, and laughter stuck in her throat. She turned to look at the man who held her, to thank him for his help. Dark eyes looked down at her, stilling the thanks on her lips. She tried to pull away, but his hand held her waist, his hold unbreakable.

She twisted around and called to Dylan. Her voice drifted into the high-pitched clamor that surrounded them. Ariel turned back, striking out at the same time. Her fist struck his face and split his lip. Still, he only smiled and licked at the blood.

He jerked her closer and pulled a knife from his belt. His black eyes widened, as did his smile, and fear struck Ariel's deepest nerves.

He threw back his head and laughed, but he choked on his own voice. Slowly his head swiveled down, the mirth stripped from his eyes. His body slumped forward, his weight nearly toppling her. Death marked his face. Ariel pulled away in horror. In that same moment, he was swept away by the jubilant crowd, leaving Ariel alone.

"There you are."

Dylan appeared beside her, startling her from her stupor.

"I didn't mean to startle you." Dylan laughed at her jumpiness.

Ariel tried to recover. It all happened so fast, then he was gone. She was certain Bryce was behind this, but this time Ariel faced his threat with a dead calm.

"Are you ready to go back to the hotel?"

Ariel nodded. In the back of her mind, memories replayed Jena's warning as they had said goodbye. "Great danger lies ahead. This time you must face it head-on; it will not go away. You cannot run from it any longer."

Abdul Hakeem watched as Dylan and Ariel disappeared down the street. He turned and nodded to his men. One continued to follow them at a distance.

*   *   *

"This was delivered this morning, Mr. Harrington."

Bryce looked up from his meal, annoyed at being disturbed. He hated to be interrupted when he ate.

"What is it?" he snapped, causing the already jittery man to step back.

"I do not know."

"Leave it there on the table. And go away. You sicken me."

Gladly, the manservant did as he was told, wasting no time leaving.

Bryce sipped his coffee, eyeing the box that had been delivered, its size a little smaller than a hat box. It was quite ornate, and this made him curious.

Dabbing at his mouth with his napkin, Bryce rose and crossed to the table. It was a beautiful, gold-leafed box with jewels encrusted on the carved lid. He opened it.

Inside was a velvet bag with a gold rope tied at the top. Bryce pulled it out. Then holding it with one hand he untied the sack with the other.

As the fabric fell away, so did Bryce's pleasure. Dead eyes stared out at nothing. He recognized the Arab he had hired.

He dropped the head back into the box and slammed the lid shut. It had taken him days to find someone to take the job, and it was all for nothing.

"All the better for it," he muttered to himself, his hand rubbing his jaw. "It's time to take care of business myself."

Bryce knew Ariel and Dylan were leaving for the coast and then taking a ship on to Bombay in the morning. Once in India, he would handle matters himself. And this time he would do the job properly.

Ariel stood on deck and watched the city disappear from the horizon. The ship's sails filled with the breeze, taking them farther out to sea.

Deep within Ariel her soul stirred as if awakening from a long sleep. She was going home. Calmness descended over Ariel. The fear dogging her dimmed in the glow of her excitement.

"You're quiet today, Ariel."

Dylan's arms slipped around her waist, and he snuggled her up close to him, his head looking over hers. Ariel reveled in the special feeling of having him close.

"Actually," he whispered in her ear, "you've been quiet since our outing yesterday."

Ariel tilted her head up to look at him. "You worry too much."

"Only when it comes to you, my love."

Her smile dispelled his worries. "Perhaps we should put your mind on more important matters."

Dylan returned a devilish grin, its intent lighting the blue of his eyes. "And what would that be?"

"Many, many things come to mind," Ariel teased.

"Perhaps we should go to our cabin and discuss this further."

"A very good suggestion."

Playfully, Dylan whisked her into his arms.

"Dylan, everyone will see," she said softly, though it seemed everyone was already watching.

"Is it against the law for a husband to carry his wife to their cabin?"

Dylan's voice had raised, allowing all those who stared at them to hear. The heat stained Ariel's cheeks, as much from embarrassment as the passion coming alive within her. "No, it isn't," she agreed, ducking her head to hide her face. "But—"

"But nothing," he interrupted. "Tell me, love, is it also okay for a husband to kiss his wife in public?"

"You are hopeless." Ariel gave over to him. Quite brazenly, she kissed him, long and lovingly. "Shall we go?"

"I believe we'd better," Dylan agreed. "Before I show them all just how much I desire you."

Chapter Twenty-Six

Dylan set the letter onto his small writing desk with a movement so smooth it did not show any of the emotions he was experiencing inside. All the street noise that drifted in the open windows faded away, overpowered by the clatter in his mind.

His eyes no longer followed Ariel about the hotel room as she unpacked their things. The warmth within him was no longer the effect of her swaying hips but a hot anger that swept through him. Yet it was quickly cooled by the chill that came with the onslaught of other emotions.

"Son-of-a-bitch," Dylan mumbled, clenching his fist. Slowly, he uncurled his fingers, flexing his hand to relieve it of the tension. He then used his long fingers to comb his hair back, frustration now clear.

He looked at the letter he had put on the desk.

Dylan's gaze returned to Ariel. He wanted to say something, but indecision kept him silent. Dylan picked up the letter and reread it, as if there were something he might have missed. There was nothing more.

Franklin's investigation had uncovered the truth. Bryce had killed the man in the park, and, in turn, this led to what had happened to Ariel in the asylum.

A shudder accompanied the realization of what this meant. Dylan studied Ariel as she stood at the window looking out at the city. Her demeanor was calm, almost surreal. It was hard for him to imagine the horrors she must have endured, the fear she had experienced that night in the park and the terror of being locked up.

Dylan, Bryce Harrington has left England. You must be careful.

Gritting his teeth, Dylan pulled his fury under control. *The time will come when I can let the anger out. Then I will kill the bastard.*

"Are you ready to go?"

The soft lilt in Ariel's voice brought him from his dark mood. The anticipation that lit her golden eyes made him smile, and he determined to chase away the bad feelings. He didn't want to ruin her day.

"Ready?" he teased, seeing the delight on her heart-shaped face.

"Yes, you promised to take me out."

Playfully, Dylan tugged her onto his lap. "Would you consider just staying in? We could have our dinner sent up." Dylan could smell the sweetness of her perfume and nuzzled closer, his lips brushing her silken neck. His tongue slid to her throat; then he kissed away the bumps he had raised.

Ariel laughed softly and pulled away half-heartedly. "Later, Dylan. I haven't been in Bombay for over two years."

Dylan refused to let her go, continuing his exploration of her throat and neck. "You know, for a jungle girl you certainly like to explore cities."

"They are exciting, if you go to the right places."

"If you go to the right places?"

Ariel nodded, her mood turning serious. "Aunt Margaret always thought the dinner parties, dances, theater and opera were the right places." A soft sigh sounded. "They held no life..But the heart of a city is life."

A wide grin spread across Dylan's face. "You are a wild one."

"Do you disapprove?"

The grin vanished, a seriousness descending upon him. "I wouldn't have you any other way. Don't you know that?"

"I do now."

"We'd best be going, Ariel. Otherwise, we will be eating in."

Ariel turned back, her head tilted to the side. "I'll make it up to you later. I promise."

"You will be held to that promise."

"I expect no mercy if I don't."

Dylan burst out laughing, then stood to follow Ariel as she walked from the room.

"No mercy," he mumbled, "no mercy at all."

*   *   *

"You're very beautiful."

Ariel looked up from the silk scarf she was looking at and smiled at Dylan's compliment, her face reflecting the fire she saw in his eyes. "Do not look at me that way."

"What way?"

"You're a beast."

This only made him smile. "A beast for my jungle lady."

Ariel frowned. "Don't tease."

"I never tease."

Ariel felt sad. The time they had spent together had been wonderful, their days filled with pleasure and their nights filled with loving. It was like a dream, but Ariel feared the dream would end soon.

Tomorrow they would start out for the plantation. She was going home. It seemed a mixed blessing now. To be home again gave her life. Yet in the shadows lurked danger—Bryce, a constant threat.

"I didn't mean to upset you."

Dylan's voice was soft in her ear, sending shivers down her spine at his closeness. "You didn't. I guess I'm feeling a little strange about going home."

"It's what you've wanted."

"No, it's what I've needed." Ariel turned to look up at him. "Don't you see? The jungle is my soul. When I'm away it is as if a part of me dies inside."

"Then why are you so sad? You should be happy."

"I am." Ariel tried to smile his doubts away. "And I'm hungry. Feed me."

Ariel whirled about, her laughter mingling with the buzz of strange dialects. She disappeared into the throng of people, leaving Dylan no choice but to follow. Easily, he played her game of hide-and-seek, her bright blue dress a beacon of color for him to chase as she darted in and out of the vendors' stalls.

Then she was there, waiting for him with a gleaming smile on her face. Her cheeks were flushed from their play, the warmth adding a sparkle to her eyes. The sun glinted off her hair, bringing the red to life, a few unruly wisps struggling free of the confining pins she had so carefully placed in the curls earlier that day. Dylan wished fervently they were back at the hotel.

A carriage came out of nowhere; a crowd of people parted hastily to clear a path. But Ariel was watching Dylan and not the commotion behind her.

"Ariel," Dylan yelled, but his cry was lost amid the noise. He saw the expression on her face change as she turned to see the four-wheeled conveyance fast upon her.

She reacted just as Dylan reached her, his hand clamping onto her arm as she jumped. He jerked her into his arms, the carriage rolling by only a hairbreadth away. She twisted about in time to catch a glimpse of Bryce's face through the window of the carriage. He was laughing.

Neither moved, Ariel clinging to Dylan, he clinging to her. He watched the carriage disappear, and a strange fear gripped him. Could it be?

Ariel finally pulled away from the security of his

arms. She attempted a casual laugh, but it came out forced, fading altogether in the end.

"I guess I need to watch where I'm going."

Dylan had an urge to shake her, to yell at her that just maybe it wasn't an accident, that maybe it was Harrington trying to kill her. He wanted to force her to say it, to say out loud what he knew she feared.

"Damn it, Ariel." Dylan went so far as to grasp her shoulders. "Don't you think it's time you told me what's going on?"

A closed look came into her eyes, replacing the fear of only moments before. "It was an accident, Dylan. What more is there to say?"

Her look, her tone and her manner were as if she'd pulled shutters around herself.

The terror of her close call left Dylan weak, allowing anger to sneak in and take control.

Finally, he did shake her. "Why are you doing this to me?"

An unusual craving hit him, gnawing at his mind. He wanted her to hurt just as he was hurting. It was unbearable; it was uncontrollable. "Damn you for coming into my life and turning it upside down. Damn you, Ariel."

He let go, then turned away, unable to look into her shadowed eyes any longer. "What must I do to make you trust me?"

Something touched Ariel, his pain-filled words dragging her from her private retreat. She reached out and touched the shoulder that was turned from her.

"Dylan, I'm sorry if I've hurt you, but . . ." She

could not bring herself to finish as she struggled with indecision.

Dylan turned back and grabbed her hand as she pulled it back. "But what, Ariel? What is it?"

"I don't know how," she whispered, the evidence of her confusion clear on her face and in her voice.

"To trust?" he pushed on. "To share? It's all part of loving, Ariel. It's time to trust in me, to share what you are carrying inside."

"In the jungle the rules are simple. To live the animals must find the strength within themselves. They depend on no other. There is no trust or sharing. It is what I know."

"Do you love me, Ariel?"

His words were so soft, so tender that Ariel felt breathless. "Yes, I love you."

He said nothing more, but she saw everything in his eyes.

Thoughts raced across her mind, the impact leaving her breathless. Suddenly, she knew it was time to rid herself of this unreasonable independence that claimed her. It *was* time to start trusting, sharing. Ariel realized she no longer walked alone. "He's here in Bombay, Dylan. He followed me to Alexandria, then Cairo. Now he's here."

Dylan forced himself to be patient and stay calm. "Who are you talking about? Who?"

Ariel licked her lips and took a deep breath. "Bryce Harrington. He killed the man in the park, and I saw it all. I tried to tell the police." Her eyes closed, but she went on. "They thought I was crazy and took me to the asylum. Bryce found out."

"That's when he decided to marry you, so you couldn't testify against him."

"Yes." Ariel nodded. "I've made such a mess of things. I should have married him and everything would have been all right. He threatened my family, but I still ran away from him."

Dylan's voice rose in anger. "How can you say such a thing? He's a cold-blooded killer." His anger was laced with pain. "But why did you run away from me?"

"He found my necklace. It must have come off when I tried to help the poor man. He threatened to take it to the police and see that I was hanged for murder. I was afraid, Dylan. I couldn't think. All I had in my mind was to come home, to return to the jungle where I could come alive again."

"I wouldn't have allowed what he threatened, Ariel. But it doesn't matter now. What matters is that we are together. It will be all right. I promise."

"No." She shook her head vigorously as she cried out in fear. "He means to kill you now, just as he killed my father."

Dylan let go of her hand. "So Bryce did kill your father."

The look on Ariel's face made Dylan uneasy. She was calm, maybe too calm.

"It wasn't an accident. He murdered my father to make it easier to get at me. Everything he did was to have me."

Dylan took her hand again, the look on his face hardening to a cold, stony mask. A rush of feelings flooded Dylan, the months of frustra-

tion culminating into one viable emotion—hatred!
What he knew in his heart to be true had eluded
him, the proof never materializing. His father had
depended on him, and he had failed.

"How do you know this?" Dylan's thoughts were
rushing ahead, trying to anticipate what he must
have missed to keep this fact a mystery. He never
expected her answer.

"He told me."

It took a full moment before he said, "I think it's
time to talk. No more lies or half-truths, Ariel. I
want the whole story. From the beginning."

Chapter Twenty-Seven

Ariel slept little that night and knew Dylan didn't either. They started for the plantation at dawn, neither speaking again of Bryce Harrington. Yet, as she neared her home, all her problems faded in the wake of a stronger, more dominant emotion. She drew in a long breath to smell the jungle and clean the city air from her lungs. It worked on her soul like magic, freeing her spirit.

Looking down at the main house, happy memories of her youth flooded over her, only to be doused by the cold reality of her losses. Just as suddenly, fear came upon her, fear from her more recent, painful memories.

Slowly, she rode on. It was time to face her ghosts.

She dismounted at the well-worn path to the tiny cemetery. It was familiar to her from the many trips she had made over the years to visit her mother's grave. Even the jungle's overgrowth was unable to hide it from her. This time, though, her visit was different. She felt like an errant child and hesitated. But Ariel knew there would be no scolding or harsh words. She would have welcomed them.

"Are you all right, Ariel?"

She glanced up at Dylan and smiled. She was glad he was there beside her. She reached out her hand to him, and he took it. Together they walked the last few steps to the old, wrought-iron gate. Its hinges squeaked as Dylan forced it open.

Fear kept Ariel from stepping into the courtyard.

"It's time to say goodbye."

Dylan's voice soothed her jumbled thoughts and gave her the courage to go in. The marker on her father's grave was new, its lettering dark against unweathered marble. Her mother's headstone showed its many years in the elements.

Memories tugged at her mind, drawing her back in time. She knelt down, then hesitantly touched the lettering of her father's name.

"It's for your own good, Ariel."

Echoes of the past swarmed over her, taking Ariel the last step backwards as she remembered their last conversation.

"But I want to stay here with you, Papa. Please, don't make me go away."

Jason Lockwood had never denied his daughter anything, especially when she looked at him in such a way, but today would be a first. "I'm sorry, Ariel. I've made my decision, and whether you like it or not, you will be returning to England with Margaret."

"Why? Why are you doing this?"

"Someday you will understand my reasons."

"No, I will never understand! You're taking away everything that is a part of me. Kala Bagh, the jungle and you. How can you possibly think it's for my own good?"

Tears blurred Ariel's eyes, and she could no longer read the tombstone, but tears could not wipe out the hurt on her father's face that remained firmly embedded in her memories. It was the only time they had ever argued.

"I refused to say goodbye." Ariel looked up at Dylan, the tears now running down her cheeks. "I knew I would be back. Nothing would keep me from coming home. Didn't he know that?"

"I think he knew but wanted the options open to you. Then, if you chose to live in India, there would be no doubt in his mind. Or yours."

"I didn't say goodbye because I never thought he wouldn't be here, waiting for me." Ariel's voice dropped to a choked whisper. "I never said goodbye."

"You couldn't have known he would die."

Dylan's words were meant to ease her mind. Ariel understood that. Instead they brought forth a terrible anger. "No. I couldn't have known he would be shot in cold blood."

Dylan brushed clean the small bench at the garden's edge, the seat nearly hidden by lush growth. He offered it to Ariel, then sat beside her.

"Franklin knows about Bryce, Ariel. Bryce's

friends weren't willing to share the guilt of what he had done."

"He is mad," Ariel whispered softly.

"No, he is merely cold-blooded."

A strange look came to her face, a look Dylan found difficult to define.

Ariel shook her head in disagreement. "No." She refuted his own statement. "A man that hunts another for the pure pleasure of killing must be mad. A man who kills to possess another must be mad. He pursues me as if I were his prey."

Dylan pulled her into his arms and she felt secure, if only for the moment. "I love you, Ariel. I'll not let anything happen to you."

Ariel pulled back and looked at Dylan longingly. "He'll follow us here, Dylan."

"Yes." He pulled her close again. "Yes, I know."

The rain stopped, as quickly as it had started. The dampness hung in the air, its clean smell washing from it the sultry heat left from the day. Dylan breathed deeply, filling his lungs with its crispness.

He wished he was able to rid himself of the foul thoughts that plagued him as easily as the air had cleared his lungs. He glanced back inside the double doors leading to their bedroom, an oil lamp casting a muted glow about the room. Ariel sat at the dressing table brushing her long hair, the lantern's yellow light bringing out the flame in the soft strands.

He was struck by her beauty, by how much he

loved her. A brooding determination shook him. He wouldn't let Bryce harm a single hair on her head. Hate heated his blood. Never had he known such a strangling emotion. It sucked the air from his lungs, took away his breath.

How he hated Bryce Harrington. How he hated the fear he had created in Ariel's eyes, the terror she had been forced to live with. The only way to take it away would be to kill him. It had come down to that. Kill or be killed. It had been Harrington's choice, and Dylan would oblige.

"Are you coming to bed?"

Ariel's soft voice sent tremors through him, immediately dispelling all the violence that churned within his body and mind.

When she slid her arms about his waist and hugged him, he thought he would melt beneath her loving touch. She laid her cheek against his broad back, her hands locking across his muscled stomach.

"I cannot sleep until you are with me."

Such simple words brought havoc to his heart. He laid his hands upon hers, the softness beneath his fingers only a promise of what was his to share.

"Do you know how much I love you, Ariel?"

He turned around so he could look down upon her beautiful face.

"I do now, Dylan. I do now."

Ariel sat up, uncertain of what had awakened her. At first, she heard only the pounding of her heart, but slowly, she was able to hear him.

"Kala Bagh."

Excitement surged through her with such force
it left her light-headed. She slid out of bed quietly, not wanting to disturb Dylan's sleep. Without
even pulling on a robe, she stepped out onto the
veranda. She waited and listened, thinking perhaps her own longing had inspired his calls. This
time his cry was stronger. He was close to the
house.

Tears blinded her, but she didn't need sight to
find her way. Barefoot, she ran across the lawn,
each step faster and lighter, each step taking her
to Kala Bagh. The groomed grass of the garden,
soft beneath her feet, turned into the rough undergrowth of the jungle. It felt marvelous.

The dewy scent of the jungle was intoxicating, the
musky perfume strong in her nose. Ariel stopped.
The denseness of the trees blocked the moon's light
as it hung low in the sky, but it took only a moment
for her eyes to adjust. Her senses were alert, tightly strung. Soft noises floated to her, serenading
her, bringing alive the soul that had slept much
too long.

Kala Bagh called to her, filling her with anticipation of their being together again. Ariel ran farther
into the darkness, fear no longer a part of her emotions. She had come home.

Bryce Harrington paused at the jungle's edge,
then plunged on. He was stunned that Ariel would
be so foolish. He followed her, the hunter taking
over. Actually, it made the chase more exciting.

It was easy to follow her with Ariel calling out
often. He didn't take the time or the care to won-

der where she was going or why; he only understood he would have her soon. Soon he would
have his revenge on her. Then he would take care
of Dylan.

He smiled.

"Ariel."

Dylan called out to Ariel, thinking she had gone
into the other room. When there was no answer,
he got up and pulled his pants on. He noticed the
doors to the garden were open and stepped outside
to see if she was there.

A nagging fear prodded his mind, but he pulled
it back. He walked out into the garden, calling her
name again. He heard no answer.

He turned his gaze to the dark silhouette of
the trees. Apprehension brought the fear forward
again. He wanted to believe she wouldn't go out, not
this late and not alone. Still, the feeling remained.

He heard the cat's cry and stopped. Its eerie
sound touched him, raising the hair on the back
of his neck. Kala Bagh called to her again and
he knew. Ariel had gone to find her soul mate.
He ran into the jungle that taunted him with the
truth.

Dylan moved into the trees, then stopped. He
needed to go back for his gun, but Kala Bagh's
cries were quickly fading. If he took time to go
back, he would lose her, so he followed the sound.

Ariel stopped to catch her breath, knowing Kala
Bagh could not be far away. She waited and
listened. Immediately, she felt the presence of

someone watching her. Every muscle in her body tensed.

She could smell him, the scent of him drifting to her sensitive nose. All her instincts came forward, preparing her for the confrontation.

Ariel felt his movements before she saw him, his hand coming from the dark shadows that surrounded her. She twisted away. His fingers clawed at her arm, ripping the delicate fabric of her nightgown and scratching her tender flesh.

Bryce's laughter echoed in the stillness, his intrusion causing the sleeping birds and animals to object in an odd chorus.

"Ariel," he called to her.

She pulled farther back into the trees shadowing her.

"You needn't run from me. I'll have you in the end." He walked in a circle, his eyes searching the blackness for her. "I always get my prey."

His voice was teasing. When she dared a look, he was smiling, an arrogant smile holding no humor. Only madness. Ariel closed her eyes and drew in a deep breath. She tried to think, but her mind was beyond thought, beyond fear or caution.

Ariel stepped out, and he slowly turned to face her. "I'll not be as easy as the man in the park."

Bryce lunged at her, but he caught only air. Ariel eluded him, but his laughter chased directly on her heels. Immediately, she heard him crash into the foliage behind her.

She could almost feel his hot breath on her neck as he remained a few steps behind. Every once in a while, he would call out to her, reminding her of his presence, of what he was going to do when he caught her.

Dawn's first light brightened the horizon, bringing the jungle to life. Birds began their morning chatter, and monkeys screeched in joyful play. All these sounds were familiar to Ariel, but her mind concentrated on the sounds that didn't belong. She paused to determine where Bryce was. The ground beneath her crumbled. The rain had softened the earth, and she started to slide down a small hill. She grabbed for vines, but they gave way to her weight.

She rolled to the bottom of the hill, coming to an abrupt halt as she hit a tree. Ariel tried to raise up but found herself face-to-face with a cobra. Its hood spread out as it reared in defense; large, black eyes stared back at her.

"Well, well," Bryce drawled, a low chuckle telling her of his delight at her dangerous predicament. "What have we here?"

When he moved closer, the cobra turned to him, then back to her. Ariel did not move.

"Now, I could shoot the snake. Or maybe I should let it do my dirty work. No one would ever suspect me if you were to die of a snakebite. But then, if I let the cobra kill you, I wouldn't have the pleasure of it myself. Nor of having you. No. Actually, I could still have you. If it bit you, you wouldn't die right away."

As Bryce fretted over his decision, Ariel slowly inched up, bringing her legs beneath her and freeing her hands.

"Then again," he drawled, "you wouldn't have

the fight in you I've always dreamed you'd have when I took you. The poison works terribly fast."

A shiver surged through Ariel as he talked about having her, taking her. She started to sway, back and forth, slowly and carefully. The cobra followed her movement.

"Then again . . ." Bryce continued.

Ariel made her move, catching the cobra by the neck. She rolled on her shoulders then jumped to her feet, at the same time tossing the snake at Bryce. He used his rifle to bat it away, firing it by accident.

Ariel pushed into the tangled vines of the jungle again, depending on its web of greenery to hide her.

When the shot echoed through the jungle, Dylan stopped dead in his tracks. The blood left his head. Fear rushed in its place. His step quickened, his pace matching the speed of his heart.

Dylan's tired legs were no longer tired, the burn in his lungs gone. His only thoughts were of Ariel. As it grew lighter, Dylan was able to move faster.

Carefully he traveled wide, needing to find Ariel before Harrington did. He must see her safe; then he would deal with Bryce.

He stopped, listening to the sounds about him. Dylan stepped back into the cover of the trees and waited. In only a few moments he heard a noise. She was coming.

As Ariel flew by, Dylan reached out and caught her, clamping his hand over her mouth. He felt her tense as he pulled her to him.

"It's all right, Ariel," he whispered into her ear. Immediately her struggle ceased. He let his hand down.

"Dylan," Ariel cried softly, throwing her arms about his neck in joy.

"Sssshh," he cautioned her, pulling her arms free. "We cannot waste time."

She nodded and motioned for him to follow.

Together they ran on.

Bryce paused, studying the trail he had been following. He knelt and examined the signs of her flight, then smiled broadly. He stood again, his hand caressing the stock of his rifle.

"So Dylan, my friend, now I have you together. How sweet." He laughed. "You shall die together."

Dylan and Ariel halted, the sound drifting to them like some spirit of evil, touching them and chilling them.

"He's laughing at us."

Ariel turned to look at Dylan with a look in her eyes he found difficult to place. "He thinks he has us," he added.

Her look remained unchanged. "And does he?"

"He has a rifle. We do not," Dylan replied honestly.

"Yes, he does."

He didn't know what to think about her mood. Dylan reached out and brushed away the hair that clung to her cheek, a fine sheen of perspiration shining on her face. "I'll go on. You stay here. Hide in the trees."

"No."

"Ariel . . ." Dylan drew in a long breath, as if preparing himself for the argument. "I'll not let you go on with me."

"*You'll* not let me."

A fire lit the smoky depths of her eyes, and he knew he had taken the wrong approach. "Please, Ariel, we haven't time to argue."

"No, we don't. So let's go."

He could tell by the tilt of her chin and the way her arms were folded across her chest that she would not be talked out of it. Dylan thought briefly of forcing her to stay behind but decided against it.

"You have no right to hold me back, Dylan. This is my home." Ariel's hand swept around, indicating the surroundings. "I'll not run again. I'll not hide away."

Dylan was confused. "What do you call this?"

Once again that strange mood came to her face. He even wondered if she was smiling.

"For now, I will lead him. For now, it's what suits me."

"I'll be damned," Dylan whispered in awe. The tiger awakened. He held out his hand to her. "Let's go."

Without warning the bullet struck Dylan, sending him reeling backwards and hitting the ground with force. Ariel disappeared into the darkness of foliage and trees.

Bryce moved into the clearing with caution, stepping to where Dylan lay. He looked about, knowing Ariel was watching.

"Ariel, my sweet," he called to her, his voice mockingly loving. "Come out, come out, wherever you are."

With great exaggeration he lifted his booted foot, allowing it to hang in the air above Dylan. Slowly, he lowered it, placing it directly on Dylan's injured shoulder. As Bryce dug his heel into the wound, Dylan yelled out from pain.

Bryce stopped, his smile widening. "Don't play at games, Ariel. We all know you'll come out. Why cause him more agony?"

Ariel understood his game of cat and mouse all too well. What Bryce didn't understand was she was not playing. She was deadly serious.

For now, he had the upper hand. For now, it suited her to give in.

Ariel stepped out of the shadows that hid her.

Chapter Twenty-Eight

"You are a smart girl." Bryce ran a finger over the smudge on her cheek. When she pulled back, he frowned, then caught her chin in a painful grip.

"You should be nice to me, Ariel. Maybe, just maybe, if you please me, I'll let Dylan die quickly, less painfully than I planned."

"How generous."

Bryce's jaw twitched as his teeth ground together in vexation. The game was not going his way. He wanted her to show fear, to cower before him and beg. Yes, he wanted to hear her cry for mercy. He wanted to see tears in her eyes, not hate.

"You won't be so cocky after I'm done with you, love. I promise you that."

A small, perfect brow arched in amusement, his words seeming to have no effect on her at all.

This brought a heat to his blood, warming him

from head to toe. He raised his hand to strike her, but she didn't flinch, even as he struck her hard across the face. Slowly, she looked back at him.

Ariel smiled.

With a guttural cry, Bryce jerked Ariel to him, taking a handful of hair and wrapping it around his fist. Defiantly, she stared him down. That made him even madder.

"Bitch. I'll take that look from your eyes."

His lips came down hard and cruel, bruising her lips. His free hand hurt her breasts, pinching and grabbing her. Her gown, already torn from her flight, gave easily as he tore it from her body.

Ariel stood like a wooden doll as he mauled her, showing no emotion, no response. Bryce's hold on her hair tightened, and he pulled her to the ground. She turned her head and met Dylan's eyes. Never had she seen such fierceness. Never would she forget it.

She closed her eyes a second, and when she opened them again, Bryce was watching her. She turned away. He twisted her head back to look at him, his eyes full of anger.

"You *are* a cold bitch."

"What is it you want? Do you want me to wiggle beneath you?"

Ariel did so. The effect it had on Bryce was immediate. "Do you want me to kiss you like this?" She kissed his chin, then brushed her soft lips against his. "Perhaps you want me to whisper words of love in your ear?"

Bryce's eyes had closed, and his breathing was ragged. She could feel him trembling beneath her touch. She moved her mouth close to his ear. "I'd sooner die than give you one ounce of pleasure." Ariel bit down on his earlobe, tasting blood when he pulled away in pain.

Bryce yelled and struck her again; this time the blood she tasted was her own. Unexpectedly his weight was lifted from her. She saw Dylan jerk him back and all but throw him aside. He grabbed Ariel's arm and pulled her up. Ariel saw Bryce going for his gun. She shoved Dylan forward, urging him to run.

Bryce's taunts followed them.

"You'll not escape me. I always get the animals I track."

Dylan shucked his shirt off as they moved through the thick growth, wincing as he pulled it off his shoulder. He handed it back to Ariel.

She pulled it on, the reddish-brown stain cool against her flesh, reminding her of his loss of blood. Ariel wished she could tend to it but knew better.

On they went, pushing themselves to go further and faster than their bodies were willing. They came upon a pond, and they both knelt down to drink.

Ariel splashed the cold water on her face and used the sleeve of Dylan's shirt to wipe it. She looked up at Dylan, his face drawn with pain.

"Can you go on?"

Dylan flashed her a reassuring smile. "It's nothing." Tenderly, he touched the split in her lip, the flesh showing a bruise. "Are you all right?"

She returned his smile as best she could without causing her lip to bleed again. "We'd better move on."

"No need."

Slowly, Ariel turned, facing immediately the barrel of Bryce's rifle. She swallowed hard, a sudden dryness coming to her throat.

Bryce clicked his tongue at her like a nagging fishwife. "Tsch, tsch. Ariel, my sweetness, I really expected better of you."

She knew what he wanted. He wanted her fear, desperation, terror. She was determined not to give him a single moment's satisfaction.

Bryce moved the barrel and nestled it below her jaw. The cruelness in his eyes showed her danger. He pressed it hard against her, the cold steel making an impression on her delicate flesh. He nudged it higher, forcing her to stand.

He looked at Dylan, and the smile returned to his face. "You are terribly quiet, old friend. Nothing to say?"

Ariel saw Dylan's jaw clench, the anger in his eyes no less than what she saw in Bryce's. But she also saw the tremendous amount of blood he had lost. The paleness of his skin alarmed her as did the sweat beading his face.

She didn't know what to do. So she said a silent prayer.

"I went to a lot of bother to have this woman. Did you know that?"

"That's what I've heard."

"Well . . ." Bryce pulled his pistol out to keep Dylan at a safe distance. Nervously, he played with the hammer of his gun, clicking it back, then releasing it, each time more fervently than before. "You of all people should understand why I had to do what I did. You were there that night when we first saw her, coming from the jungle in the rain."

Ariel's eyes riveted up to look at him, her surprise clear.

"Didn't you know I was there?"

Her face showed her answer.

"You saw only him." Bryce jerked his head in the direction where Dylan stood. "You saw only him!"

She held her breath, his thumb working the hammer faster and faster, each click of release causing her to jump as he continued to wave it in Dylan's direction.

"No matter. I saw you."

He ran the back of his hand over his mouth, still holding the pistol. He rubbed the bristles of his unshaven chin, the rifle still beneath hers. "What were your thoughts, Christianson? What were you thinking when she appeared like an angel from the mist, her movements so like the tiger that walked beside her?"

Bryce turned to Dylan, waiting for his answer. "What were you thinking?" he yelled again.

"I wondered if she was real or a vision of my imagination."

This made Bryce laugh, a sick, twisted sound that caused the barrel to shake against her jawbone.

"How sweet." He mocked them both. "Do you want to know what I thought?"

Ariel closed her eyes.

He prodded her with the weapon, causing her eyes to open. "I knew then and there that I would have you. And nothing, nothing would stop me."

Bryce's look turned serious as he turned to Dylan again. "What is it like to make love to her?"

Dylan took a step forward but stopped when Bryce pulled the hammer of his handgun back again. "I asked you a question!" The pitch of his voice was shrill. Ariel could see Dylan was about to answer, but she broke in with her own reply.

"You'll never know what it's like, Bryce. You don't know how to make love."

His hand gripped the trigger tighter, his teeth ground together in fury. "I've had plenty of women, Ariel. I know how to please."

"You've had women," Ariel said clearly, ignoring the pain the steel caused her as the pressure increased, "but you've no idea how to please a woman."

Ariel dared a quick glance at Dylan, praying he would stay put. *Not yet,* her mind cried out to him. *Not yet.*

She heard Bryce draw in a long, deep breath, and she could see his hands shaking.

"So," he wheezed, his voice lower and even more deadly. "I don't know how to please."

He seemed to be thinking. "But I'm sure you know how to please a man with all the practice you've had of late. Tell me, Dylan, is she as good as a whore?"

Carefully, he moved the gun down the length of her throat, then across her shoulder. He used the tip of it to part the shirt, the cold metal seeking out the swell of her breast, coming to rest on the rosy tip. He played with her nipple, sliding the barrel over its peak.

A sick feeling rolled in the pit of her stomach.

"How about," he drawled out slowly, lazily, "you showing me how you've pleased Dylan, Ariel."

She didn't move, a new fear churning inside her. The barrel moved further down, passing over her stomach, each inch of flesh quivering beneath it.

Bryce's breathing became ragged, his eyes now glazed with lust. He lowered the steel to the soft inner flesh of her thigh, inching it up to the delicacy he craved.

Ariel's knees went weak. She sank down on them, fighting the bile that had risen in her throat.

Bryce tossed aside his pistol and twisted a handful of rich, auburn hair about his hand. Then he threw away his rifle too, quickly replacing it with the knife he carried. He twisted Ariel about for Dylan to see, stopping him in midstep as the blade dug dangerously into her throat.

"Don't try it, Dylan. I'll kill her. I'll slit her pretty little throat."

Ariel wished he would.

Bryce seemed satisfied that Dylan would behave. "Ariel, dearest, since you're already on your lovely little knees, you can begin your lessons on how to please a man."

The point of the blade drew blood, the warmth trickling down between the fullness of her breasts. Her own sweat stung her eyes, and she blinked to ease the discomfort. The grip on her hair tightened.

"Please me, sweetness, or I will see Dylan suffers for it."

Dylan couldn't hear what Bryce was saying. Bryce had lowered his voice for Ariel's ears only. He knew his strength was flowing from him with each drop of blood he lost. He was light-headed, his movements slow and cumbersome, his thinking just as sluggish.

He wanted to kill Bryce Harrington with his bare hands, if necessary. Never had he felt so murderous. Yet as hard as it was, he kept still. The blade of the knife against Ariel's throat kept him at bay.

Frustration turned into an agonizing pain as Bryce's hand forced Ariel closer to him, his intentions clear.

Dylan died a thousand times over as she reached up to undo the buttons on Bryce's trousers.

"No!" Dylan cried, anguish deep in the single word.

Bryce's gaze came into contact with his, stopping Dylan once again. Ariel cried out as the knife's tip again pierced her flesh, a trickle of blood running down her neck.

"Come on, Dylan. Come stop me."

Dylan couldn't move. Fear for Ariel kept him frozen in place.

"No?"

Bryce was taunting him.

"Where were we, Ariel? Oh, yes. You were about to show me your talents."

Once again, Ariel worked on the buttons, her shaking fingers clumsy and slow. Bryce's impatience became strained.

"Christ almighty, woman, a man could lose interest by the time you get started!"

He jerked her head back, holding it at an alarming angle. He unbuttoned his pants, the bulge within drawing her fearful gaze. He only laughed.

"You look as frightened as a virgin on her wedding night. But we both know you are not a virgin. Actually, the way I see it, you prostituted yourself to Dylan for his protection. So it should be a trivial thing to do so again."

Suddenly, the jungle was pierced by a tiger's angry cry, its closeness unnerving. Bryce looked away, and in that second Ariel reacted, her bunched fist slamming into his unprotected groin. She rolled away from the knife's edge, the tip only grazing her flesh.

Dylan was beside her before Bryce even knew what was happening. He pulled her to her feet, then moved toward Bryce just as he went for the rifle. Ariel saw Bryce's hand clasp the butt and bring it around to clip Dylan on the jaw, reeling him backwards.

The scream of the tiger deafened them again. Ariel grasped Dylan, trying to pull him away.

"He has a gun, Dylan." She tugged at his resistant form.

Bryce drew the weapon up and took aim.

"Please, Dylan," she screamed in horror.

Dylan lunged at Bryce, his feet lifting off the ground as he flung his body across the distance separating them. The rifle went off and Ariel heard his flesh tear away, the blood confirming her fears.

"Run, Ariel!"

She saw him bowl Bryce over, the impact of his body's weight taking him down. Dylan did not get up. Only Bryce did. Ariel's gaze met the cold gray of his. A chill shook her as she saw his smile creep back. He reached down and picked up his knife.

"He's dead, darling."

"No!" Ariel cried, sinking to her knees, denying his ugly words. "No!"

"Now it's your turn."

Bryce moved towards her, slow and deliberate. Ariel tried to stand but couldn't, her shaking legs unable to hold her. She crawled into the brush, Bryce only a few steps behind.

"You've nowhere to hide, Ariel. I can find you so easily. Too easily, really. I'd hoped for more sport from you. After all, you are the jungle girl, or something like that. That is what they said, isn't it? All the gossips with all their whispered secrets."

Ariel felt his nearness.

"It's just too easy," he repeated, only inches away.

She scrambled away, but he grabbed her foot, slowly pulling her to him. Ariel twisted about and kicked at him, her free foot landing a blow to his chest. This stunned him, taking his breath away, giving her the second she needed. Her hand came into contact with a rock, and she brought it around, slamming it down onto his skull.

This caused him to let go, slumping back in pain.

"Ow," he whined, then chuckled. "Good girl," he yelled out, the chuckle turning to full-blown laughter.

"Good girl," Bryce repeated, watching her disappear into the dense growth of trees. He dabbed at the wound on his forehead, then looked at the blood on his fingers.

"Bitch," he whispered, wiping it from his fingers.

He stood and casually looked around.

"Run, sweet thing. Run for your life."

Ariel stopped, his words grating on her nerves. She closed her eyes, trying to think. Anger kicked in, prompting her survival instincts back to life. Heat pumped through her cold veins, and the thoughts in her mind floated away as the persistent beat of her heart took over. Steady and strong, it filled her with its rhythm.

She drew in a deep breath, then opened her eyes. She was ready. Bryce was close, and he made no effort to conceal himself. With quiet ease, Ariel scaled the tree she stood near.

Bryce moved into view, then stepped beneath her. She held her breath.

"Ariel," he called out, "your trail stops here."

He walked in a tight circle, checking the dark shadows as he went. "Not in here," he continued to chatter at her. "Not here!"

It irked her he was enjoying himself so much.

"Now, you didn't dig a hole and crawl into it. So . . ." His head swiveled up, his eyes shadowed and cruel. "You must be up there."

Before she thought, Ariel dropped down on him. Her cry of fury echoed through the dark jungle as she landed on him, her nails digging into the flesh on his face. She locked her legs about his waist, keeping him from flinging her away. He sank to his knees and pulled her head back dangerously as he brought the blade of his knife back to her throat.

Ariel let go.

Bryce pushed her back onto the ground, his body heavy on hers, her legs still around his waist. He freed her hair so he could make better use of his hand. Slowly, enjoying her predicament, he ran his hand up her leg and over her naked hip.

"I considered just killing you and being done with it. But since you seem so obliging, your open legs so inviting, I think it will wait." His hand found her breast, the fullness of it pleasing him.

He bent his head down and bit the buttons off her shirt, then spat them on the ground, freeing her lovely body to his view.

"How can I resist such beauty?" His tongue licked her nipple. Ariel couldn't keep from shuddering.

"I would like to think, sweet Ariel, that you shiver from delight."

"Or," Ariel whispered, "it could be from repulsion. Which do you think?"

She felt him tense and took satisfaction from that.

"I'll show you what it's like to be with a man."

Bryce pulled his pants open, freeing the hardness within.

"It's time for you to pay, bitch."

Ariel felt his weight fall upon her, and she whispered in his ear. "You aren't man enough, Harrington. What lies between your legs is a joke."

"Shut up," he screamed in her ear, causing her to flinch. "Shut your filthy mouth."

Bryce struck her, then kissed her hard. He pulled back, then licked the blood from her lip. His hips moved on her, then he poised himself above her. Ariel closed her eyes.

"Look at me, Ariel."

She kept her eyes shut.

His hand grabbed her by the chin, his grip hurting and cruel. "Open your eyes. I want to see your eyes. Open them!"

Slowly, she opened her eyes.

"Good," he almost purred. "I want to see the look in your eyes as I have you and take pleasure from your body."

His hand moved from her chin down to her breast, then down to the curve of her waist and on to her hip. "You are the most beautiful woman I've ever seen. It will be a shame to kill you, but kill you I must."

He leaned down and sucked her nipple, his breathing coming in short, gasping breaths. Ariel felt the bile rising in her throat.

"Look at me," he cooed. "I want to see what you are thinking as I taste the sweetness between your legs."

For the second time, Bryce was lifted from her and thrown aside. Dylan stood above her, bloody and torn, but alive.

Bryce rolled up onto his feet and took a step forward. He stopped dead.

"Kala Bagh," Ariel whispered. The tiger crouched only a few feet away. The cat's scream rang out.

The great Bengal and Bryce jumped at the same

time, the man's knife flashing, the animal's fangs bared.

"No." Ariel moved to interfere, but Dylan stopped her.

Man and beast rolled about in a twisting mass of fur and flesh. Only a moment passed. Bryce's movements stilled. The knife fell from his hand. Kala Bagh gave his prey one last shake, the strength of his jaws crushing his victim's throat.

Once again the cat's cry echoed about them, this time in victory. Then silence fell upon them.

Kala Bagh stood over the lifeless body, Bryce's blood marking his fur. Ariel stepped forward, drawing his golden gaze.

"Kala Bagh," she called his name, her voice shaking with emotion.

"He may not know you, Ariel."

Dylan's warning fell on deaf ears. She refused to believe that, unwilling to even consider the possibility.

"How could he forget any more than I have? We are one in spirit."

"It's been a long time," Dylan argued.

Ariel moved closer.

"Please, Ariel."

She did not listen.

"Kala Bagh, I've come home."

The cat growled, his paw clawing the air.

Ariel started to cry, tears blurring the image that was so much a part of her. "Oh, Kala Bagh, my friend, I did not want to leave you. I loved you."

"Ariel, please, come away." Dylan reached out his hand to her, pleading.

Sobbing now, Ariel touched her hand to Dylan's but hesitated as Kala Bagh moved away from the body. He walked toward her, and she pulled her hand away from Dylan and turned back to wait for Kala Bagh.

Kala Bagh reared onto his hind legs, snarling and pawing the air. Then he placed a massive paw upon her cheek. Her tears ran into his fur, and she covered his paw with her own hand.

"You remembered me, my friend."

Kala Bagh turned away, then disappeared into the dense growth.

"Kala Bagh," Ariel called out, then started to follow. Dylan stopped her.

"No, Ariel. Let him go. He's no longer yours." Dylan wiped away her tears. "Just as you are no longer his."

Just then, Kala Bagh reappeared, and by his side was a tigress. He came forward, but the female remained cautious and stayed close to the cover of the trees.

"He has a mate," Ariel whispered.

"Just as you have," Dylan said softly. "Now you both have another in which to share your spirit. You are no longer alone, Ariel. And neither is Kala Bagh."

With a bittersweet sadness, Ariel watched her friend return to his mate. Together the cats moved back into the trees, but Kala Bagh turned back one last time and growled a soft, final farewell to her. Ariel understood.

"Goodbye, my friend. You shall be in my memories forever."

Dylan took her by the arm. "Let's go home."

"Can we stay a while before we go back to England?"

"I think our home is here, Ariel."

A broad smile lit her face. "Have I told you lately that I love you?"

"How about . . ." He tried to smile but it ended in a wince. "How about you show me at home?"

"*If* you survive," Ariel teased.

"Don't you worry, love. I'll not let these scratches hold me back."

"Promise?"

"Promise." Dylan held out his hand, and together they walked away. Ariel was home, an old love in her heart, a new love by her side.